72 Hours of Insanity: Ant

Volume 5

Presented by

The Writer's Workout

Copyright © 2018

www.writersworkout.net

Dedication

This anthology is dedicated to those who wrote and those who didn't for each week of the 2018 Writer's Games;
to the families of the participants for their unwavering support and understanding;
and to the judges and their families for taking this journey with us.

Note from the Editors: The following entries have been published as received from the winners. Though our team of editors do suggest changes in some places, these stories represent the amazing work that writers produced within the 72-hour time frame and we strive to maintain the integrity of the original submission. As such, you may find typos or grammatical adjustments that were not updated following the editorial process. We feel these errors do not take away from the work but in fact, showcase just how strong our winners are: they managed to produce quality work on such a short deadline.

INTRODUCTION	7
THE FLAVOR OF GRIEF	10
LEMON SCENTED BLEACH	15
ONE NIGHT IN OLD TOWN	20
BRUISES	35
MADAME DOLCE	38
THIS TOO WILL PASS	48
THE WOLF AT THE DOOR	60
OVER THE TOP	68
FORBIDDEN INTIMACY	76
CRYING WOLF	84
A COMMON BOND	90
DRESSED TO KILL	100
CORRINE JI'S STORY	109
MOM LIFE	114
REFLECTIONS	120
THE STAINED GLASS RIVER	125
STAY CLOSE TO THE FIRE	133
THE VIRGIN STRETCH	137
THE PENANCE	143
PLAIN JANE	152
LOVING YOU BEST OF ALL	159

SINS OF THE FATHER	166
INFINITELY PRACTICAL	173
TIME IN PLACE	183
THE SILENT WATCHER	192
LEFT ON THE SHELF	204
BIOGRAPHIES	208

Introduction
knock knock

Oh, hello! I hope I'm not bothering you. Can I talk to you today about The Writer's Games? Based on our records, you bought an anthology this year.

What records?! Oh, don't worry about that. Do you know about the Games? A little? Well, let me tell you all about it.

The Writer's Games is a free 2-month-long writing competition where writers of all skill levels compete in different Events. Each Event has a specific prompt participants must write towards and they have 72 hours to complete their entry.

Please, don't close the door!! I know that might sound daunting but it really is fun!

Participants must register in advance and all Events are kept secret until the designated time of the reveal. But I haven't even told you the best part!

Every entry receives unbiased feedback from a group of amazing judges. So, not only do participants get to stretch their writing muscles, they also get help honing their craft. You get feedback no matter if you place in an Event or not.

Are their prizes? Oh, you bet there are!

If a story places anywhere from 1st to 5th place, it is published in our annual anthology.

Deep breaths. Deep breaths. I know being published is always so exciting. Do you think you'll try out next year? Yes! Oh that's great!

A portion of the proceeds from the sale of the anthology goes to the group that brought The Writer's Workout together: The Office of Light and Letters, the group that runs NaNoWriMo. First, second, and third place winners also have an interview placed on our site and get a ton of writerly goodies!

I know! Those are some amazing prizes, right?

One last thing before I leave you. Make sure you take a look inside this year's anthology and all the extraordinary winners from 2018. We had entries in every genre. From fantasy to romance to mystery. Here are the writers that won. We hope you enjoy them as much as we did.

Thank you so much for purchasing a Writer's Games anthology! Happy reading. Goodbye.

waves and trips over a pebble

-Sarah Perchikoff
Writer's Workout Director of Brand

IN ABSENTIA: Some of the best stories revolve around people you've never met. For this Event, write a story around an absent character that is referred to but does not appear directly. They should affect the plot in a significant way, and their absence should be part of what advances it.
Core Concept: planning; show, don't tell

The Flavor of Grief
EB Stark
First Place

When Bobby Greeley broke his arm in the summer of 1970, I knew my prayers had been answered. Not that I'd prayed to the man upstairs to break Bobby's arm—he wasn't bad for an eighth grader—but the Lord works in mysterious ways according to Gramps, and if that's the way He wanted to work it, who was I to question?

All summer Ma and Pa had been watching Archie Bunker lob insults at anyone within earshot, as if that made for good entertainment. Gram and I couldn't stand the show. She for different reasons than I, but it's something we agreed on, and we hadn't agreed on much since Gramps had passed the year before.

I'd spent most of the break in my room, drooling on the pages of the Schwinn catalog I'd borrowed from the Huffs. The catalog had a permanent bend across the spread that touted their new Diamond Jubilee series. That's where I got my first look at the glorious green *Pea Picker*—the dreamiest bike I'd ever laid eyes on. More dreamy than Bobby Greeley's Huffy Dragster, even.

I took the catalog to the dinner table with stars in my eyes one sticky July evening. With my twelfth birthday only two months away, I'd been certain a few hints were all it would take.

"If a boy had one of these," I'd said and sighed—long and deep to give it time to sink in— "he wouldn't ever need another thing in his whole life, I imagine."

Ma and Pa exchanged glances.

"I'd imagine some boys are lucky to have a bike at all," Gram said as she dropped a ladle of Great Northerns over cornbread.

I scowled. She was just sour I didn't appreciate the rusty ole hand-me-down she'd given me after she sold Gramp's house.

"But it's huge and ugly and—"

"It rides, don't it?" Pa said with one eyebrow raised.

I cast my eyes to the floor. "It's a lady-bike."

"Well, I'm sure we could find a lady, then, who'd be happy to take it off your hands."

I was so sore at them, I'd skulked to me room, plate untouched,and sought the comfort of my pillow. It was a huge, overstuffed bundle of cotton that had seen me through even the toughest nights after Gramps' ordeal.

After dinner and evening chores, Ma had slipped into my room before going to bed herself. She ran her fingers through my hair like she'd done when I was little, sending shivers of glee down my back.

"You know your Pa works awfully hard just to put a roof over our head and food on the table," she said. "And now that we've taken Gram in, there's an extra mouth to feed."

"It's not fair." I tried not to pout, but I felt my mouth pull at the corners despite my best efforts.

"That's how the whole county's been feeling ever since the plant shut down," she'd said.

I didn't know much about the plant shut-down that had wreaked havoc on so many families in our town, but I did know a thing or two about cinnamon disks, and every time I saw one, I resented Gram a little more.

"Why'd Gram have to come here, anyway?" I punched my mattress.

Her mouth dropped open. "Would you have your own Grandmother live on the streets?"

I lifted the sheet over my head to cover the shame that burned my cheeks.

"For a bicycle?" Her voice rose with each syllable, ending in a pinched squeak.

"It's only a hundred dollars, Ma, and Gram don't eat that much."

Ma shook her head, and I couldn't bear the disappointment in her eyes. "Might as well be a million, son, when you ain't got none to spare."

I'd stayed awake long after she went to bed that night. A summer breeze fanned the room with wafts of lilac from the bush out front, taking the stifle out of the air. I'd just started a conversation with Gramps in my head when the curtain rustled in my peripheral. "Is that you, Gramps?"

I strained to hear his voice amongst the cicadas' songs, but nothing could get past that thunderous hum.

I crept to the window and whisper-shouted for them a shush. They didn't go down even a decibel, let alone stop.

And then a whiff of cinnamon floated in on the breeze.

I tensed.

"Is it really you?" I gripped the window sill and strained to see by the light of the moon. "I'm not afraid, Gramps."

I could handle it, I assured myself. Whatever form he might choose to take, I didn't care.

I *needed* him.

I needed the man I'd spent every summer of my youth with; the man who'd taught me to bait a hook and helped me catch my first fish; who wiped my tears when I'd made one bleed retrieving the hook.

The man who took me to every baseball game the Chiefs played on their home turf and went to bat for me any time I got into trouble at home.

A bird alighted on mom's feeder in the front garden—*a bird in the middle of the night?*—and I remembered the seeds. Gramps had sent a message, and I received it loud and clear. I ran to the kitchen and pulled a chair to the front of the fridge, reaching up to the cupboard no one used.

Still there.

I grinned and ran all the way back to my room, clutching the bag of sunflower seeds as though they held a secret power. And while they may not have been Jack's beans, they did possess a certain magic.

Like Gramps had taught me, I spilled a few into my mouth and broke them open with my teeth. After working the seed out of its casing, I curled my tongue into the shape of a gun barrel, sucked in as much air as I could hold, and shot the shell so far it rustled the leaves of the lilac bush yards away.

"Whoa. Did'ja see that one?" I chuckled and shot another. Then again and again. I could sense him there with me—could smell the sharp aroma of cinnamon. I imagined he was making his own deadly shots in the ether around us.

Turn by turn it went, just like we'd done so many times in the past, when talking was too hard, and instead of spittin' ugliness and negativity, we spit seeds until the flames of discontent had burned their way to ash and life seemed a whole lot less muddy.

"If you were still here, I know you'd find a way to get me that bike," I said finally, when the blaze had died down and only a flicker remained.

Gramps had always been a church-going man, and he would have told me to pray for it, but I didn't believe in that stuff Gramps believed in.

I spit another seed. *Thwop.* The bush rattled.

"But instead of you, I'm stuck with Gram—and all she does is take, never give." *Thwop. Thwop.*

"Double-tap," I whooped as whispery as I could manage. I grinned myself silly at the accomplishment and imagined the reaction I would have gotten if Gramps was *truly* there. High-fives and floats from A&W—that's how we would have celebrated.

A cricket took up song just below the window as another breeze pushed past, bringing with it a hint of root beer and vanilla. I closed my eyes until I tasted it on my tongue, let it slide down my throat in a delicious swirl of sweetness. I held and savored it until the creamy root beer turned hot on my tongue; sweet and hot like—*cinnamon*. My eyes popped open and I spat, trying to get rid of the horrible taste of the memory.

"I can't forgive her." I choked the words out. "Even though I know that's what you want, I can't do it."

I spat again and raked fingernails over my tongue, trying to rid myself of the cinnamon-disk nightmare that had stolen the sweet reverie of an evening with Gramps and our shared seed therapy.

"Her whole life she worked in a hospital," I said and swallowed the tears that crawled up my throat. "So how do you choke to death on a piece of candy when you're married to a nurse?"

My throat filled with the tight strangle of contained sobs, building so much pressure, they threatened to release at any moment.

"She didn't save you," I gurgled and dove into my pillow. "So she may as well have killed you." The boiling point came before the last words were out, so the explosion was too much even for my overstuffed pillow to contain.

My bedroom light flicked on and gentle hands found their way to my back. They stroked and caressed, dutifully silent until the entire kettle had released its steam, and I pulled away from the pillow I'd soaked with a river's worth of tears and snot.

When I turned, Gram was there, holding her own pillow. She pulled my soiled one away and put hers in its spot. The kindred look in her eyes said more than any words could have and understanding fell on me as though a heavy veil had finally lifted.

I didn't know much about how to do it, but I felt moved to pray in that instant, so I did. I didn't pray for forgiveness. I didn't pray for my soul. Heck, I didn't even pray for that bike, but Gramps had told me one time the Lord knows the desires of our heart. Coincidence or not, Mrs. Greeley had called Ma the very next morning and asked if I could take over Bobby's paper route for six weeks until his arm healed.

Five weeks later a shiny green *Pea Picker* sat in my driveway, commanding the attention and adoration of every kid in the neighborhood—and soon to be everyone at Kelly Junior High School.

Gram came out to see me off that first morning I'd ride the dream machine to school.

"Mighty fine bike you've got there, boy," she said with a wink.

Seemed our distaste for Archie Bunker wasn't the only thing we agreed on, after all.

Lemon Scented Bleach
CE Snow
Second Place

Maribell cut the peanut butter sandwich on the diagonal and arranged the halves on a plate like a butterfly. Humming to herself, she set lunch on the table and cleared away the untouched breakfast dishes. Lips twisted in a rueful grin – Basil hated oatmeal, refused to eat it – she took the bowl over to the stainless steel, double sink. After scraping out the congealed mess she opened the tap and flipped on the disposal.

Unseen blades hummed, and for a moment she wondered what it would feel like to stick

her hand in. Would it crunch, like the time she'd accidentally dropped in a chicken bone? She shrugged and turned it off, then set the bowl in the other side of the sink. The dishes could wait until later.

Maribell had one foot on the stairs when a buzzer caught her attention. She turned and headed into the laundry room. Opening the dryer, she grabbed an armful of clean clothes and hugged them to her chest. She breathed in the clean, lavender scent. It was the closest she got to a spa treatment these days. Dryer sheets aromatherapy. She snorted and dumped the load on the top of the washer, then started to fold.

Laundry was a never-ending battle for a mom of a toddler. Countless, adorable pairs of tiny shorts. A hundred little socks with no matches. A small t-shirt with a reddish blotch on it. Cherry kool-aid? Maribell frowned as she dabbed spot remover on the splotch. She threw it into the washer for another round and prayed the stain hadn't set.

It was Basil's favorite shirt, the one with a funny yellow cartoon character on it. He'd been wearing it on their annual summer trip to the beach. It had been a perfect day filled with ice cream cones and sandcastles and the squeals of laughter when foamy waves crashed over their toes.

Maribell wished she could recapture that feeling, back when they'd been so blissful. Before that knock came at the door. Before her backside went numb sitting on a flimsy folding chair, dressed in all black. Before two strangers, in crisp blue coats and shiny brass buttons, handed her a folded flag while "Taps' played in the background. As if all that bullshit, Marine Corp ceremony could help her explain to a three-year-old why Daddy wasn't coming home.

She sagged into the pile of laundry and let the warm fabric smother her sobs.

When the tears played out, Maribell sniffed and, unthinking, rubbed her eyes with the closest thing at hand. A dark smudge came away on the white ribs of a mateless sock.

"Dang it!"

She sighed and grabbed the spot remover again. Wearing mascara was pointless. It was a race each day to see what would set her off, tears spoiling her careful applique. But makeup was a habit, and all the righteous grief pamphlets and nosey advice givers advocated for sticking to a routine. Besides, there was Basil to think about. He didn't need to see a washed out, lifeless, zombie of a mom.

She scrubbed at the black mark. It wasn't budging. A bubble of laughter tickled her throat. How could a few tears melt 'waterproof' mascara, but the extra strength stain remover was useless? Maribell squashed down the laughter, ignoring its hysterical edge, and grabbed the bleach.

The bottle was a cheery white and yellow with bold letters splashed across the label. *'Fresh new scent'* and *'Made with real lemons!'* Maribell clucked her tongue.

"What a world. The bleach is made with real lemons, and my iced tea is artificially flavored."

She twisted off the cap and inhaled. Chlorine and lemon fought for dominance and the scent made her lightheaded. She wondered what it would taste like. Would it burn going down, like the whiskey she hid on top of the fridge? The plastic bleach bottle trembled in her hand and her thoughts buzzed. Eyes watering, she shook her head.

Buzz. Buzz. Buzz.

"I'm coming!"

Maribell thunked the bottle down, bleach slopping over her hand, and dashed to the kitchen. She arrived just in time to see the pre-school's number flash across her phone display before the screen went dark. Fire prickled her skin. She ran water over her hand and waited for her phone to ding with a new voicemail. It never did.

Perhaps after a half-dozen messages, the teacher had finally realized she wasn't going to return his calls. She didn't have the energy. Didn't they understand she couldn't send Basil back to school? It was just too much right now.

The water soothed her reddened skin, cool against the bleach burn. Maribell glanced down. Dishes were piling up – it was her least favorite chore. It was easy to leave crusty bowls in the sink, fill them with water, and tell herself they needed to soak.

A jelly-gummed knife caught her eye and her stomach roiled. Basil hated jelly, especially strawberry. How could she mess that up? She grabbed a dish towel and patted her hands dry before spinning around to double check the sandwich. She sagged and flopped down in the chair. Just peanut butter. Tears pricked her eyes and she blinked them back. Stupid.

No, not stupid. Exhausted. She barely slept. The bottle of untouched sleeping pills mocked her each night when she brushed her teeth, but she refused to take them. They made her feel fuzzy. She was a single mom now; she needed to stay alert. For Basil.

Maribell gathered herself and stood. She turned her back on the sink and the butterflied sandwich and crossed into the living room. In contrast to the growing pile of dirty dishes, the large common room was tidy. Almost too clean. She looked around for something to straighten. With a vigorous thump, she fluffed already plump throw pillows and restacked the coasters on the coffee table. She glowered at the bookshelves, the titles neatly arranged, side-by-side. A finger trailed across the lowboy came away dust-free.

Something neon yellow peeped out from under the couch.

"A-ha!" Mirabell pounced and fished out a toy truck. "You belong upstairs."

Triumphant, she marched towards the front hall. At the foot of the stairs she hesitated. A fat, brown spider lounged on the bottom step. For a moment she considered squashing it. No. She was teaching Basil compassion for living things. Spiders and ants got relocated outside. Flies were swished out open windows.

Maribell waffled. Basil would never know. A quick stomp and a swipe of a paper towel, and there'd be no evidence left behind. No. She'd trained herself not to swear, even when little ears weren't listening. She could do the same here.

With a suppressed shudder, Mirabell grabbed an unopened bill off the end table and coaxed the hairy monstrosity onto the envelope. She studiously ignored the big red letters shouting – *final notice.* They wouldn't dare turn the lights out on the widow of a war hero.

Taking care not to drop the spider, she carried it to the back door. She twisted the knob, whipped open the door, and shook the intruder out into the yard. As she did, something leaning against the side of the house shifted and fell against the step with a thump.

Maribell jumped back, startled. Her good garden spade, caked with dirt, lay sprawled on the ground.

"Basil!" She stomped back through the living room, into the front hall, and headed up the stairs. "How many times do I have to tell you – Mommy's garden tools aren't toys?" She strode down the hall. "Basil?"

Maribell pushed open the door to her son's room. It was dark and stifling with the drapes drawn and windows closed.

"Come on, buddy. It's time for lunch."

The lemony scent of bleach burned her nose. "Basil?"

Despite the stuffiness, a shiver ran up her spine, as if the spider was back, feather touch footsteps crawling across her skin. She threw back the curtains to let golden sunshine flood through the window. The light pooled across the floor, illuminating a discolored spot on the carpet. The room was empty. Shiver forgotten, sweat trickled down her back.

Something dark fluttered at the edge of her memory. She pushed it away.

"Basil! Where are you?"

Urgency pressed her feet in motion and she flew down the hall. The dark thing pursued her, whispering horrors in her ears. Lies.

Frantic, Maribell checked all of Basil's favorite hiding places. Under her big four poster bed, in the hall closet, behind the sofa. He wasn't there. He wasn't anywhere. Her heart raced as panicked bile clawed its way up the back of her throat.

Feeding on her terror, the shadow grew. It loomed over her and forced fractured, bleach-coated images into her mind's eye. They stabbed like shards of glass.

A stained t-shirt.

The muddy spade.

A poorly cleaned carpet.

She grabbed her head and moaned, "No, no, no..."

The dark thing laughed. *Yes*. It showed her a knife in her hands. Not smeared with strawberry jelly, but dripping blood. She remembered the clatter as she had, dispassionate, dropped it in the kitchen sink.

Maribell staggered into the master bathroom, legs leaden. Her head pounded and her ears rang with the silent echoes of a child's screams. In the mirror, a stranger with hollow cheeks stared back at her. Smudges of mascara ran beneath flat, expressionless eyes. Grey. Like Basil's.

On the edge of the sink, an orange plastic bottle called to her. A siren song of oblivion.

She shot a stern look at her reflection.

"We should put those away. Basil could get into them."

Don't worry. He knows he's not allowed in our bathroom.

"When do little boys listen?"

Well, then. Get rid of them.

Mirabell's reflection nodded in approval as trembling fingers reached for the pill bottle. It took several tries to open the childproof cap. Yellow ovals spilled into her palm and she swallowed them dry.

Good, good. All of them now. It's dangerous for Basil to find even one.

"Don't you say his name."

Mirabell choked down the last of the sleeping pills and stumbled from the bathroom. The hallway swam in her vision and she lurched against the wall. Behind her the shadow thing stalked her. Silent. Waiting.

Fingertips tingling, she lurched forward on feet disconnected from her body. A fog descended and she shook her head, trying to clear her thoughts. Basil's room. She had to reach Basil's room. The floor rippled and she pitched forward onto her knees.

Wordless, the dark creature urged her onward. She crawled over the threshold.

Sunlight streamed through the window. Dust motes danced in the beam, flashing like tiny, whirling stars. The train car bed, the over stuffed toy box, the sneakers with tangled laces faded from view. She had to cover the discolored spot on the rug, that one thing out of place in Basil's perfect sanctuary.

Maribell inched forward to curl across the damning stain, spotlighted by the afternoon sun. Its warmth didn't touch her skin. Her breath slowed. As the world went dark, her last thought was that the carpet reeked of lemon scented bleach.

One Night in Old Town
Paul Webb
Third Place

The rain beat straight down onto the dark and winding Edinburgh streets. It rattled off the slate roofs and ran in rivers down the tarmac, forming great puddles wherever the roads stopped sloping. MacLellan splashed his way through the storm, hunched as deep into his trench coat as he could manage, his fedora pulled down firmly, but still the cold water found a way inside his cheap suit. His feet were so wet he had long since given up avoiding the great torrents of water rushing down the gutters. *What a night to be out in*, he thought with a grimace as another icy drip ran slowly down his back.

Up ahead he could make out the Square, dimly lit by the single, flickering street-lamp. Here on the border between New Town and Old Town electricity still worked, but only just. Another figure was hunched almost out of sight at the edge of the circle of light, MacLellan stopped as he reached the lamp and waited underneath it, watching the sheets of water lashing down through the orange glow. After a few moments the figure strode towards him and into the light. He was tall and broad and wearing the same hat and trench coat. It's what they all wore; an unofficial uniform of sorts.

'Ahh,' said the man as he extended his hand. 'How did she get you involved in this then?'

'I was in the unfortunate position of owing her a favour,' MacLellan replied as he shook the man's hand firmly. 'The kind I couldn't refuse to return if you take my meaning.'

The man nodded with a knowing smile, droplets of water running from the rim of his hat. 'It's good to see you again MacLellan, even if it's in this kind of a situation. How long's it been anyway?'

'Good to see you too Galbraith. Nearly eight years, and it's not nearly been long enough.'

Galbraith nodded again. 'Yeah, we all thought you'd made it out permanent. Damned surprised to see you walking out of the shadows to meet me.'

'Well don't get used to it, it's just this once. I repay the favour then I'm gone again, that's the deal.'

'Good for you, I hope it works out that way,' Galbraith said. 'It'll be nice working for you again this once though. Just like the good old days right?'

'Yeah, right,' MacLellan replied, though he didn't have too many good memories himself from the old days. Galbraith had just been a rookie back then, capable but never a stand-out. 'You won't be working for me though, not this time. I'm here in an unofficial capacity, no badge, so you can take the lead.'

A gust of wind rushed across the Square, whipping the rain into the side of their faces and they both turned their backs to it, now looking up the hill towards the electric lights of New Town, and the imposing, well-lit Ministry building sitting on top of Calton Hill. They stood in silence for a few moments as the storm raged around them before MacLellan spoke again, without turning to face his old friend.

'So, can you tell me anything about why I've been dragged out from my nice warm home to tramp around these wet old streets again?'

'I can't say I know much,' Galbraith said. 'But I can tell you one thing, I haven't seen the Top Brass this worked up for some time. Maybe not since the Coolidge Case. And if they've brought you back in...'

Galbraith's voice trailed off, but MacLellan knew what he meant; something big must be coming, and he already knew it was something he wanted no part of.

The harsh metallic ring of a payphone stopped his thoughts in their tracks and both men turned towards the sound. After the second ring Galbraith took a deep breath and walked back into the shadows at the edge of the Square. MacLellan stayed and watched him step inside the old, red phone box. The faint white light above the phone painted Galbraith's face a sickly colour; the rain-streaked windows blurring his image. He waited for the fourth ring to finish before picking up the receiver.

MacLellan felt the cold dampness of his shirt as it stuck to his back. Water ran in a constant trickle down his nose and he tried to wipe the drip away before sinking both hands deep into his pockets. He already felt every one of his forty-nine years. This was going to be a long night.

Galbraith had hung up and was leaving the phone box when MacLellan glanced back across from under his hat. The big man's face was stony; his brows knitted into a deep frown.

'That was the Head of the Ministry herself,' Galbraith said after a moment. 'They received reports last night of a disturbance.'

'A disturbance?' MacLellan replied, raising an eyebrow. Even minor disturbances in the Old Town were uncommon these days. Ever since the Registration and Disempowerment Programmes had been brought in there were far fewer users than there had been in his early days in Investigations; and those that somehow escaped detection tended to avoid drawing undue attention to themselves thanks to the heavy punishments usually given out.

'Yeah, a Category Five,' Galbraith added. 'Suspected unregistered user. A young girl of around fourteen.'

'A Category Five and they left it a whole day before following up? That doesn't sound like the Ministry to me.'

'The sense I got was that there isn't anybody else in Investigations with your level of experience in this sort of case. I think they wanted to wait until you were back in before they investigated.'

'Like I said, I'm not back in. Just this one case then I'm gone.'

'Sorry Mac, you know what I mean. Anyway, we're to investigate, apprehend the individual responsible, and then return them to the Ministry for processing.'

MacLellan winced at Galbraith's last word; he knew all too well what that would mean for the suspect.

'Fine,' MacLellan said. 'Did they at least give us an idea of where to start?'

Galbraith smiled in his simple way.

'I've got the address of the person that reported the disturbance right here,' he said, gesturing to the investigation report he was trying vainly to shelter from the rain with his body. 'His name is...Damn I never know how to pronounce these old Scots names. Dub? Dove?'

'I believe the "b" and "h" are normally silent in the rest of Scotland. But most Old Towners would say "Dove", said MacLellan, peering at the report. 'A little education goes a long way in this job.'

'Well, you're the brains of this operation. How long since you set foot in the Old Town then?'

'Not since I left the unit,' MacLellan replied.

They both turned away from the lights of the New Town and set off down the hill towards the Old Town, which looked like a sea of darkness by comparison, broken only by the faint glow of the occasional gas lamp.

'Well, not much has changed,' said Galbraith.

MacLellan laughed through his nose and put his head down.

The address Galbraith had been given was in Wester Portsburgh, for a small dwelling above a shop on Spittal Street Lane. They stuck to the main road along the border as they crossed the town, turning south only when they had to. The streets of the Old Town were as wet and deserted as those in the New, but here the shadows were deeper and the air more charged with mystery. They followed the trail round under the shadow of the great cliff of the castle, where the Lord of the Old Town had been allowed to remain after signing the Anti-Magic Act some two decades ago. Lanterns were hung from the rock at intervals, and between these the faces of gargoyles, carved long ago, leered at them as they passed. It was so long since MacLellan had been here that he started slightly when one of them spoke.

'You're not welcome here,' the troll-like face jeered.

'Go back up the hill where you belong,' hissed another.

'Or what?' laughed Galbraith, raising his middle finger to them, which met with a chorus of sneers and abuse until the two men reached the road.

At the last of the gargoyles, a huge, ancient-looking face, MacLellan paused then turned to it.

'What news from the night, Eagna?'

The great eyes peered out from under their hooded lids, then opened wide in recognition.

'MacLellan!' Eagna said. 'It has been a long time, and still you are not welcome, nor will you ever be.'

'I know that,' MacLellan replied. 'I don't plan on staying longer than I have to. Any help you can give me will speed me back.'

'Well, in that case,' Eagna's voice lowered and MacLellan leaned in to listen. 'I see there is a hunt on tonight. She will be caught, but I do not think it will be by you. There is treachery in the air, I can smell that as clear as the fumes that drift in from your New Town.'

'Good to see you remain as cryptic as ever Eagna.'

'Information is only as useful as the person interpreting it,' Eagna replied and the stone face grinned. 'We'll be seeing each other more often again MacLellan.'

'Not that I don't miss your ugly mug Eagna, but I don't think so. So long,' MacLellan said, turning away.

'Go home!' Eagna shouted after him as the two men walked away, followed by the laughter of several of the other nearby gargoyles who then echoed the sentiment in their own choice words.

MacLellan was lost in his thoughts, pondering Eagna's words, frowning so deeply that his brow had become etched with lines, and he didn't notice the incredulous look on Galbraith's face.

'You talk to them?' Galbraith asked after they had turned off on the road leading to Spittal Street.

'Aye, from time to time,' MacLellan replied. 'We need all the help we can get down here, even if it doesn't always make much sense at first.'

'And you trust them? I mean, why would they help us?'

'Hmm,' MacLellan thought for a moment. '*Trust* isn't exactly the word I'd use. But they know more about what goes on round here than we ever will, and there's truth bundled up somewhere in all their curses and riddles. They're always right in the end, even if it takes me too long to see it.'

They walked on through the Old Town gloom in silence, passing rows of shops closed up for the night, and houses where the dim glow of fire and candle light peeked out around the edges of thick curtains. MacLellan was preoccupied with the gargoyle's words and kept his head down. Nothing it had said had sounded good, but then it never had done before either. That the girl would be caught gave him mixed feelings. He felt slightly nauseous about it as he knew what it would mean for her. But at the same time he wanted the job to be done so that he could return to his wife and daughter. The cosy warmth behind the curtains of every house only made him miss them even more.

His train of thought was interrupted as he stopped instinctively at the entrance to Spittal Street Lane. His feet had walked these streets so many times during his years as an Investigator that he seemed to know every twist and turn without thinking, even after all this time. Looking up through the rain at the ornate sign hung high on the wall of the the street corner building he felt as though he had never been away. Galbraith had stopped alongside him but now they continued down the narrow lane, keeping a cautious watch on the shadows lurking beneath the overhanging buildings. Galbraith checked the report slip and then stopped at the foot of a set of winding iron steps.

'This is the place,' he said, motioning at the small wooden door at the top of the steps. 'How do you want to play this?'

'You take the lead,' MacLellan replied. 'Like I told you earlier I have no badge, so no jurisdiction.'

Galbraith led the way up the stairwell, their hard-soled footsteps echoing off the metal and round the alleyway. At the top MacLellan stood back a little as his partner rapped loudly on the door three times. They waited and listened. From somewhere inside the building they could make out the sound of feet shuffling on a wooden floor; locks clicking and clunking; the rattle of a chain. The door cracked open a couple of inches then stopped. The dirt-streaked face of an old man with the long nose and chin of a native Old Towner peered out at them through the narrow gap.

'Mr. Dubh? We're Investigators with the Ministry,' Galbraith said, unfolding the wallet and holding up his identification for the man to inspect. 'You reported a disturbance last night, we've come to ask you some questions about it.'

'Yes, yes, what do you want to know? I'll tell you everything,' the old man stammered.

MacLellan could see the man was terrified, it didn't take a genius to spot that. Plenty of residents of the Old Town would be anxious at a visit from the Ministry late at night, but this seemed more than that, especially as he was only recounting the details of a report he had already made. Something wasn't quite right. It was difficult to tell in the gloom but it looked to MacLellan as though the old man had been worked over very recently. There was definitely some bruising half-hidden under the smears of dirt.

'So, where did you observe the disturbance, Mr Dubh?' Galbraith asked.

'Over by Greyfriars,' the old man replied. 'Last night, just after the twelve bells had sounded.'

'And what did you see exactly? Could you give us a description of the user?'

'Shadows!' Mr. Dubh replied in a whimper. 'Bad magic, the kind that was illegal even in the old days. In the cemetery. I didn't stay to see, I just ran.'

The old man was visibly shaking now, and MacLellan leaned forward.

'It's alright, Mr Dubh. You're safe now, we're not going to hurt you.'

The man recoiled a little, back into the shadows of his house, the crack in the door narrowing.

'I've told you what I know,' his frightened voice spoke from behind the door. 'I can't tell you any more, now just leave me alone.'

The door closed before Galbraith could wedge his foot inside and the two men looked at each other.

'We could always kick the door down,' Galbraith said with a grin.

'I don't believe we have a warrant,' MacLellan replied. 'Besides, I think he's told us all he knows, and I don't think we're the first people he's talked to. Did you see his face? I've seen bruises like that plenty of times after interrogations.'

'He certainly didn't seem too pleased to see us,' Galbraith added. 'So what next?'

MacLellan looked up at the night sky, still black with clouds and full of rain. He sighed.

'After this weather I doubt there'll be much left to see, but we might as well check out Greyfriars,' he said. 'There's more going on tonight than just this though, I can feel it.'

'Careful,' Galbraith laughed, 'Or they'll be investigating you as a mystic as well!'

MacLellan took one last look at the door to Mr. Dubh's house hoping to see something useful but shook his head and followed Galbraith down the stairs and back along the alley.

It was only a short walk along the Wester Porter road to Greyfriars, but the rain seemed to be getting worse and both men were soaked to the skin by the time they left the well-maintained cobbles and followed the path up into the Kirkyard. The church here made an effort to keep the ground consecrated, but even so, entering an Old Town graveyard at night was not something to be taken lightly. The heavy iron gate glinted with its flaking silver paint. MacLellan pushed it open as carefully as he could, but it still creaked ominously and the two men shared a glance of trepidation before stepping through.

The gate clinked shut quietly behind them as they stepped carefully among the graves, following the flagstone path. MacLellan watched the pale blue wisps flicker into life above the graves as they passed by. He already felt that they weren't welcome here.

'Let's not spend longer here than we have to,' he whispered. 'You take the West Yard, I'll cover the rest. Meet back here in ten minutes. Shout if you need me.'

Galbraith nodded but said nothing. He had become noticeably quiet since they had entered the Kirkyard, but still he dutifully headed off down the hill until he was swallowed up by the night. MacLellan watched him go then surveyed the tombstones around him. He walked a quick tour of the yard, searching the ground by the deathly pale illumination of the grave lights as they appeared. At last he found what he was looking for. A small pile of grey dust at the foot of one of the graves, sheltered by the branches of an ancient yew and not yet washed away by the rain. He bowed his head by way of apology to whatever spirit might still be attached to the grave as he knelt down and scooped up some of the dust in his hand. He dabbed a little on his tongue. Just as he thought: ash and salt, the usual remains from a summoning spell. He brushed the rest of it from his hands and noticed something else next to the pile. It looked like a footprint in the wet earth, a print from a shoe he would recognize anywhere.

'MacLellan!' hissed a voice from behind him and he was on his feet in an instant, whirling round with his heart pounding.

'Jesus, Galbraith!' he said, suddenly short of breath, leaning with his hands on his knees. 'Are you trying to give me a bloody heart-attack?'

'Sorry, sorry!' Galbraith whispered back. 'Are you okay? There's nothing down there but these damned spooky lights and a statue on a tombstone that I swear was moving when I wasn't looking. Did you find anything?'

'Evidence of magic use. And this,' he said, crouching by the footprint again. 'Recognize it?'

'Looks like one of ours,' Galbraith said, leaning over.

'Exactly. I'm really starting to think we're not the only ones looking into this case.'

'Well, you know the Ministry, they don't like to say too much, even to us.'

'That's true, I guess,' MacLellan replied and then stopped, catching movement out of the corner of his eye. His voice lowered to a barely audible whisper. 'I think we've outstayed our welcome now. Time to leave.'

Galbraith followed his gaze and could see the shadows behind several graves starting to twist themselves together and creep towards them.

'What are they?' Galbraith croaked.

'I have no idea. A side-effect of whatever magic was used here I would guess. Let's go.'

They backed away slowly from the shadows, a prickling sensation of fear following them with every step until they passed through the silvery gate and MacLellan shut it behind them. As he did he noticed a jet-black cat sitting on top of the wall, looking down at him with deep green eyes. It watched them both as they walked away, then padded along the wall and disappeared.

'God, I don't think I'll ever get completely used to this place,' said Galbraith after heaving a sigh of relief. 'Can we find somewhere to eat now? I'm starving.'

'Yeah alright, I could do with getting out of this rain for a bit.'

'Waverley Cafe?'

'Now it really is like the old days,' MacLellan forced a smile then followed his partner as they trudged north along the muddy roads back towards New Town.

The splashing roar of traffic hit MacLellan like a crashing wave as they reached Princes Street. He found to his surprise that a part of him already missed the peace of the Old Town night. Flickering electric street lights cast their orange glow onto the road and the pavement, helped by the lights from the shop windows which shone out even while they were closed.

Waverley Cafe was the only place on the border with Old Town that stayed open most of the night. As they ducked inside MacLellan blinked at the glare of the fluorescent neon lights, hanging up his hat and coat at the door, then following Galbraith to a table by the window.

'Two coffees and two bacon baps please,' Galbraith called to the middle-aged woman behind the counter. She nodded at him then disappeared into the kitchen. 'So, not much to go on so far eh. What's our next move?'

MacLellan sat back in his chair, looking himself over and coming to the conclusion that there was now no part of him that was still dry.

'I guess we head back to Greyfriars and knock on some doors,' he said as he wrung his tie out onto the floor. 'Somebody else must have seen something, though I doubt anyone will want to talk to us about it.'

The waitress reappeared from the kitchen with a tray. She placed it on their table with a tired smile.

'Let me know if you want anything else boys.'

They smiled back at her then turned their attention to the coffee. Galbraith had finished his first cup and was halfway through his bap before he spoke again.

'Do you think we'll catch her then?'

'I don't know,' MacLellan replied, looking him squarely in the eye for a few seconds before continuing. 'A part of me really hopes we don't.'

Galbraith frowned back at him over the edge of his newly-filled coffee mug but said nothing.

'Do you actually know what will happen to her if we do catch her?'

'Not really,' Galbraith replied. 'I mean I've heard the rumours same as everyone, but it's not my business. I just do my job and go home at the end of the day, I'm happy with that.'

'Ah, the joys of ignorance,' MacLellan shook his head. 'I *do* know. That's why I left, when it went too far. You see, the lucky ones are the ones you have heard about. Taken from their parents, stamped with a barcode, then rehomed away from the Old Town so they can't use their magic. But the ones the Ministry deem too powerful, well, they are taken away to a "facility" where surgeons remove the section of their brains responsible for their magic. After that they are returned to their parents, though they are usually capable of little more than staring and drooling.'

Galbraith shifted awkwardly and swallowed his mouthful of bacon and bread. MacLellan couldn't tell from the blank look on his face how much he really cared.

'Is that really all true?' Galbraith said at last.

'I'm afraid so partner,' MacLellan replied, fishing into his inside pocket for his money clip then placing a tenner on the table. 'Come on, let's bang on some doors. This night has to end sometime, and then I can go home.'

They threw their coats and hats back on and headed out into the rain again, walking back along Princes Street. Before they even reached the bridge over the railway leading back to the Old Town MacLellan heard footsteps behind them. Before he could stop himself he glanced over his shoulder and saw a short, thin man in a raincoat a little way behind them.

'Follow me,' he said to Galbraith as he quickly scanned the road for traffic. 'I want to check something.'

With that he took Galbraith by the arm and jogged across the street heading into New Town.

'What's up?' Galbraith asked as they reached the pavement on the other side and took the first road leading off the main street.

'Don't look but I think we're being followed. Just stay with me and be ready.'

MacLellan managed a quick glance back to make sure the man was still behind them, though a little more distant now, then ducked into a narrow, unlit lane. Galbraith tucked himself into a dark corner as MacLellan walked slowly on. Sure enough the man followed them into the lane, moving quickly to try and keep up. Galbraith stepped out from the shadows behind him, gripping his arms like a vice and pushing him up against the wall to one side of the lane.

'You were right Mac,' Galbraith called over as MacLellan came jogging back. 'Want me to break some fingers?'

'Let's hear what he has to say first,' MacLellan said looking the man over. It wasn't anybody he recognized.

'MacLellan,' the man gasped. 'I've been looking for you.'

'Well, now you've found me, so what do you want? And you'd better spit it out quickly, my friend here is pretty anxious to break something.'

'No, please, I'm here to help,' he glanced nervously back down the lane towards the road. 'I know the girl you are hunting tonight, but it's a trick, you're looking in the wrong place.'

MacLellan nodded at Galbraith and he released his grip on the man.

'So tell us what you know,' said MacLellan.

'No, there's no time!' the man replied. 'Come with me now, please!'

MacLellan searched the man's face but could find only desperation. This felt more like walking into a trap than anything ever had before, but something in the man's expression made him relent.

'Okay then, lead the way, but you go first, and remember how happy my friend here would be to break every bone in your body.'

The man nodded then broke into an awkward trot to the entrance of the lane, stopping only to urge them to hurry. MacLellan and Galbraith followed on behind.

'Do you trust him?' Galbraith asked as they turned north, moving further into New Town.

'Like hell,' MacLellan replied. 'But we don't have much else to go on so let's see where this leads.'

The man stopped at a pedestrian crossing, waiting impatiently for the lights to change. MacLellan and Galbraith hung back keeping a close watch on everyone they saw. The lights turned to red and the beeping of the green man beckoned them across the road. The man strode out and didn't even see the car lurching out of the queue of traffic with a screech of tires. MacLellan froze as the car roared past sending the man rolling into the air then landing with a crunch on the hard tarmac. The car was out of sight before MacLellan could even reach the broken body.

'Call an ambulance,' he shouted back to Galbraith. 'And get the damned police down here!'

He crouched over the man as a cluster of bystanders began to gather around. He was still breathing, but only just. He managed to reach up and grip MacLellan's lapel.

'Go...go home,' he managed to gasp out before his eyes glazed and his breath stopped.

MacLellan stared down into the man's lifeless eyes before closing them softly with the palm of his hand. Before the bystanders got too close he quickly patted down the man's coat and pulled out his wallet. He rifled through it as he walked back to Galbraith. There were a few notes and coins but, other than that, only a single piece of paper with an Old Town address on it.

'Cops and paramedics are on their way,' Galbraith said. 'Though I'm guessing both are too late?'

'Seems that way,' MacLellan replied.

'Did he say anything?'

'He told me to go home.' MacLellan said, holding up the piece of paper.

'Not the first time we've been told that tonight,' Galbraith laughed. 'What's that?'

'A lead,' MacLellan replied. 'We're heading back into Old Town.'

It didn't take them long to find the address in a little alley just off High Street, and they slipped through the shadows towards it. The nearest gas lamp was on the road around the corner and they could move here without being seen. There were no lights on in the house, and a quiet knock on the door received no reply. MacLellan took off his hat, made a fist inside it, then tapped hard on the glass window of the door. The smash and tinkling of glass was lost in the wind and the rain but still the two men listened hard for any movement inside. They heard nothing so MacLellan reached inside and unlocked the door.

The house was small, just a single room with a small bathroom attached. They crept inside and MacLellan drew the curtains. Galbraith pulled out a couple of chemical torches and shook them, handing one to MacLellan. They produced a soft glow, nowhere near as bright as an actual torch, but they were better than nothing, and even batteries wouldn't work this deep in Old Town.

They worked slowly around the room in opposite directions. It didn't look to MacLellan like the kind of place the man had lived. There was no bed, just a heap of blankets; no wardrobe either. A saucer of milk sat in the corner of the room but a quick sniff revealed it had been sitting there a while. A desk in the corner was strewn with colouring pencils and crayons. She was here then, MacLellan suddenly felt sure of it. Were they trying to keep her hidden? Where were her parents? Killed by the Ministry he supposed. The summoning spell in the graveyard made ominous sense then. He looked through some of the drawings on the desk, then he picked one up and looked closely. A girl, a cat, and a white bird. A dove? His face creased into a soft smile as his brain made the connection. Mr. Dubh! Did that little old man take a beating from Ministry interrogators without saying a word? But why would he phone in the disturbance? Maybe it would make it look like he was assisting, then he could divert attention away from her. It was possible. If that was the case then he had seriously underestimated the Ministry's level of suspicion and had paid for it with some nasty bruises. He guessed the poor man lying dead on the road had been trying to get him away from Old Town so they could move her somewhere safe. He glanced over at Galbraith, then carefully folded the picture and placed it in his coat pocket.

'You reckon she was here then?' Galbraith asked from the other side of the room.

'Yeah I do.' MacLellan replied.

'Not anymore though,' said Galbraith after fishing around in the small bin then handing two ticket receipts to MacLellan. They were for the afternoon steam train today, bound for London. 'Seems like she's long gone. Left Edinburgh at least, probably in London by now. Wouldn't you be if you were being hunted by the Ministry?'

'I guess so,' said MacLellan, but he doubted that was the case. It wasn't easy for a user to voluntarily sever themselves from magic. He patted his pocket carefully. If he had to guess, he would say that she was hidden in Mr. Dubh's house. He doubted that would be the end of it, but at least she was safe for now. 'Well then, we should go and make our report.'

Leaving the abandoned house they strode north together, back towards the station and New Town. The rain had eased a little now, though it no longer mattered to MacLellan as he was wet through, and he allowed himself a smile knowing he had done what was asked of him but had managed to let the girl remain free. They were heading for the Ministry but had barely made it back into New Town when a payphone began to ring as they approached it.

'I hate how they do that,' Galbraith said as he went over to answer it.

MacLellan leaned against the phone box and waited for him to finish. A few minutes later Galbraith emerged and smiled.

'That was the Head again,' he said. 'She says you can consider the favour fulfilled. Feel free to go home.'

He wasn't quite sure why, but MacLellan suddenly felt sick. The thought of the Head of the Ministry telling him to go home. She never said anything without meaning, and there was something sinister behind this he felt certain. The man had told him to go home too, but he hadn't even listened. So had Eagna.

'Are you okay Mac?' Galbraith asked. 'You don't look so good.'

'Shit!' MacLellan said under his breath. 'I've got to get home.'

He turned and ran, faster than he had run in years, flat feet pounding along the pavements as he wound his way through the empty night streets, up into the cheap district of New Town, the only place he'd been able to afford a house after leaving the Ministry. His lungs burned and his heart pounded inside his chest but he kept on going, even though he knew really that it was in vain.

He saw something was wrong even before he reached his front door. It still hung slightly open and he burst through to find his home had been ransacked. Everything had been turned over or smashed or strewn over the floor. He raced into the bedrooms but they were empty.

'Evelyn? Cora?' he shouted into the confusion that used to be his home, but he knew there would be no answer. He buried his face in his hands as he staggered to the kitchen and then looked up at the table, the only thing still in its usual position. He walked over to it. Sitting on top was his old badge and gun along with a note, printed on Ministry-headed paper.

"An eye for an eye; a girl for a girl. Your wife and daughter are quite safe. They will be returned to you when you hand over the location of the user. We shall expect to see you back in work from Monday. Welcome back MacLellan. Yours, The Head of Ministry Affairs."

Galbraith arrived, red-faced and panting, and found MacLellan still standing in the kitchen. He took one look at the badge on the table and the state of the house and knew what it meant.

'Damn, I'm sorry Mac,' he said between gasps. 'I guess nobody ever really escapes the Ministry. What are you going to do now?'

'Not much choice,' said MacLellan with a sigh. 'I'm okay though, you get yourself home. I guess I will be seeing you again after all.'

Galbraith nodded and picked his way back out through the wreckage which had been MacLellan's perfect life. MacLellan took up his gun and badge and slipped them into his coat pocket alongside the drawing he had hoped to keep secret. He wondered how they knew, but then, this was the Ministry after all. He walked slowly to the front door, desperately racking his brains for a way out of this and there, at the end of the driveway sat a little black cat with deep green eyes. MacLellan walked over to it, reaching down to stroke its head.

'I really hope you are what I think you are,' he said softly, feeling a little foolish. 'But if you are, tell Mr. Dubh to take your mistress and get out. I'll stall them as long as I can. They should leave Edinburgh, at least for a while, I'm sorry.'

The cat looked up at him, blinking its eyes at him slowly then turned and disappeared at a run. MacLellan watched it go then set off for Calton Hill and the Ministry to deliver his report.

Bruises
Dominique Goodall
Fourth Place

No more bruises, no more lies. No more fake stories of falling down the stairs, of being clumsy. We were free now.

And yet…

Every movement makes me flinch. I expect to hear the creaking of the floorboard, a grunt of anger. The meaty smack of a fist. It didn't matter that he was *gone* now. We still walked about on tiptoes, breathlessly whispering our conversations during the times when he'd be out. Days had passed, the police had gone… but he still haunted our every breath.

The good times had been few and far between. Times when he'd been my dad, and not the bad-tempered monster who had literally used his belt across my legs for the smallest, often imagined, infraction of his *'rules'*. And still, I hadn't been the one to deal with the worst of it. That was my mother. Infinitely strong yet cowed and as soft-spoken as ever.

Even when bruises had flowered on her pale skin, she hadn't made a sound. It had been afterwards, just the the lightest sound of sobbing whenever the beating was done. The fact that we were free now hadn't sunken in. She didn't want to antagonise him, even though he was gone, and he wasn't coming back. The police had promised me that. They had taken great pains to mention that he was gone for good. That he wouldn't hurt us again.

That fact was all I had to go on, without guilt hitting me. My mother had scrubbed the bloodstains out of the worn, discoloured carpet. The amount of times I'd seen her doing it before, perched on her knees, despite bruises and grazes, often with one eye swollen shut, was uncountable.

The bowl of bleachy water, the scarred, prominent knuckles, reddened by hard use and hot water – they were all familiar to me. I hated that I could see such things as usual, but the ring of bruises around her throat, blacker towards her narrow chin… they made everything worth it, everything I'd done… If I had to choose between my parents, she would win, every time.

As I laid in bed, I brought my knees up to my chest, clutching at them tightly, listening as my mother cried. I didn't know if it was in relief – or if she feared for me. After all, my mother wouldn't ever fear me, that was one thing I knew. If she flinched a little when she saw me, if she couldn't meet my eyes – it was because she was hiding her relief that I had been stronger than her.

I had done what she couldn't do.

Strange though. No matter how many times I showered and soaked myself,in the first two days, I still felt dirty. Like I was like *he* was. I'd scrubbed my hands until I'd bled, until my sobs were so loud the bathroom echoed with them.

And still, she didn't come to help me. What had I done? How could I make things better? There were so many hours spent curled into a corner of my bedroom. All I could do was hope his heavy footsteps didn't hit the floor, that my door didn't creak open… that he didn't yell at me.

I hadn't done anything to deserve what he had done to me. To my mother. We were better off without him. Why couldn't she see it? Every time he'd hit her, every time he beat me until I couldn't move, she'd held me afterward and promised me it was the *very last time,* and that *she'd look after me better next time.*

She'd failed. I'd had to get rid of him for us. I could ignore the fear in her worn-out eyes. She'd feel better in a week, in a month. He wasn't coming back, and nothing could be done about that. And yet, I'd not feel better until I had her arms around me.

Creeping out of bed, after the third night of not being able to sleep, I knocked on her door. I'd not heard her cry tonight, so she could be asleep. Or she was like me, too scared to move, too paranoid in case he came back.

"Mum?" I opened the door slightly, poking my head in the door. I could hear her breathing speed up, even as she stayed almost resolutely still. "Mum? Are you awake?" I kept my voice low, not wanting to startle her. She was so cold toward me, and I had no idea why.

"Go back to bed, Leah. You need to sleep." She didn't seem like my mum. She was held away from me. I didn't know what I'd done wrong. Tears slid down my face, hot and unchecked, as I stayed at her door, staring at her shadowed shape in the large, mostly empty bed.

"Go to bed already, will you?! I don't need you staring at me with *his* eyes!" Her hoarse voice grew in volume as she shouted at me, and I slammed her door.

I didn't need her to hear me crying as I ran back to my room.That was why she couldn't look at me, why old bruises and broken bones were preferable to spending time with me. I was the reason why she spent hours scrubbing a house she'd kept clean for fear of him hurting her, hurting me. I curled up in bed, wrapping my arms around my legs and ignoring the sharp pains of bruises, old and new, pressured by the touch.

I couldn't even let myself cry. My throat had closed up, and my stomach ached. I'd done everything I could to help her, to help us – and the hate in her voice made me feel as though it hadn't been necessary.

Why was there blood on my hands, when I'd been protecting her? I couldn't puzzle it out, not even when I couldn't fall asleep, still flinching whenever I heard a movement – but this time, it was my mother that scared me, not the haunting spectre of my now-dead father.

I couldn't help but wish I still had his metal baseball bat, to keep myself safe. But the police had taken it as evidence.

What more evidence did they need than the bruises on our skin, and our shattered lives?

Would she ever look at me again, and not just see him?

Madame Dolce
KM Shapiro
Fifth Place

  Carrie shook her head as she looked at the invitation in her hand, the same one she had received in the mail twice in the past three weeks, and had declined to respond to.
  "Madame Dolce insists, m'lady," said the driver of the Town Car, who Carrie assumed was some sort of butler, given the fanfare that surrounded this mysterious affair.
  "That's great and all, but I have no idea who Madame Dolce is or why she would invite me to her dinner party," Carrie withheld her frustration for the time being. "I have a family that needs to be taken care of. I can't just abandon them on a whim."
  "M'lady, you've had plenty of time to consider the invitation. I would hardly call that a whim." He held the door open and, for the third time since he arrived, motioned for her to get in.
  "Stop calling me that. And I didn't reply for a reason. Usually people take that as a 'no' and go about their lives," Carrie said as she shuffled her feet to go back inside.
  "Madame Dolce doesn't take no for an answer," replied the Butler.
  "Then Madame Dolce needs to grow up. Temper tantrums are not attractive in adults," Carrie said. She turned her back on the butler and walked towards her front door.
  "There is some incentive, m'la-.. er, Mrs. Adams," said the butler, a hopeful note in his voice. Or maybe that was desperation. Carrie couldn't tell. "A monetary one, if you will." Carrie stopped walking and turned her head.
  "What makes you think I can be bought?" she asked with a hint of anger, although she was a little flattered. Nothing like this had ever happened to her before. Of course, she wasn't going to let the butler see that and give him a reason to continue pursuing the matter.
  "It's no secret your family is struggling. Your husband lost his job six months ago and you're barely keeping your head above water."
  "Actually, it is a secret since we haven't told anyone except a few close friends. How the hell did you know that?" The

conversation had just gone from annoying to suspicious, and Carrie was ready to bolt.

"Madame Dolce has eyes everywhere, m'lady," he said with a smile. Carrie ground her teeth at the formality and noted the eeriness of his expression.

"So she spies on people. Yeah, that's great incentive," she said. Her stomach churned, suggesting she go back inside, but she had to admit the temptation of having a permanent positive balance in her bank account was outweighing the risks, whatever they were.

"Not spying. Vetting, I suppose," he said. "She is very particular about who she invites into her home."

"Why does she want to pay a perfect stranger to have dinner with her? This doesn't add up." Was she actually considering this? No, it was ridiculous.

"Madame Dolce does not give explanations, m'lady. She gives orders. And my orders are to bring you and the other guests to the dinner party, no questions asked."

"Well, I have a lot of questions, and if she can give demands, then so can I," Carrie said boldly. She didn't know to what extent this Madame Dolce would go to get what she wanted, and perhaps Carrie should have been more wary of whatever consequences would arise should she refuse to submit to this butler and the woman giving him orders, but for the time being, she was standing her ground. It didn't register initially that the butler said others were invited, though that may not have swayed her decision one way or the other.

"It is a substantial amount of money, Mrs. Adams. I would think about that before declining her invitation a third time." He gestured to the open door of the Town Car and Carrie hesitated. Her mind raced with risks and benefits, weighing an invitation to a stranger's house against struggling to make ends meet. She had no way to verify what this butler was saying was true, but what did she have to lose? It would only be a matter of time before she lost her house, her car, her financial freedom. She sighed as she looked at her house, the one she and her husband had turned into a home for themselves and their three children, the one she knew she could never say goodbye to without an exorbitant amount of tears.

"I... okay... I'll go," Carrie muttered with trepidation. "Just let me tell my husband." The butler nodded as he glanced at his pocket watch. She hurried inside to give the news to her husband, leaving out a few key details that he would have used to persuade her not to go, like the offer of money and the stranger trying to drive her to a place she had never been before. That done, she returned to the Town Car a few minutes later, ready to be taken to Madame Dolce.

    The Town Car pulled into a large, half-circle driveway. Carrie stepped out of the car and spent a few moments staring at the Victorian mansion. The large bay windows, complete with decorative stained glass, gave her a glimpse into a formal sitting room filled with a variety of antique furniture, but no people. The towers lit up the night sky, drowning out the stars. She had no doubt this woman was rich given everything that had happened so far, but being in the presence of the monstrosity was haunting, and reminded her that she really had no idea what was going on here.

    "This way, please," the butler said. He guided Carrie onto the wrap-around porch that led to the front door and into the foyer, where four guests were waiting. A large, hand-painted portrait of an elderly woman hung on the wall, and Carrie assumed it was of Madame Dolce. "Dinner will be served shortly. For now, please enjoy cocktails and hors d'oeuvres." Several people were walking around with trays filled with food and drinks, encouraging everyone to take something. There was an awful lot of food for just six people, but Carrie had a feeling Madame Dolce had a tendency to go overboard.

    "Are you a friend of Madame Dolce?" one of the other guests asked as he casually strolled up to Carrie.

    "No," she said awkwardly. "Are you?"

    "Nope. Never met the woman," he said. "Doesn't look like any of us have."

    "And yet you all still came here?" Carrie asked. She wondered if they, too, had been offered money in exchange for company.

    "I was told there would be some great food here," he replied. Food? He came here for food? "I own a booming restaurant. Well, I did, until my business partner ran off with my accountant and half the money. Madame Dolce promised connections with the top chefs in the industry, along with a generous donation. I just couldn't turn that down."

    "I see," said Carrie.

    "I'm Rob, by the way," he said and held out his hand with a smile. The sudden gesture caught her off-guard, but she regained her composure and shook his hand.

    "Carrie," she said as she shook his hand. Was it important who these other people were? And where was Madame Dolce?

"It's nice to meet you, Carrie," Rob said. The other three followed Rob's example and came over to introduce themselves. After little tidbits of conversation, Carrie came to the conclusion that no one really knew what they were doing there, only that some old lady desired company and was willing to bribe others who needed something just to get it.

"I told that man if Madame Dolce can keep my ex-husband in prison, I would attend a dinner party every night," said Jane, the only other female guest.

"He said she would help my sister get custody of her son," said Andre.

"She offered to pay my gambling debt. I didn't even hesitate," said Carl.

"Do you often divulge personal information to total strangers?" Carrie asked. She couldn't believe what she was hearing out of the others. "You just met us no less than an hour ago and you're telling us about your addiction."

"Odds are I'm never going to see you people again. What does it matter if I tell you or not?" Carl replied.

"Ahem, your attention please," said the butler who had picked up Carrie. "Madame Dolce sends her apologies, but she is going to be late. However, she insists you begin dinner without her. This way to the dining hall, please." The group looked at each other, then followed after the butler. He motioned to the multiple chairs seated around an antique table. Carrie hesitated, fearing she would break the chair if she sat down too hard. She knew nothing about antiques or if it was even appropriate to use them as furniture rather than as decoration.

One of the house workers, a short woman with her dark brown hair up in a bun that was covered by a lace doily, brought out a metal serving tray and sat it in the middle of the table, then lifted the lid. Laying on the bottom was a single note, with a swirly border, folded in half and standing upright. The five of them looked at the note, but none of them moved. The same worker who brought out the tray picked up the note and began to read.

"Welcome to my home. I do hope you are enjoying yourselves. Please eat and drink to your heart's desire. My sincerest apologies for being unable to join you for dinner. I look forward to speaking with you over dessert. Yours truly, Madame Dolce."

She replaced the letter on the tray and took the whole ensemble back through the double swinging doors she came from.

"Well that's a shame. Bring on the food!" said Rob.

"Wait," said Carrie. "Doesn't anyone else find it strange that she left a note saying she would be late?"

"Maybe she wrote that as a backup. You know, in case she actually would be late," said Jane. The double doors opened and copious amounts of food were brought to the table, much more than five or six people could eat in one setting.

"Now this is what I'm talking about," said Rob as he piled his plate high with food and immediately began to dig in, completely ignoring which fork to use first. Then again, did anyone really pay attention to that? "This is some gourmet stuff, here. Exactly the kind of food I'm looking to serve."

Carrie watched the door, anxiously waiting for someone to announce that Madame Dolce had arrived. She had had her doubts since the beginning about the validity of the butler's claims, but no one had asked her for anything in return other than to come to dinner. If this was a scam, someone was doing it wrong. It bothered her that no one else seemed concerned about Madame Dolce's absence. All of them had something important on the line, and she was the only one impatiently waiting for the exchange she was promised.

They finished dinner with no sign of Madame Dolce. Carrie could tell the others were getting antsy. Carl was occasionally glancing at the door, probably wondering the same thing she was. Jane had stopped eating after the third course and was checking her phone repeatedly, though for what reason, Carrie didn't know. Rob looked at his watch more times in one minute than Carrie had all day. Andre was the only one who actually asked members of the staff where Madame Dolce was.

"Who invites people to a dinner party and then never shows up?" Andre asked to no one in particular. "Are we really going to get the things she promised or was this just some game?" His agitated voice broke the uncomfortable silence, but he asked the question that was on everybody's minds.

"She will arrive as soon as she can, I can assure you," said the butler. For all they knew, he was lying through his teeth and she was deliberately avoiding the party.

"We've been here for over two hours and the only communication from her has been that damn note," said Carl. "A note, I might add, that she probably didn't even write herself."

"If you would please be patient, sir. Madame Dolce values both her time and yours. She is rarely ever late, and she did send her apologies," the butler said.

"Does that mean she'll get here before the party ends?" asked Rob.

"Considering what she promised each of us, it might be better if we didn't get upset that she isn't here," Jane said. "Our futures depend on us staying here until she says we can leave."

Carrie didn't want to admit Jane was right, but she was. Each of them had something on the line, some more life-altering than others. If they had all decided to leave, she would have been the first to get up and get the hell out of that mansion, but she would leave behind the opportunity to provide her family a comfortable life with no financial worries. She didn't exactly have the luxury of turning that down. So she, along with the others, waited around the table until dessert was served.

Most of them weren't even hungry anymore. The four course meal in addition to Madame Dolce's lack of an appearance had left a bitter taste in their mouth that wouldn't be disrupted by chocolate truffles and gourmet tiramisu. Upon the butler's insistence, they stuffed themselves full of the desserts placed in front of them. Rob miraculously found room to eat more, and spent the rest of the time at the table talking about his restaurant. Towards the end, another tray was brought out and placed in the middle of the table in the same fashion as before. The bun lady picked up the note and read a second time.

"I know my absence has startled some of you. I send my apologies a second time for being unable to attend dessert. You are in good hands with Gerard. Please ask of him whatever you need. A post-dinner salon is scheduled for which I hope to be present. Please enjoy some after dinner drinks until my arrival. Yours truly, Madame Dolce."

"Okay now this is getting ridiculous," said Andre. He pushed his plate away from him and stood to leave. "This whole thing is a hoax, isn't it?"

"Please calm down, sir. Madame Dolce will indeed be here as soon as she can," Gerard said in a hurried voice. As eager as Andre was to leave, he was eager for everyone to stay.

"Is she even real?" asked Carl.

"Of course she is!" replied the butler.

"I want to talk to her, then," Jane said. "If she's real, then you can call her up and put her on speaker phone and we can all calm down."

"Well, um..." Gerard fumbled over his words. "She cannot be reached at the moment." He lowered his eyes and stared at the floor, disgruntled at the position he had been put in by Madame Dolce.

"What does that mean, exactly?" asked Rob. "How has she been communicating with you then? Obviously she spoke to someone or else she wouldn't know we've been 'startled by her absence'."

"Madame Dolce has eyes everywhere, sir," said Gerard.

"You do realize that doesn't make us feel any better, right?" said Carrie. "In fact, I think it makes us feel worse. You're telling us she can't be reached, but she's been watching us this whole time? The gig is up. We're leaving."

"I'm staying here," Jane said. "I'll wait if that means I can have peace and quiet for the rest of my life." Jane's words calmed everyone down enough for them to leave the dinner table and navigate to the parlor.

"She's right. We have to think about what's at stake, here," said Carl. "If this Madame Dolce really is going to do what she promised, we have to wait."

"You're really banking on this being real, aren't you?" asked Carrie. The question was irrelevant. They all needed it in some way or another.

"You say that as if I have a choice," Carl replied. "It's either this, or my family loses everything. My wife will leave and take the kids. I'll have nowhere to go. I can't not trust this woman, whoever she is."

Carrie said nothing in response. It was true that Madame Dolce's gift would make her life better, there was no denying that. But her life was currently being controlled by someone she had never met, and her faith was dwindling.

Gerard ushered them the rest of the way into the salon, where drinks were already waiting for them. He sat them next to a curtained bay window in oversized chairs around a large, stone fireplace and encouraged them into conversation about anything other than Madame Dolce. That only lasted for so long, and soon the conversation again made its way back around to their mysterious host who had yet to show her face.

"Why is she doing this?" asked Rob. "Why pick five strangers to have dinner at her house, only for her to never show up, and then give us all something that will change our lives drastically?"

"Because she's old and wants company?" replied Andre. He took a swig of his drink and leaned back in the comfy leather chair.

"If she wanted company, she would be here with the company," said Jane as she, too, took a drink.

"Does it really matter what her agenda is?" asked Carl.

"You mean to tell me you're not the least bit curious?" asked Carrie. She poured herself another glass of scotch, determined to not leave the mansion sober if she could help it.

"Of course I am, but not finding out isn't going to change what I need from her," Carl said.

"What we need is to get out of here before that butler murders us," said Rob as he looked over his shoulder. The six-paneled double doors were closed, and everyone assumed Gerard was on the other side listening in. "I've seen these movies before. I know how this ends."

"Don't be ridiculous," said Carrie.

"Think about it," said Rob. "She lured us here with fake promises and delicious food. Gerard has kept us here, convincing us however he can to not leave. We're either slaves or roadkill."

"You're such a delight to talk to. Did you know that?" said Jane. She downed her third drink and poured herself another. She and Carrie were standing next to the fireplace admiring the books in Madame Dolce's collection. Some of them were original first editions worth tens of thousands of dollars. Carrie wasn't an avid reader, but even she knew she would never see some of those books again after leaving the mansion.

The door opened and the bun lady walked in with an identical silver tray.

"You're joking, right?" asked Andre. "She still isn't here?"

She lifted the lid and began to read a third note.

"I do hope you have all enjoyed yourselves. It has truly been a delight sharing dinner with you, despite my absence. The favors I promised you are already in progress, and I am sure your families will reap the benefits."

In the middle of the sentence, Gerard and several other staff members entered the salon.

"Do realize that nothing comes without a price. I would like to introduce you to the others I have helped in the past."

"I told you this was going to end badly!" said Rob, who backed into a corner to escape the staff.

"Will you stop doing that?" asked Carrie, who was holding onto Jane as if that would save them from what was about to happen.

"Doing what?" asked Rob.

"Being insufferable!" yelled Carrie. Carl and Andre had joined Rob in the corner, desperately searching for a bookshelf door or a statue that also served as a switch for a hidden passage, but finding the only entrance blocked by the staff.

"Each one of them was given a favor by me. In return, they pledged dinner. And servitude. Please take this time to get to know your fellow employees. They each serve at my pleasure, as will you."

"I don't know about you, but this doesn't feel very pleasurable!" screamed Andre.

" I wouldn't upset them if I were you. Don't you remember what the butler said? She has eyes everywhere," said Jane, her voice shaking. Carrie watched the staff close in on them, and her only thoughts were of her husband and children, the very reasons she had for doing this in the first place. Would it be better for them if she submitted and let them have the life they deserved? Would they be okay? A husband without his wife, children without their mother… would they be okay without her? They would adjust. And maybe one day there would be a chance to see them again.

"I welcome you into my home. Do not dawdle, for we have another dinner party to plan. Yours truly, Madame Dolce."

Event 2

REMEMBER WHEN: History comes to life when coupled with fictional characters and a little research. For this Event, choose from the provided list of historic events, create your own characters, and write what happens on this day in history.
Core Concept: cohesion, research

This Too Will Pass
LS Fellows
First Place

Juan Medina had lived his whole life in Luarca where white houses formed an S-shaped cove sitting between sheer cliffs. Since Spring 1918, his town - The White Town, as it was known locally - had lost over four hundred inhabitants.

'Four hundred, Juan, and there seems to be no end in sight,' said fellow doctor Alberto Guardado as they trudged home after another day of mounting deaths and little else.

'So much for the three-day fever,' said Juan as they passed the historic quarter of Luarca and crossed the small river that divided the town in two. 'Today, I have seen patients complaining of sore throats and headaches in the morning, only for their malady to develop into the most vicious type of pneumonia I've ever seen by the evening. Lately I've seen far too many cases of people - friends, colleagues and even entire families - falling prey to this beast of a disease.' He stood on the narrow bridge that would take him home and looked out to sea, his shoulders sagging and dark hair sinking beneath his collar as he leaned on the grey-white wall. The lighthouse offered the only light as dusk crept in, cloaking the chapel and the cemetery in the ephemeral gloom that had become commonplace with summer a distant memory. Not even the sea breezes could banish the whiff of death from the air.

'Indeed, I fear we have not seen the end of this. And your poor wife must be frantic at the thought of bringing a new life into this chaos.' Dr Guardado patted Juan on the back, the intention to offer support but the motion instead causing Juan to slump further forward and bump his weary chest against the centuries-old white stone, hand-cut from the cliffs by pickaxe-bearing stonemasons.

'I can't believe only one year ago my wife and I were honeymooning in Lastres, watching the glorious sunsets from San Roque embrace both the ocean and the mountains in the distance. I joked that her smile was as stunning as those sunsets.'

'The sun, surely?'

'That's what Reyes said, but our Spanish sun can be too harsh at times whereas sunsets represent beauty and tranquillity.'

'You should have been a poet, my friend.'

'She says that, too. It was so peaceful, Alberto… and now we are to be parents. What should be such a delightful experience fills me with dread.' Juan stretched out his neck, massaging it with his fingers. 'All this disease scares me. My wife, on the other hand, is the epitome of calm; every day her serenity amazes me. "To worry would harm the baby. Besides your mother worries enough for all of us", is all she says with a smile. Always with a sunset smile, you know.' A soft chuckle slipped from his lips as he recalled the twinkle in his wife's eyes, so distinct from the mania with which his mamá greeted him daily.

'It can't last forever, Juan.'

'We'll run out of patients if it doesn't end soon.' Juan pushed himself off the wall and resumed his homeward journey.

'Ah, the gallows humour of the medical profession,' Alberto said, 'is that all we have left?' His voice cracked as they reached the end of the bridge.

'It feels like it.' Juan paused, his limbs too heavy to move, his thoughts too sombre to voice. 'See you tomorrow then. Sleep well, my friend. We have yet more challenges ahead.'

He waved at the agreeing Alberto before each set off in opposite directions.

Juan approached the family home. The former fisherman's cottage as built by his grandfather was now a sprawling three-storey, four-bedroomed house with extensions on extensions.

"If you can't build out, build up" had been his grandfather's saying, a mantra reinforced by his wife, Juan's abuelita, reluctant for her sons to leave home. Juan's father, despite turning his back on the fishing industry, had inherited the building twenty years ago when his papá and two brothers were sacrificed to the sea during a freak storm. Juan's grandmother had lived with them until her own demise while he was away studying medicine in Barcelona, following in his papá's footsteps.

The curtain twitched as he walked up the gravel path. His mamá, nervous at the best of times, now wore paranoia as an overcoat and practised gossip as her religion. She tapped the window once, then again, the rat-a-tat-tats a warning to him that frenzy awaited.

'I'll be in shortly, Mamá. After I've changed my clothes.' He took the side path to the utility room at the back of the house where he undressed and slipped on a clean shirt, socks, and freshly laundered trousers, hurried on by the chill of the bare floor and stone walls. This routine, a recent development to avoid carrying germs into the home, gave him thinking time.

What had happened now, to warrant his mother's current fixation?

He placed his worn clothes into the rattan basket, closed the lid and slid his socked feet into an old pair of his father's fur-lined moccasins.

Look at you, Juan Medina! Not yet thirty and already in slippers.

He had no time to ponder his predicament; his mother was at the back door, the key turned in the lock - another necessity to keep out uninvited and unclean visitors.

'Juan, son, come inside quickly.'

Barely had he crossed the threshold than she presented him with the latest *Boletín Oficial* from the authorities.

'Look! They have cancelled the Fiesta de San Ramón because of this awful disease. Cancelled it! For the first time, well, since time began. What next? That we should become prisoners in our own homes?'

Juan struggled to suppress his laughter. Did she not see the absurdity of her comment? She hadn't left the house in weeks other than to tend to the garden and pick vegetables.

'It's for the best, Mamá. All across the country they have closed schools, markets, and concert halls in an attempt to prevent the spread of this disease. It was inevitable they would call a stop to the parades eventually. Large crowds anywhere will not halt this disease.'

She huffed and turned to stir the pots atop her stove.

'You don't need to tell me about the markets. There is nothing to sell. There is nobody left to pick fruit, let alone take it to market. Had it not been for the wisdom of your grandmother to cultivate the herb garden and grow enough vegetables to sustain her family, then you'd be …' she waved a spoon at him, tomato juice dripping from it, '… well you'd be starving as well as condescending. Your father reads the newspaper. He tells me what's going on. But never, never did I think it would come to Luarca. Not like this.' Her face, shiny from perspiration, reddened further as she leaned over the bubbling pot. 'It's an omen, I tell you. An omen.'

'Sorry, Mamá. I didn't mean to suggest you were ill-informed.' He dipped over the pot, sniffing in the delicious aroma of tomatoes and fresh basil. 'Mmm, smells wonderful, as always.' He kissed her brow, knowing a loving smile and forgiveness were not far away. His mother might hold a grudge with the authorities, but for her children she had nothing but love, albeit often coated in impatience.

'I'll just pop up to see Reyes. We'll join you for supper in—'

'Ten minutes and not a second longer.' She continued stirring, holding back the forgiving smile he'd expected.

He raced up the stairs like a whippet chasing a rabbit, hearing the clinking of cutlery behind him. He reached the door and tapped before entering.

Reyes sat in a faded blue armchair, her feet resting on a matching stool. The scent of lavender stung Juan's nostrils.

'Evening, cariño. You're late today. How's it been?' The soft smile she wore upon his arrival paled as frown lines puckered her forehead. She put down her embroidery and rose to embrace him.

'You look lovely, as usual,' he whispered. 'How do you stay so calm when my mother does her headless chicken impression downstairs?'

Her laughter tinkled, like a babbling brook in a cave of darkness.

'There's one advantage to being over eight-months pregnant. She makes me rest, and won't allow me to run up and down the stairs like my "loco" husband.'

'She called me that?'

'And more, but I swore an oath of silence. Seriously, Juan, I keep telling your mother I'm not ill, but she's so old-fashioned.'

'I'll remember you said that when the baby is born. I have a feeling mother will be your best friend then.' He winked, and squeezed her tightly. 'She forgets you're a trained doctor, too. That you might know better than the old wives' tales. Such a thing was not possible in her time.'

Reyes flushed, her chin dipping a little.

'She doesn't forget a thing, Juan. In fact, she never ceases to remind me how fortunate I've been. I'm certain your mother believes my family's wealth bought me my place alongside you at the university; that it was nothing to do with a change in the law allowing women to finally study medicine. Yes, yes, I know,' she dismissed his wide-eyed glare with a flutter of the hand, 'women of your mother's generation had it much harder, but can she not see things have changed? In her words, I should count my blessings for my good luck. Luck, I ask you, luck!'

'Hey, I was only just telling Alberto how calm you are, despite all this death and disease around us. Look at you now.'

'You're right, it seems silly that only your mother can raise my blood pressure given our current circumstances. Forgive my nonsense. Shall we go to supper? I promise I'll be a dutiful wife.' She giggled.

'That I cannot wait to see. In my mother's defence, she did lose two daughters in childbirth, and with Raúl off fighting in France, despite her screaming "it's not our war" at him until the day he left, she's guarding her nest.'

'I know, my love. I'll be sure to mind my lucky manners in her presence.'

'You are incorrigible, my dear Reyes, but we should go down now, Mamá said ten minutes …'

She hooked her arm in his and they descended the stairs, purposely treading carefully so as not to incur Mamá's wrath.

After supper, Mamá gathered up the plates to wash up. For once Reyes's offer to help was accepted and she jumped to her feet, open-mouthed, and followed her mother-in-law into the kitchen.

'Slow down, Reyes. There's no rush,' said Mamá as she put down the dirty plates and shut the door.

Juan's gaze bounced from the closed kitchen door to his father, whose dark eyes narrowed on producing a letter from his pocket.

'From Raúl?'

'Yes, but your mother hasn't seen it yet. Oh, he's fine,' he said in response to Juan's fleeting look of terror. 'You recall, back in May, when the ABC periodical first mentioned this fever could be a pandemic?'

Juan bowed his head, having been shown the newspaper headline during a meeting of all medical staff at the hospital.

'They are calling it "Spanish Flu", mainly because our country has been the only one brave enough to advise its citizens of the widespread nature of the beast.'

'I heard it came from France,' said Juan. 'What does Raúl have to say?'

His father's lips twitched.

'Reading my mind again, son? Well, he confirms that line of thought. Says the disease has ravaged France, but they are too cowardly to tell their people.'

'They are at war, Papá. The French have enough to contend with.'

'But they should not be blaming it all on us when it is their promiscuous soldiers and the movement of troops across the land that has enabled its dissemination. Here in Spain, our King died of this fever, and those ... filthy scoundrels blame us. It's not on, Juan. Not at all.'

'The truth will out, Papá. It's more important to save the lives we can than to dole out blame. That gets us nowhere.'

'Well, yes, you're right. I'm angry, and ... don't tell your mother ... I've been asked to pitch in at the hospital. I don't want her to know the severity of it. No more than she can see with her own eyes, anyway. I've been censoring the reports in the paper to keep the worst from her. If she asks you for information, please spare her the harshness of it all. Imagine how she'd react if she knew everything. *¡Dios mío!*' He raised his hands to his head. 'It does not bear thinking about.'

'Okay. I'll warn Reyes, too. But what exactly does Mamá think we're talking about now?'

'Oh, she thinks we should talk to the council about the San Ramón fiestas. It's all she can think about.'

'Seriously? How are we supposed to fix that?'

'Don't you worry. I'll spin her a story. Just remember, keep the real facts to yourself. She hasn't been out of the house since the market closed, so she's relying on the bulletins and me for her updates. Shush, now, here she comes. I'll cheer her up with Raúl's letter... parts of it anyway.' He got up and went to the kitchen, squeezing past Reyes who joined Juan at the table, her head tilted and raised eyebrows hiding beneath her glossy fringe.

As she sat, her dark curls bounced off her shoulder. 'What was that all about?' she mouthed to him.

'Later,' he replied, putting a finger to his lips.

'Coffee, anyone?'

Mamá carried a tray of espresso glasses, her husband carried the coffee-pot and, unbeknownst to his wife, had tucked a bottle of cider under his arm.

'I think a little celebration is in order. Juan, fetch some more glasses. I have a letter from Raúl that I've saved until now.'

'Since when?' Mamá elbowed him and he winced.

'Uff! I picked it up this morning. Now, let's raise a glass and then I'll read it to you.' As was tradition, he held the bottle high up and took a glass from Juan, keeping it as low as possible. The time-old method of oxygenation caused bubbles to rise to a frothy top, and he rushed to fill the other glasses.

'To Raúl, may he be home soon.'

They repeated the toast in unison and drank the cider in one sip, quietly revelling in the sharp dryness of the region's finest beverage.

Taking his seat, Papá proceeded to read the letter, following the words with his finger. Juan grinned inwardly. His father was a cunning old fox, but a wise one nonetheless. Just imagine if Mamá could read the awful news for herself. Papá wasn't lying to her, really; he was saving her from the horrors of war and disease, and the rest of them from her intense paranoia.

That night, in bed, he told Reyes of his father's little trick. Initially outraged that he'd kept the news from her mother-in-law, she had to agree that his reasoning was solid.

Walking to work the next day, Juan passed council workers in anti-germ masks spraying the streets with chemicals. Queues of sick people blocked the entrance to the hospital and he had to fight his way through the crowds. Some no longer had the strength to stand and collapsed into the gutters. Inside, the staff were overwhelmed, doctors and nurses worked to breaking point, many themselves struggling to keep on their feet.

Juan saw his father amid a team of retired and student doctors brought in to offer relief.

What would his mother say, if only she knew?

He waved, catching the older man's attention. Papá zigzagged across the reception area, dodging patients whose skin bore a lavender hue and sidestepping others with mahogany spots over their cheekbones. For both groups, symptoms signalled a shortage of oxygen, and death was imminent. A young man, around Juan's age, fell to the floor between father and son, spluttering for air, his face blue as suffocation ended his life. The Medina men carried him across the foyer to a room bearing a handwritten sign: Morgue.

'He worked at the bank,' said Juan's father, 'I saw him only a few days prior and he struck me as being in fine health. His mother ran a stall at the market.' He whistled a breath. 'This is far worse than I imagined.'

'Papá, you might need to prepare mother for this. I don't think you can keep it from her now.'

'I'll talk to her tonight.' His face blanched. It was impossible to tell whether it was caused by the scenes in the hospital or by the thought of telling his wife the truth about the devastation the disease continued to cause.

'Reyes and I will be there. Hopefully we can soften the blow a little.' He patted his father's arm. 'I must go. I've been asked to do some home visits now the cavalry has arrived.'

'A few old men and fresh-behind-the-ears medical students!' His father scoffed. 'Hardly the cavalry, son.'

'You are to me, Papá, and to the rest of the staff. Now, go get a mask, and be sure to wash your hands between patients.'

'Yes, sir,' his father saluted him with a half-smile.

Juan traipsed across the village to the chapel to meet the local padre. The Church had been inundated with requests for funerals, which had been limited to fifteen minute services while bodies piled up in warehouses. Even the Church bells were prevented from tolling the dead to avoid alarming the population further, a factor that had played into his father's hands.

Cemetery keepers could not keep up with the demand for plots. Some families resorted to digging their own graves but there was a shortage of coffins.

He saw the padre in conversation with the local undertaker and a distressed woman almost on her knees.

'Please, please, let me put him in this sack, at least.' The woman held out a Hessian sack, normally used to hold flour. 'Please don't bury him in a mass grave, not without something to protect him—'

The padre spoke in a hushed breath, urging the undertaker to grant the woman's wishes, and once an agreement had been made he stepped around them to talk to Juan, who had kept a dignified distance from the sobbing woman.

'Doctor, good to see you. This promises to be a difficult day for you. I appreciate you taking the time. So many of my parishioners have been unable to seek medical help.' He shook Juan's hand and guided him towards a narrow path leading away from the chapel.

'We've had plenty of difficult days already, Padre,' said Juan, his sharp tone an instinctive response to the religious man's lofty attitude. 'The hospital has been overwhelmed and this disease shows no sign of abating.'

'We must put our faith in the Lord and trust he will deem us worthy to be saved. And to bring an end to all this, of course.'

Juan lowered his head and stood back, allowing the padre to lead the way. The horrors he'd witnessed in recent months had tarnished his faith, and he had neither the will nor the words to engage in any form of debate. He followed the padre in silence to the first house in a row of cottages, similar to his family's own but without the extensions.

'Señora Garcia has lost three children to the fever already. It's a miracle she has survived herself, but here she is, caring for her husband now.' Padre rapped on the door, and when it opened he stepped back to allow the doctor inside.

'After you,' he said, holding his hand to his mouth.

Juan flinched. A shiver tiptoed down his spine.

Trust in the Lord, indeed. You're a hypocrite, Padre!

The Garcia home was sparse, devoid of clutter. A washing line ran through the kitchen from which hung ribbons of seaweed and eucalyptus leaves drying over the stove.

'I keep the curtains closed,' said Señora Garcia, lighting up a candle and passing it to Juan. 'Seen far too many funeral processions coming up that hill. My husband thought one was coming for him, so —'

Juan gave a thin-lipped smile.

'It's fine. I can see well enough.'

He examined Señor Garcia and, finding no signs of infection in his lungs or an elevated temperature, asked what she had been treating him with.

'I boil up the seaweed and eucalyptus and get him to inhale the vapours several times a day. Then I make tea from the liquid once it's gone cold and add a drop of punch for sweetness, and to disguise the stink. *¡Madre mía!* Pardon the language, Padre, but it smells like the pits of hell.'

Juan forced himself to keep a straight face as the padre gave a condescending nod.

'We've not got much else, Doctor. The markets are closed, supplies are running out, but we can always find a spot of alcohol. Thank the Lord my own father used to bottle it himself once the summer fruit harvest was over.'

The padre squirmed again, which cheered Juan enormously.

'My grandma was the same, except with vegetables, not fruit," said Juan. 'Her parsnip liqueur was something special. Pretty sure we'd find a few bottles around the house if we looked. Is it just the two of you here now, Señora?' He'd spotted a pile of baby clothes piled high on a wooden kitchen chair.

'Yes, Doctor. My only surviving child Elena had a baby three months ago. She went to stay with her husband's family in Madrid because of all the sickness in the village. I fear it's as bad there now.' Her eyes brimmed with tears. 'The baby, a boy, came early you see. I thank God every day the boy survived. He was born here, in this very room. I delivered him myself. He was so tiny. I washed him, wrapped him in a blanket, and put him in a shoe-box behind that there stove until the doctor arrived. He truly is a miracle baby, Doctor. I pray they're safe now. We haven't heard from them for a while.' She dabbed at her eyes with the corner of her apron.

The padre shuffled his feet and then cleared his throat.

'Well, we had better move on, Doctor. I'm very pleased to see you doing so well, Señora Garcia. By the way, there will be a special Mass this weekend. I hope you can make it. It'll be a shorter version, given the fact I'm run off my feet with funerals.'

Juan gasped at the man's insensitivity and all but shoved him outside, saying goodbye to Señora Garcia and her husband over his shoulder.

'Could you be any more offensive, Padre?' he whispered after pulling the front door shut behind him.

The man shrugged and stared at Juan, oblivious to any transgression he might have made.

'Where next?' Juan snapped, and continued his visits without speaking to Padre other than to ask for directions and introductions.

After a twelve-hour stint, only three spent with the sanctimonious padre, Juan made his way home. Weariness stole the power from his limbs, and the idea of his mother going all shades of "loca" did nothing to spur him on.

She wasn't at the window this time. No curtain twitching. No rat-a-tat-tat on the glass. He headed for the utility room and changed clothes, and was heartened to hear the key turn in the lock of the back door.

His mother, flushed of face with beads of sweat on her brow and more towels than he knew they possessed over her arm, greeted him between short intakes of breath.

'Reyes … baby … coming.'

He sped around her and raced up the stairs to find his father wearing his anti-germ mask and standing at the foot of the bed, holding his arms out as though to catch a ball.

Reyes lay on their matrimonial bed, laughing so much the bed shook.

'What's going on? Papá, get out of here. Give her some privacy.'

'I am a doctor, son,' he said, though his words were somewhat muffled by the mask.

'Juan,' said Reyes, 'we're teasing you. See, there's a sheet over me. I'm completely decent, but aren't I lucky to have two doctors in attendance?'

Juan exhaled noisily.

'But the baby is coming?'

She nodded, smiling her sunset smile.

'Yes, soon. I'm glad you're here.'

'But, Mamá looked so flustered. I thought I'd missed the birth, and then I saw Papá standing there, poised to catch—'

'I'd have stepped in, if necessary, but I am more than happy to wait downstairs with your mother. You know, for that chat—'

'You're going to tell her now?'

'Tell her what?' said Mamá, piling more towels on Reyes's faded blue chair.

'Nothing, cariño. I'll be in the kitchen if you need me.'

'Your supper is plated. Yours too, Juan. Be off, and let the women do their work.'

Reyes nodded at him to go.

'It'll be hours yet. Eat. Take a nap. You've had a hard day by the looks of it.'

His father steered Juan back down the stairs and into the kitchen.

In the early hours of the morning of October 6th, Serena Medina Lopez arrived to the jubilant screams of her grandmother and the exhausted relief of her mother. Juan and his father, who had fallen asleep downstairs safe in the knowledge that Mamá had everything under control, climbed the staircase two steps at a time on hearing Mamá's shrieking.

Nursing the swaddled baby in her arms, Reyes sat up in bed, her brow dotted with perspiration that brought a glow to her face. Juan moved past his mother to perch on the side of the bed, stroking his baby's cheek and kissing his wife's head. Mamá had retreated to the doorway and now stood alongside her husband. All would suffer aching jaws from smiling so much, but at long last they had good reason to be positive. A new-born child, barely minutes old, had already enriched their lives and given them hope for the future.

EPILOGUE:

In spite of an increased number of deaths that month, cases reduced in November. Soon after, the Health Department was able to declare the epidemic in the province over, although it still raged across the world.

A few weeks later, Raúl returned from France to meet his niece, arriving at the chapel just as the daughter of Reyes and Juan was baptised. For the first time in many months, the bells rang in celebration of the most recent addition to the village.

The Wolf at the Door
Danielle Kiowski
Second Place

Henri trembled as he entered the strange wood of Gévaudan. He told himself that it was from the chill of the rain, but in truth the day was hot and the muggy rain offered little relief. The clouds cast no shade, but seemed to filter out the virtuous part of the sun's rays. What remained was a sickly yellow light that bore down on the rocky ground. The drops of rain that soaked the hem of Henri's skirts turned to a cloud of steam that sent sweat trickling down his back and legs. Mist blanketed the ground and wound between the trees, giving the forest an ominous air that was amplified by the nervous beating of Henri's own heart in the face of his mission. He was there for the hunt.

The company arrived in Saint-Flour after dusk a week before. The men nodded in their saddles after a long day of riding, but as they neared the town they perked up at the sound of revelry from a tavern on the outskirts, where civilization prodded the wilderness of the forest. Henri grinned at the prospect of a good meal and a flask of wine. They had ridden on through supper at the commander's insistence. He was itching for a chance at the reward, and the men weren't complaining. Some were nervous about what they might find, or what might find them, in the open field so close to their destination. Others, like Henri, were eager to get on with their work. Henri was amused by the fanciful reports coming out of the backwoods of Gévaudan.

"Nothing but a lot of noise over a wolf," Henri said to Jean-Paul, who chuckled, but touched a hand to the cross hanging at his throat and cast a glance into the woods surrounding the trail.

"Not you, too?" Henri chided his friend.

Jean-Paul coughed. "They say it has the eyes of the devil," he murmured, face reddening.

"This is France," Henri continued. "If we can survive the wilds of America, surely we have nothing to fear on the soil of our own country."

"The outcome of that was nothing to boast about," Jean-Paul

said.

"It was still an adventure, my friend. Why, I've seen you face down a bear twice the size of any wolf!" Henri laughed.

Jean-Paul did smile at that, though face paled at the memory and a shiver ran down his back. He sometimes woke up in a sweat, heart racing at the memory of the beast bearing down on him. When he slept he still saw its yellow eyes inches from his own and smelled the stench of salmon on its breath. His gun had saved him that day, but he was keenly aware of how thin the border was between man and the destruction of nature.

The tavern was attached to an inn where the men took a room for the night. Henri and Jean-Paul settled in for a drink and a hearty meal of stew with crusty bread.
Henri fixed his easy grin on the innkeeper, who narrowed his eyes in return.

"What do you know of this beast?" Henri asked.

The innkeeper grunted and plopped the stew down so that it sloshed on the rough-hewn table. He walked away and sat at a corner table with a pair of grizzled men that Henri guessed must be locals. They all hunched together and spoke in hushed tones, casting alternating glances at the newcomers like they were keeping a watch.

"Friendly town," Henri said.

"He lost a niece," said a voice behind him. He turned to see two women standing near their table. Jean-Paul stood and bowed politely to the ladies. Henri sat and stared, his mouth slightly agape. It might have seemed like a consequence of his realization of his inappropriate lightheartedness about the town's burden of tragedy, but in reality that realization had never made it to his mind. He was stunned by the girl who had spoken. She had already turned away, but in profile her face was even lovelier, with dark eyes set into pale skin and framed with glossy chestnut tresses.

"So you two are here to hunt the beast?" said the other woman, her voice breathless with awe. She slid into the bench next to Jean-Paul. "You must be so brave." She blinked several times at Jean-Paul, who choked on a mouthful of stew.

Her friend flashed her eyes upward in a brief roll and perched on the end of Henri's bench.

"My name is Yvette," the lady next to Jean-Paul cooed. "And my cousin is Marguerite."

Marguerite nodded curtly and looked out the window.

Yvette wanted to hear about their mission.

"No one has ever seen the beast and lived," she said. "How will you find it? Do you know how to kill it?" She leaned forward and dropped her voice to a whisper. "Aren't you afraid?"

Henri smiled at her questions. "Why, of course not," he said. "This beast is nothing compared to the terrors that we fought on the American frontier."

His reflexive charm overcame his befuddlement and he told her a rousing tale, much embellished, of Jean-Paul's showdown with the bear. In his telling, the bear bulked up to twice its real size. It accomplished this feat by becoming a verified man-eater, the terror of the French army until the brave Jean-Paul brought it down. Of course, he had help from his brave friend Henri, who shot the monster in the heart. It was so fierce that even this expert shot couldn't finish it, but it broke its concentration just long enough for Jean-Paul to get off a fatal shot before it could make him its next meal. Yvette stared up at Henri with eyes the size of wagon wheels, casting shy glances at the blushing Jean-Paul.

"Come on, Yvette," Marguerite said, after about an hour. "It's time we were going." Yvette stuck out her lip in a pout but stood to go. Henri and Jean-Paul stood. Yvette kissed Jean-Paul shyly on the cheek.

"For luck," she said.

Henri turned to Marguerite. "Can I see you again?"

She fixed her dark eyes on him and pressed her lips into a line.

"You should concentrate on the beast," she said.

"And then?" he ventured, but she was already walking away.

The company convened the next morning before dawn in front of the cathedral of Saint-Flour. The church tower loomed out of the dark mist, its black stones making it darker than the predawn sky. The commander wore an expression to match, his face a mask of solemnity.

Henri checked the load on his pistol, eager to begin the hunt. He looked around for the commander, but he had yet to appear. Probably supervising the armament, Henri thought.

Two junior men came into view from the direction of the tavern. They hauled a wagon behind them. It groaned under the weight of its cargo.

The commander strolled behind the cart.

"Fall in," he called. Henri frowned and looked at his pistol once more. He shrugged and tucked it into his holster, and he fell in next to Jean-Paul on the march into the forest.

The morning sun burned the mist away and beat down on the men. They stopped a short distance into the woods, and each man took an armful of meat.

They lined up in front of the commander, who held a jar and a wooden spoon. He worked down the line, sprinkling a scoop of powder onto each slab.

"Mind that you don't touch this," he called down the line. "It's a powerful toxin. Just three grains will poison a whole well." The commander had heard the local legends. He did not yet know what they were up against, but he would take no chances.

He dumped a spoonful of at least fifty grains on the slab of meat that Henri held, and Henri held his breath. With the poisoning complete, each man walked fifty paces from the cart and staked the slab of meat into the ground. Henri felt dizzy by the time he dropped the poisoned bait onto the grass, and he whirled away from it panting. The commander marked the locations on a map of the country and they moved on.

Before midday, the meat turned slimy and started to stink. Setting the traps became hot, disgusting work.

The following morning, the men walked from trap to trap. The first two were empty. As they neared the third, they could see a tuft of fur blowing in the breeze that swept over the rise. They rushed toward it, but once they grew close they could see that it was only a badger that had the misfortune to come across an easy meal. The men deflated and trudged on. Most of the traps were empty. The few that had caught anything had small scavengers. At each circle they collected the rotting meat from their stakes. In the first one they tried to bury them, but the digging was slow in the rocky ground, so the commander sent the two youngest men jogging back to town to collect the wagon. As it filled with meat the odor of rot settled into the company and a cloud of flies hung in the air around the cart. Any hope that the men had for a successful venture drained away with the heat and the drudgery of the day.

The last circle of traps was set in a small hollow. They were almost standing on top of it before they could see inside. The tallest of the company, a youth who had just enlisted a month before, let out a whoop. A giant wolf lay in the center of the hollow. Foam lined its muzzle where the poison had done its work. It was a huge animal, easily twice the size of a normal wolf. The men slapped each other on the back, but no one took a step toward the beast.

Henri laughed at the cowardice of his compatriots and stepped right up to the body. He crouched next to it and grinned back at the company.

"The great Beast of Gévaudan," he called. "A wolf after all."

The animal let out a wheeze and heaved upward, snapping its yellow fangs at Henri's throat. He shouted, taken aback that the thing was not dead, and jumped back. It snarled and lunged toward him, but its back legs were unmoving on the ground. He fumbled for the pistol on his belt and sent a bullet between its glaring eyes. It collapsed, shuddered once, and moved no more. Henri stood frozen, staring at the body. Then a man laughed, and soon the whole company was bowled over. They tossed the beast on the heap of meat and headed back to town.

The commander selected Henri and Jean-Paul, the two most senior veterans, to haul the carcass into the inn. With a flourish, they dropped it onto the bartop and stood back, arms outstretched in pride. The innkeeper looked at the remains of the giant wolf, his face expressionless save for a flaring of the nostrils as the scent of decay from the beast's fur reached his nose. He turned and disappeared into a room behind the bar. Henri and Jean-Paul stared at each other in confusion.

"No pleasing him," Henri said. Jean-Paul shrugged.

Then the innkeeper burst out of the doorway in a cloud of dust that smelled of damp. He held a bottle in front of him in triumph. He wiped the layer of dust off of the crystal and popped the cork. Jean-Paul, the son of a merchant in Paris, gasped when he saw the label. The innkeeper's stony face cracked and shifted into a smile. "Only the finest for the heroes of Gévaudan," he said, and poured three glasses.

"To those we've lost," he said, raising the amber liquid in a toast. His eyes shone with tears as he added, "and to you, my friends, for those we won't lose."

Henri and Jean-Paul stationed themselves on either side of the beast. The townspeople filed into the inn, clambering over each other to see the famed monster. They bought drinks for the heroes and reached out gingerly to touch the wolf's fur. Those who had lost loved ones to its maw brought tokens to lay by the table, turning the inn into a makeshift altar in memory of the victims. Word spread quickly, and soon the people of neighboring towns added to the mix. Everyone wanted to see the terror and ensure for themselves that it was really dead.

Henri watched the crowd for a sign of Marguerite. He ran over tales of his bravery in his mind, imagining how she would gasp when the wolf came to life and snapped at him. She appeared outside the window with Yvette and his heart leaped, but she looked in at the crowd, shook her head, and disappeared. Yvette flitted through the crowd and planted a kiss on Jean-Paul's cheek. He blushed and the crowd cheered.

The men gathered at the front of the inn late the next morning. A few, the most junior men, loaded supplies into the carts. Several nursed headaches, leaning against the tavern walls to catch the shade of the overhang of the roof. A keening sound filled the air and they squinted their eyes closed against the pain. The sound grew louder and the men that were doing the loading stopped their preparations. It rose to a scream and Henri opened his eyes through a fog of pain to see what was causing the commotion.
Yvette ran into the crowd, gasping and clutching at the constriction of her corset. Jean-Paul went to her and held her shoulders to steady her.

"Marguerite! She's—" she broke off into a wail and pointed toward a field where a herd of sheep milled around in confusion.

Henri's head cleared as fear ripped through his chest. He sprinted ahead of the others and found her lying in the field, limbs askew. Her dark eyes stared up into the overcast sky and her chestnut hair was clumped with the black blood that soaked the ground around her. The beast had ripped her throat with its fangs and sliced through her side with its claws. Henri fell to his knees and took her slender fingers in his hand.

"This was no wolf," he whispered.

"We need volunteers," the commander said. The men stood at attention next to their abandoned preparations for departure. Most of them stared at the ground. Henri swallowed hard and stepped forward.

"You knew the girl?" the commander asked.

"Yes, sir," Henri said.

The commander considered for a moment. "Ah yes, you were the first to her."

"Yes, sir."

The commander looked Henri up and down, taking in his slight build and reddened eyes. Henri puffed himself up as much as he could, trying to look like a man who could face down a beast.

The commander nodded and gave a grim smile. "You will be perfect."

Henri was to be live bait. The commander determined that the beast had a taste for maidens, so they gave him a dress of Marguerite's to wear. It grazed his ankles and the bodice had gaps in the lacing to accommodate his larger frame, but her delicate scent still clung to the fabric.

The men of the company gathered in a line to see Henri off into the woods. They hung their heads as he passed, looking like mourners by a graveside. Henri shook each man's hand, his usual jokes gone. Jean-Paul stood at the end of the line, with Yvette next to him. He pulled Henri into an embrace and pressed the cross that he wore into his friend's hand. Henri met Jean-Paul's earnest gaze and nodded his thanks. Yvette, like Henri, had lost her playfulness. She set her trembling jaw in defiance. "Good luck," she said. Her voice broke and Jean-Paul steadied her.

Henri turned away before her fear could stir up his own and weaken his resolve. He made his way into the forest. His eyes darted from shadow to shadow, straining to pierce the gloom lurking between the trees. Deep in the heart of the woods, he found a seat with his back to a trunk and spread out Marguerite's skirts around him. Henri checked the load of the pistol and sat it in his lap. Then he settled in to wait. His mind drifted back to Marguerite, lying broken in the field, and shuddered at the power of the beast that lurked in the darkness.

The beast leapt at him from nowhere, materializing from the shadows of the river bank where he had looked just a second before. He grabbed for the pistol and fired a shot right into its gaping mouth. The force of the bullet knocked it back and it rolled into the tall grass. It stood and shook itself off. Then it crouched for another attack. It was bigger than the wolf that the men had claimed credit for, and more powerfully built, with a stocky torso and rippling muscles in its thick legs. Its fur was reddish and matted, and its eyes—eyes of the devil, Jean-Paul had said, and Henri knew in a flash that the legends were all true.

The beast let out a roar and flew through the air, fangs gleaming as it lunged at his throat. There was no time to reload, so he covered his face with his hands, clutching the cross that Jean-Paul had given him in one fist. He smelled its hot breath as it knocked him to the ground, coppery with blood. Its massive weight crushed his chest, and he struggled to inhale, but the air lodged in his throat. His lungs burned. He stared into its burning eyes and opened his mouth in a silent scream.

The flaming depths of its eyes engulfed Henri. He lay mesmerized, even as he felt the monster rip at the dress with its fangs. His mind filled with the memories of all of the shameful moments of his life, played in burning silhouette like a demonic puppet show — the lies, the boasts, the bravado.

The beast let out huffing breaths as it sniffed and pawed, searching for the innocent blood that the scent of the dress promised. It nosed at the cross still clenched in his hand and snorted with disdain, coating Henri with a spray of droplets. It swatted the talisman out of his hand and leaned down to glare into his eyes once more. He felt the flames of its eyes burn a mark on his soul. Then it bounded away and he was alone, bruised but whole. Marguerite's clothes lay scattered around him and the outline of a paw print singed purple on his bare chest. He stared into the swirling mist after the beast and dreaded the day when he would meet the devil again.

Over the Top
Tony Kelly
Third Place

Bullets whizz past overhead. Too many to see. Too many to count. Endless. A ubiquitous volley piercing the air above, one continuous sheet, a barrage of lead, a blanket of death. A horizontal guillotine judging a generation and finding them all guilty.

The sound is the only way to sense the imminent destruction. A subtle, subdued thwip, thwip, thwip, as tiny instruments of death pierce dirt or wood without purpose. Or pierce flesh, with disastrous purpose. The cacophony of concussive clatter, gunpowder explosions both near and far, must shout to drown out that silent sound of piercing lead.

A long whistle skrees out above it all. Thomas listens for the signal. Over the top? Are they mad? The Gerries haven't even let up on the barrage yet. Over the top means death.

Thomas clambers up the dirt embankment. He teeters on the edge of the trench. Jackson, standing right next to him, pitches forward. Johnny, on the other side, falls backward into the trench. Forward and back. Forward and back. A rocking motion of life and death...

Forward and back. Forward and back. Despite the sea's best effort to keep Thomas unconscious, a body and mind must eventually counter the continuous, subtle rock-a-bye-baby pitch and roll. Even an exhausted body and a battered mind must come to the surface eventually.

Thomas wills himself to a sitting position, bracing himself against the pitch and yaw of the Atlantic Ocean. He wipes the sweat from his forehead. His core temperature spikes despite the chill throughout the boat. If the last few nights are any indication, his dreams will be prompting fevers for the foreseeable future.

The Great War is over. Thomas survived.

Perhaps survived is too strong a word. Survival implies action. Instinct, at the very least. Neither action nor instinct placed Thomas on this ship. Blind, dumb luck got him out of the trenches, to Brest, to the docks, to the ocean. Thomas did not survive. Thomas escaped.

Despite his fatigue, Thomas forces himself above deck. The brisk wind does little to cool him off, but he relishes it just the same. Because there are sights and smells he never expected to see again. Like the sight of sky. Or the smell of air. Things he doesn't deserve to experience again. Not because he was a bad soldier, but because nobody deserves to experience anything anymore.

But he's here, whether he deserves it or not.

A vast horizon of blue sits before him. For the first time in months, the horizon holds hope. The future is uncertain, but at least it is a future. A week from now he will see something that felt like an eternity away only a week before. Boston. And beyond Boston, a train ride home. And beyond the trainride home could be anything. Or nothing. And either thing is something to look forward to.

His great adventure, which turned out to be neither great nor an adventure, is over. A week from now, his past will be behind him. He bundles up against the wind and coughs.

Gas. A greenish yellow layer of terror, blanketing the the fog of war with a fog far deadlier. With a terror more complete. A bullet is a bullet is a bullet. Death by that kind of wound is instantaneous. Gas doesn't have the decency to kill. Even to maim. Gas suffocated. Gas smothers. Gas makes you turn your rifle around backward and pray for the gratuity of death. A silent prayer. Nothing can be said aloud.

Franklin didn't put his gas mask on in time. Fumbling with his gun, mixing up the signal, readying himself in position when he should be covering up. Heading for low ground as the smell of chlorine assaults his throat.

In the real world, Thomas never tasted the mustard. But in dreamland, it is all too real. Franklin's mouth is his mouth. His tongue expands, searching for moisture, something cool in a world afire. The smell of burn, the taste of burn. Swallowing, inhaling, drowning. Franklin's eyes bulge out. His nose bleeds. Thomas's mouth coughs.

Choking. Suffocation. Choking. A cough. A separate gasp for unfettered air that will never come. Watery eyes, drowning on solid ground. Cough. Choke. Cough.

Thomas awakes with a start. Cough. Cough. The gas is here on the boat.

No, it's not. But the rattling in his chest makes it seem so. A lot of soldiers on this boat are coughing. Sympathy coughs. A reminiscent choking to commemorate all of those who would never breathe again. Phlegm dislodges from Thomas's throat. His chest constricts, trying to find air. He swallows the mucus back to its source.

"Gas never caused phlegm," Thomas says as he turns onto his side. He doesn't know who his statement is intended for, but a nurse, who is checking on a soldier on the next bunk, turns to engage him.

"Were you ever gassed?" The nurse says. As she approaches him, he reads the word "Betty" on her nametag.

"No. By the time we entered the war, gas wasn't very effective. We practiced gas masks on the first day of basic."

Thomas tries to laugh, but the phlegm makes its presence known once again. His chest is tight. Getting a full breath is difficult, as if his lungs have forgotten what to do with real oxygen. He sits up and starts to feel around for his handkerchief.

"Why were they still using it, then?"

Thomas scratches the stubble on the back of his neck and thinks about her question. He doesn't have an answer. He doubts the higher-ups had much of an answer, either. If they did, it had certainly never trickled down to the rank-and-file. You didn't ask why anything in those trenches happened the way it did, you just followed orders.

"Terror, I suppose. Bullets are scary. Artillery is daunting. But the worst thing those'll do to you is kill you. Gas is a whole 'nother level. Gas might kill you, but it might just suffocate you. I've seen some people die instantly from a bullet. I've seen a guy with a shredded chest still have a peaceful look on his face. The only thing you ever see in a gas victim is the eyes. Bloodshot eyes. Eyes coming out of their sockets. As if the oxygen, blocked from its normal routes, is trying to find a new orifice to breathe through. Gas isn't war. It's terror."

The nurse stays silent for a bit. She nods. Thomas knows she's seen pain. She's seen death. A nurse knows every ounce of the brutality of war.

"This flu is a terror."

"Flu?""

Nurse Betty nods again. "It knows no rules. It cripples and maims and eats away at the healthy."

"The one from Spain?"

Betty shrugs. "I don't know."

"I thought that was just a ruse to keep us on our toes."

"It's real, alright. We've already had one soldier die on this ship and I count at least two more in the serious stages. Such a shame to survive all of that and then..."

Betty trails off, not knowing what more to add.

"Do you think I might have it?"

Betty looks up into Thomas's eyes, takes in his pale face. Thomas tries to hold in his breath, a trick he had learned against the gas. Even while wearing a gas mask, instinct forces you to hold your breath when the mist spreads across your eyesight. But it was easier to do against the mustard. The swallowed cough tickles its way up out of his lungs. Thomas tries to disguise it as a rasp.

Betty shrugs again. "Pray to God that you don't or you might never see your home again."

The dugouts are the worst. Cramped. Crowded. Concave. On the surface, in the trenches, a smell is there and then gone. With twenty soldiers cramped into a sardine-can twenty feet under the ground, every smell from 1914 on still lingers. Body odors of living and dead. Human and rat.

The rats are corpulent from the ample supply of corpses to feed on, but that doesn't stop them from stealing your food. They have no need to dart quickly or stay hidden. They move slowly, no shame, standing amongst the soldiers with little regard for nature or hierarchy or survival. Having seen what's above, the soldiers have little effort or interest in killing the creature. Save the savagery for the Gerries across no-man's land. Let the rodents be rodents.

Every sound from above reverberates tenfold. A distant explosion becomes a rasp of thunder. A strike closeby shakes and squeals like a Chicago El-train. When the shell hits overhead, it escalates to the San Francisco Earthquake. Dirt falls from the ceiling. The walls become the floor, which becomes the ceiling.

When the shelling stops, Kevin still hears it. He's still rocking back and forth. The rest of Thomas's platoon is back to the present, putting their bunker back together. Kevin is still lost in time. Like a dream. None of his senses are working. He doesn't shake out of it soon enough, and he never comes back. He joins the long line of the injured who are not injured. Rooms full of soldiers without a scratch, but who are wounded nonetheless. In some far-off field, but still trapped in the underground room.

The tight, constraining, claustrophobic tomb of a room.

Thomas darts awake. He can't breathe. He's trapped in another tomb. Not of earth, but of steel. Just as crowded as the dugouts. Cots and bunks scattered across the room, each filled with a moaning, shaking soldier. Ravaged not by the guns of the Germans, but the virus of the Spanish.

He can't stay trapped in here. He needs to escape. The fresh air awaits him up on deck.

He tries to stand, but really only sways. Vertigo. He's never had an issue with his balance before, but he's heard of it. The sickbay lists, but not to the standard cadence of the sea. Walls become floor become ceiling. Thomas's stuffed head is providing the role of the artillery now.

Still, he refuses to succumb to the shellshock of the flu. He manages to find the door. Focus, lurch, focus. Once outside, he'll smell the air of freedom. A reminder that the war is over.

"Where are you going?"

Betty appears in front of him, blocking his visual access to the real world. She is wearing a mask, a thin white gauze over her mouth and nose. Not the full gas mask that Franklin failed to get on in time. The virus won't get in her eyes. They're no longer at the front, but the dangers are no less present.

"Just need some fresh air."

"We talked about this yesterday, Thomas."

"We did?"

"You cannot leave the quarantine room."

Thomas looks around.

"But all of these people are contagious."

"As are you."

She puts subtle pressure on his shoulder and his knees buckle. They have forgotten how to stand, having ducked for too long under bullets. Now the death lingering above him can't be ducked under. Can't be jumped over. His legs are no use. The assassin is smaller than a bullet and knows its target with a heat-seeking accuracy that a weapon of war could only envy.

Thomas slumps back to a sitting position on his bed, which, despite his many meaningful strides toward the door, is still directly underneath his bottom. He tries to stand again, but cannot break through the powerful force on his shoulder, the vice-like of the diminutive nurse.

"Why don't you go back to sleep, Thomas?"

The last thing he sees is the thin white mask saving a life that is not his.

No-man's land should be the worst experience of the war, but it isn't. Three feet away, it is absolute hell upon earth. But here in this shellhole, the war is paused. No crowded dugout, no distant latrine, no bullet whizzing past your sandbag position. If you can ignore the dead bodies in here with you, it might as well be a vacation. Precious minutes off of the full-time job or trench warfare.

Trench means life. Over the top means death. A shellhole is the only chance for uncertainty.

No place to run to if that whine of incoming artillery approaches a little too close. But maybe that's why it's so peaceful out here. No place to run. No use being on your toes. You might as well just stare straight up into the cloudy sky overhead and wonder if it's true that the artillery creates its own weather system.

Or maybe God doesn't want his light to shine upon this Hell that we've created.

The smell of death is much worse out here. Morbid wounds, festering lesions, vacated bowels. While the smell of death can be removed from the trenches, out here the corpses remain to fester. Johnny took some shrapnel in the stomach before he fell back into the trench. He was dead before he hit the ground, his body stretchered to the reserve trenches and his guts buried within minutes

When Jackson took a bullet going over the top, he bled out for five hours, alternately screaming and moaning and whimpering within earshot for hours. His body's still there, maybe ten yards away, months later. Nobody's taking him away. No stretchers in no-man's land. And Jackson's not the only corpse out here. French and English, too. Even German. They're all out here, some of them right here in this shellhole with Thomas. Smelling.Rotting. Their guts unburied. And that's where they'll stay for the duration of the war. Until one side or the other, or maybe both at the same time, throw in the towel.

The trench means life. Over the top means death. Johnny taking shrapnel, falling back from the precipice. Jackson with a bullet, pitching forward to slowly rot. The corpse beside him in the shellhole.Franklin failing to put the gas mask on in time. Kevin rocking back and forth after the shelling stops. The trench means life. Over the top means death. Johnny. Jackson. Franklin. Kevin.

The trench. Over the top.

Boston.

Thomas can see it now in the distance. Maybe not the city itself, but he can make out a thin shoreline against the horizon. Massachusetts. The United States of America. Home.

"Thank you for bringing me out to see it," Thomas says.

"It's the least I could do," Betty answers from beside him. Her face is bare. "Besides, you're no longer contagious."

"Is that normal?"

"Yes. A virus makes you sick and then moves on. That's how it survives."

"At least..." Thomas coughs, then rasps in a big breath. "At least something's learned how to survive in this new century."

The two sit in silence. The nurse wraps herself against the ocean wind. The soldier doesn't seem to notice.

"How many have we lost?"

"Five have died since we left France. But ten more are infected, like you. I don't know if they'll let us disembark in Boston."

"I don't... I don't think I'll make it to Boston."

"Don't give up hope. You made it through the war. If anyone deserves to make it home."

Thomas shakes his head, but stops when the vertigo hits.

"Nobody deserves to go home. That's what this flu is."

"How do you mean?"

"We sowed Hell on this Earth, and now God is reaping. Nobody is supposed to survive going over the top. It's blind luck that I made it this far."

"This isn't just killing soldiers. Civilians back home are getting it, too."

"Exactly." Cough, cough. "The civilians are the ones who started the war. Got us involved. Johnny. Jackson. Franklin. Kevin. So many good people... You go over the top, you die. The world… The world went over the top."

The ship goes down one crest, then up another. Boston remains just as distant. Thomas feels the heat in his forehead, feels the constriction in his chest, feels the churning in his stomach. The only thing he no longer feels is the fight.

"Can I do something for your pain?"

"No. I know the pain will be gone soon. It's not as bad as it was yesterday. Did I tell you I took some shrapnel in my leg?"

"Really? I didn't see a wound."

"Maybe… Maybe it wasn't me. Someone else. I'm having...trouble remembering. I saw so much."

Betty puts her hand in its usual spot on his shoulder.

"But you made it through."
Thomas starts to nod. It turns into a slump.
"I made it…over the top."

Forbidden Intimacy
CE Snow
Fourth Place (tie)

The market reeked of death – blood and musk and rotting flesh. Eugénie held a linen handkerchief to her nose and averted her eyes from the grey and brown furred corpses stacked like cordwood across the square. Uniformed dragoons congratulated each other on the successful hunt. Eugénie studied them from beneath the brim of her straw hat while pretending to be interested in the sachets and talismans at an herbalist's stall.

Where was he?

A dark-haired soldier limped through the crowd, a bloodied bandage wrapped around his head and her breath caught in her throat. His fellows clapped him on the shoulder and murmured well wishes. As he brushed by Eugénie, their eyes met.

"Mademoiselle." He nodded and she sagged against the booth.

Brown eyes, not grey.

Eugénie turned back to the herbs. She reached out to examine a sachet of wolfsbane, but her hand shook. Glancing around to ensure no one had seen the tremors, she dropped the charm and clutched the handle of her basket.

Oblivious to Eugénie's distress, the toothless crone behind the table pushed a braided wreath of rye toward her.

"If ye have no faith in wolfsbane, try the rye. To wear 'round your hat. Certain to keep The Beast at bay."

A guffaw from behind Eugénie made her jump.

"Come now. There's nary a wolf left in the province. There's no need for Mademoiselle to waste good coin upon your witchery."

Pierre's deep voice gave flight to a flock of woodlarks in her stomach. She turned, pressing her palm to her middle, and glanced up to find him grinning at her, grey eyes twinkling. Heat flushed her cheeks and she dropped her gaze. Beneath the table their fingers met, skin whispering against skin in forbidden intimacy.

Eugénie snatched her hand back and spun with the stiff rustle of petticoats.

"Good day, Monsieur."

She sniffed, then hid her smile behind the handkerchief and took off at a brisk trot through the market. She didn't dare look over her shoulder as she wove through the thin crowd. These days, even by daylight, many kept close to home. Without needing to see, she knew Pierre followed. Boot heels struck the uneven cobbles behind her, with the familiar cadence of his long-legged stride.

Beyond a farmer's cart displaying a mound of wrinkled turnips, Eugénie checked to see if anyone was looking, then slipped into a deserted alley. A moment later strong arms wrapped around her waist and twirled her around. She squealed then buried her face in Pierre's broad, uniformed chest and breathed in his scent, an intoxicating tangle of sweat, gunsmoke and the faint tang of horse.

"Oh, my love. I feared for your wellbeing."

With a feather touch, the tall soldier trailed a finger across her collarbone, teasing. She shivered and swatted at him with faux disapproval. Her smoldering eyes divulged the lie.

"Fear not, sweetling. I'm difficult to kill." With a rapacious grin, he pressed her against the alley wall, hip to hip.

"But, The Beast—"

He cut her off, halting her words with a kiss, then spoke against her lips, "The Beast is dead."

Pierre's hands made themselves busy along the edge of Eugénie's bodice. He caught her bottom lip between his teeth, sharp pinpricks of pleasure. She whimpered and gathered the willpower to turn her head, smoothing her features into the stern reproval she didn't feel.

"Hold. It's unseemly." She didn't push him away; despite the indecency she longed for him to continue.

He froze and his bold smile faded, leaving his expression serious. "Come away with me, Eugénie."

"Come away with you? Where?" She frowned up at him.

"Captain Duhamel is of a mind that The Beast has been killed in the hunt." Pierre tucked a wispy curl behind her ear. "We're no longer needed in Gévaudan. The Dragoons are being sent home."

A wave of cold washed over Eugénie.

"My father will never approve."

"Buggar his approval!" Eugénie's eyes widened at the outburst, and he softened his voice to a gentle pleading. "We can marry in secret, then you can return home with me. Better a common soldier's wife in the great city of Clermont-Ferrand, than shipped off to some fat merchant in bucolic Langogne."

Pierre left a trail of butterfly kisses along her jawline and a thrill of recklessness rippled up her spine. She nodded, unable to find the breath to speak her assent.

"On the morrow, meet me at the abandoned miller's cottage at sundown." With a groan he pulled away and put a deliberate, decorous space between them. "I'll arrange a priest. Neither your father nor His Majesty's army can part what God has bound together."

The tall dragoon pressed a chaste kiss upon her brow then turned and strode from the alley, a jaunty spring in his step. Eugénie scrubbed her sweaty palms on her skirts. She straightened her hat and set out for home, heart aflutter.

"Whatever are you doing, child?"

Eugénie wobbled on the stool and grabbed the window frame for balance. On tiptoe, she reached up and yanked a bundle of waxy green leaves from the eaves.

"Taking down the mistletoe, Father."

"Your mother would be horrified by your wild antics. God rest her soul." He reached out a hand. "Come down from there."

Eugénie allowed him to steady her as she leapt lightly to the floor. Her father patted her cheek and shook his head.

"First you insisted we hang these pagan talismans, and now you're taking them down?"

"The danger's past, Father. The Beast has been killed."

The lanky man scowled, caterpillar eyebrows drawn down over narrowed eyes.

"And how do you know that? I told you to stay away from Duhamel's men. A genteel maiden of your station does well not to be seen cavorting with ruffian soldiers. Think of your reputation."

"Father!" Eugénie arranged her features, eyes wide and lips rounded, masquerading shock. "I do not *cavort*." She squashed down a prickle of guilt. "It was all the gossip in the marketplace today."

Her father clucked his tongue and tucked her hand in the crook of his arm.

"In the marketplace. With no escort, I imagine. Again."

Frowning, he steered her into the parlor and settled her on a plush settee, then sank into a straight-backed chair. For the first time Eugénie noticed the lines around his eyes, the silver threaded through his dark hair. She wriggled on the plump cushions, shamed by her selfishness. How could she leave him alone in his dotage?

Her father cleared his throat. "I've hired on a girl."

Eugénie blinked. "For what?"

"To help take care of things once you're gone." He folded his hands on his too-thin lap.

Eugénie clamped her teeth together to keep her jaw from dropping. Her pulse raced. How had he known?

"You know I only want what's best for you, Eugénie." He unfolded his hands and picked at a nonexistent spot on his sleeve. "I've arranged for a very generous dowry."

Lightheaded, Eugénie opened her mouth to speak, but her father raised a hand to stay her.

"I'll hear no argument, child. You leave for Langogne in a fortnight."

Pierre's words danced a chaotic jig in her head – *shipped off to some fat merchant in bucolic Langogne.* Her fists bunched in her skirts.

"Father. What have you done?" The words came out in a breathless whisper.

"Monsieur Blondeau is well respected. Solid. Dependable. He'll temper your willful spirit."

"He's dour and a decade my senior!" A wail built in the back of Eugénie's throat. She swallowed it down. "I won't do it."

Her father's eyes hardened. "You'll do as you're told."

Face flushed and eyes flashing, Eugénie gathered her skirts and fled the parlor to the sanctity of her bedchamber. Slamming the door behind her, she strengthened her resolve. She had a journey ahead of her and less than a day to prepare for it.

When a quiet knock came at her chamber door some hours later, Eugénie, engrossed in plotting how to slip from the house undetected on the following evening, didn't answer. Her father, too much of a gentleman to barge into a lady's boudoir uninvited, did not intrude.

Pierre glanced out the window. He needed to depart or he'd never make the old miller's cottage by sundown. It was unchivalrous to make a lady wait. A warm, dreamy feeling swelled up inside him. Eugénie. She was so lovely with her ringlets as glossy as raven's wings and dark eyes that snapped with laughter and intellect. He admired her fiery spirit – from the moment he had met her in the marketplace, a genteel lady haggling like a fishwife, and nary an escort in sight. No demure milksop would do. Despite the fact that a wealthy merchant's daughter was beyond his station, he had to have her. He had reached for a burning star and, for a wonder, hadn't been singed.

A knock on the door interrupted his daydream, and a page boy poked his head into the room.

"Pardon Monsieur, but Captain Duhamel is assembling the dragoons in the common room."

For a moment Pierre hesitated. He could use the commotion as opportunity to tiptoe out the inn's back door. Would his comrades notice his absence? He shook his head. The Captain was not a wordy man. Best see what Duhamel wanted, then slip away after. Pierre sent Eugénie a wordless plea to forgive his tardiness.

A roar hit him as he entered the common room. The other dragoons shouted and laughed, telling jokes and swapping tales of beauties awaiting them in Clermont-Ferrand. Spirits soared high, for with the destruction of the vile Beast of Gévaudan the soldiers were eager to ride homeward.

From his corner near the window, Pierre watched the sun inch towards the horizon. He folded his arms across his chest and forced himself to lean against the wall, instead of pacing the room. His feet itched to move while he waited for the Captain to appear.

A pale faced serving girl kindled a fire in the wide fieldstone hearth. As she passed by Pierre, he saw a sachet strung around her neck by a leather thong. Noticing him looking, the wench tucked the talisman into her bodice. She looked away, her gaze sideling to the window and eyeing the lengthening shadows. The girl touched the concealed charm and hurried from the room.

Wolfsbane. Pierre was sure of it. He smothered a laugh at her provincial ways. The Beast was a wolf, not some ridiculous magical creature to be repelled by a pocket full of leaves. Besides, the dragoons had hunted down every last wolf in the province. There was nothing left to fear.

The door burst open and Captain Duhamel stalked into the room. His usual jovial demeanor was dampened, shoulders curved as if he carried a great weight. Their leader's face pulled tight, lips pressed together in a straight, thin line, and Pierre stood up straight. Gooseflesh danced across his arms.

"Dragoons." The Captain's voice was somber and silence fell at once. "I have just received word. We shall not be riding home on the morrow."

Quiet murmurs rippled through the room as the men exchanged glances.

"Early this morning, a young swineherd was found on the outskirts of town, his throat torn out." Captain Duhamel paused and Pierre held his breath, willing his commander not to speak the words. "His Majesty is threatening to replace us with the wolf-hunter, Jean Charles d'Enneval, for The Beast still roams free."

The hum of angry voices faded to a low buzz in Pierre's ears. Outside the window, the mauve and lavender twilight lost all color. A tremor ran through him.

"Eugénie!"

Elbowing through the crowd, Pierre rushed past Captain Duhamel. He barely registered the shocked expression on his commander's face before sprinting towards the stables, shouting for his horse.

Eugénie pulled her cloak tighter around her shoulders as she picked her way down the track towards the river. The light was fading and her heeled boots were treacherous, the rough trail covered in loose stones and ankle grabbing roots. It had taken longer than she had anticipated to escape the house, with her father hovering and the new chambermaid packing her things for the journey to Langogne. The trip Eugénie wouldn't be taking. She smiled to herself and hurried onward, eager to join Pierre.

When the path forked, Eugénie paused to get her bearings. Left to cut through the forest. Right to follow the river. Both choices led to the abandoned miller's cottage, the former more direct than the latter. Ignoring the growing darkness, she took the wooded trail.

Beneath the trees, twilight deepened. She hesitated, eyes adjusting to the premature night. An uncanny hush blanketed the forest, as if the woodland creatures were holding their breath. No whisper of wind stirred the canopy, no sleepy dove cooed, not even the scurry of tiny feet amid the underbrush broke the silence.

Eugénie's heart thumped. Despite the quiet, a sense she was not alone made her skin crawl, like an army of spiders marching up her spine. The weight of an unseen gaze bored into her. Unsettled, the feeling urged her faster.

In the darkness, something kept pace, gliding from shadow to shadow.

Eugénie bit back a yelp and raced down the path. The forest came alive. Knobby branches reached for her, plucked at her cloak and snarled in her curls. She jerked her head and the sharp sting, as hairs ripped from her scalp, drove her onward.

A huff erupted from the darkness, a whuffle of anticipation is if the creature stalking her breathed in – and savored – her pain.

The heel of Eugénie's boot caught on a root and she tumbled forward to land, sprawled upon the path, in a tangle of full skirts and layered petticoats. Winded, she tried to stand and fire shot up her calf. She pitched backward, her twisted ankle unable to support her weight.

Between the trees, a pair of cruel eyes fixed on her, shining with a ghoulish orange glow. Eugénie scrabbled backward, her mouth open in a noiseless scream, her breath caught in her chest, as a monster emerged.

Wolf-like, but not a wolf, The Beast stalked forward on enormous paws, its long claws scraping in the dirt. The creature's coarse fur was the color of shadow, blending into the night and a stiff ridge of bristles ran down its spine ending in a bushy tail. It loomed over her, close enough that its musky scent filled her nose. The Beast remained eerily still, lips peeled back in a silent snarl.

For an eternity it studied her, saliva dripping from dagger-like fangs. A mewling cry froze in Eugénie's throat, paralyzed under the monster's hungry gaze. The creature's tail thrashed, its whole body trembled with power, taut like a coiled wire waiting to spring free. Glowing eyes still fixed on its prey, one pointed ear twitched. The faint sound of pounding hooves echoed through the forest.

Pierre! Eugénie drew in a ragged breath.

When The Beast pounced, Eugénie found her voice and screamed.

As the last sliver of sunlight disappeared, Pierre drummed his heels on his horse's flanks. Galloping down the darkened trail, wind whipped at his face, knocking his hat from his head. He didn't look back. Ahead, a fork split the path. Without hesitation he jerked the reins left. There was no question that plucky, reckless, foolish Eugénie would have taken the shorter track through the forest, where The Beast was known to roam. The horse plunged beneath the trees.

A shriek shattered the night, then cut short.

"Eugénie!" Her name ripped from his throat. For a moment it lingered, the sound bouncing against the canopy, before disappearing into the night. Only the syncopated rhythms of hooves and heartbeat remained. Pierre urged his mount faster.

They hurtled around a bend to find a vast, grey shape blocking the trail. The horse reared and Pierre catapulted through the air. He landed in a crumpled heap on the hard ground, dazed. Rolling to avoid flailing hooves, he found himself staring into Eugénie's dark, vacant eyes. One limp arm stretched toward him, entreating. Accusing.

The horse screamed when the silent monster leapt past it. Pierre struggled against a furred boulder on his chest, desperate to reach Eugénie's motionless form. Legs thrashed, hands clutched at air. As fangs closed around his throat, Pierre's wail transformed into a gurgle. All he felt was regret that he'd arrived too late for them both.

A fat moon climbed above the treetops. Its light filtered through the canopy, dappling the trail silver, glistening off pools of crimson. Two hands, one large and calloused, one delicate and pale, lay motionless, a hairsbreadth apart, as if they could just reach each other, skin whispering against skin in forbidden intimacy, they could forestall their fate.

Orange eyes reflected the moonlight, as a bloody muzzle pointed to the heavens and howled. Not a hunting cry, but one of triumph. Its challenge rang through the breathless forest. The woodland creatures huddled in their burrows, the local crofters barricaded their doors, reminded once again that The Beast of Gévaudan owned the night.

Crying Wolf
Dominique Goodall
Fourth Place (tie)

1764
Mercoire Forest, Eastern Gévaudan, France
It was taboo, yet I couldn't resist. Drool built up in my mouth as I peered around a tree. She was so clear, so oblivious. So weak. A grumble in my stomach added to the irritation I felt as I watched my prey. Surely no one would notice, or at least care, if one little human didn't skip her way home, reeking of cattle and sweat? I knew that the cows, at least, had caught my scent. They stirred restlessly in between the trees, especially as I moved forward, gliding on large paws.

I was as large as the calves they had gathered in their midst, an advantage of being what I was. They knew that I was supreme, that my strength was far greater than theirs; but I sought easier prey this time. Flicking my tongue across my canines, I found myself grateful for the red and black pelt which helped me to merge with the trees around me. She was still lacking wariness as I trod closer, a growl rumbling in my chest but chained to my throat. I couldn't warn her.

Couldn't risk anyone else hearing what I was going to do.

Head lowered, I slunk around trees, ignoring the bulls as they gathered in front of me. They would be protecting their females, their calves. I merely wanted their captor. Wanted to feel easy meat fill my stomach. It didn't matter that I'd been warned away from humans by my parents, so many times. The longing was too much to ignore.

I savoured the scent of fear building in the herd. It buoyed my hunt, heightened my anticipation… made me hunger more for her.

When I revealed myself, she shrieked, a sound so shrill that I flinched, shaking my head so hard my ears bounced off my skull, but I continued to advance. I wrinkled my lips back from my muzzle, a snarl rampaging through my body. She smelled like she'd taste wonderful. My stomach cramped, angering me even further, strengthening my body.

The bulls wheeled at me and charged. I fled backwards, putting trees between myself and the cattle which stamped and shook their horns at me threateningly. I ran behind a tree, darted to

another and attacked again – but they were there. Howling my disappointment, I fled away from her desperate screams.
"*La Bête! La Bête!*"

1764
Somewhere in Gévaudan
"You aren't meant to go near humans in your skin! If they find out we are here, they will hunt us down and kill us! How stupid do you need to be?!" I flinched from my father's voice. He snarled at me, his anger clear in the bristling of his coat. I could hear the clicking of my mother's claws around me, impacting the stone and scraping sparks into the air. "If you want to spend time among them, then do it as a *human*, not as a chasseur, a loup." *Hunter, a wolf.*

So I had permission to linger among the humans, but only when I was one of them, and as weak as they were… though I wore fur on the inside, in my real shape. Still, I had to try and convince him. I was so sure we could do this, and no one would know anything.

"They'd be so easy to hunt though, father! They have no way of hurting us, and they cover so much of our land now. They steal the food from us, so we go hungry!"

"That doesn't matter. They outnumber us, but we will outlive them all! There is no need for us to kill humans. The longing, the temptation -- we all deal with it. The whole pack knows how hard it is to fight our instincts. We all do it. Whenever I go to the village for supplies for winter, I must resist the urges. We can't let them hunt us and kill our wildkin." He snarled the words out, and as his gaze shifted, I felt teeth slice into my shoulder, my mother's body flinging me to the ground.

I deserved this punishment, but the longing simply grew. I needed to kill someone, to feel their flesh part beneath my teeth. They would be nothing to me. With every blow, every splatter of my blood, I moved my baleful gaze around. Only one of my litter, my brother, watched me. The rest turned their backs to the punishment, and an idea formed slowly…

Maybe I didn't need to hunt alone…

June 1764
Les Hubacs, Langogne, Gévaudan
I'd failed before and been punished. I was back to find more prey. I wasn't alone this time. I brought my brother with me, letting him see just how the temptation lingered to teach them how to fear

us. I growled softly at him, before he could speak, my ears pricked upwards.

"You know mum and dad will kill us for this, right?" He whined the words softly, but I continued toward the village.

"They can try and tell us not to, but humans are weak. We only wear their skins sometimes, when we need something. They are prey." I growled the words out insistently, tail wagging above my hips. I was excited to hunt. Excited to kill. I'd been watching the humans ever since I healed from the double punishment of my parents. They didn't believe in using our true-forms like this.

I enjoyed the sense of power it gave me over them.

It was… more than invigorating. It buoyed me up and made me more aggressive. My tongue creased my lips before I moved forward, leading my brother with me. Prey always made me a little more aggressive. Bumping into my brother's hip, I drew in the scents of humans. The village was thick with the rank scent of unwashed humanity and the livestock they shared space with.

He pressed closer to me, fearful of the humans. I wasn't, I knew better. They were too weak to worry us.

"Just watch. You'll see how easy they would be for food. Nothing more than prey!" I growled, hunger getting the better of me. We slunk into the tall grass, one on either side of the worn track that they had walked into their surroundings. They weren't prepared for us. She wasn't prepared for us. I could see she was on the cusp of becoming grown. The clothes she wore were so ornate they covered her from shoulder to foot, but that left her throat open. A dress, petticoats, shoes with buckles on them -- likely her first from the admiring gazes she kept casting upon them.

The hooded, short cloak she wore was something I wanted for myself, in the little longing way I had for the human shell I had to don at times, when we had to evade anyone's attention. That would all change now. I would try and save the cloak if I could.

I shuddered with excitement, stomach lurching. I knew how to hunt, how to kill. I was prepared for this. My tail lashed languidly, stirring the tall stalks of grass slightly. The moment she noticed, I could see in the way she moved, in the tenseness of her shoulders. My eyes narrowed upon her, thick coat bristling with excitement as she walked a little faster, her chest heaving as she drew in a sharp breath.

My brother moved closer, his coat a touch less dark across his back. I shuddered with delight, hunger a visceral thing of smell and taste. I enjoyed the sensations, let it heighten the anticipation until I was stalking along the path beside the girl. She was not the girl that I wanted first, but she was easy to get to. Weaker. She had no protection.

My brother lunged first, impetuous and impatient. I let him have his fun, worrying at her ankles and nibbling on her calves when she fell. There was silence around us as she screamed. I didn't fret a moment. She was nothing, they were nothing to me. The villagers were human. Weak and stupid, they had no idea what we were doing now. They couldn't hear her frantic pleas for 'mère et père'.

When I grew tired of her screams, I sank my teeth into her throat and drank her blood. When her gurgles faded, that was when I buried the clothes covering her stomach and glutted myself on her flesh.

My brother fed at my side, our growls fading into contented sighs when we left the carcass behind us, retreating into the tall grass that surrounded the village. From there, we could doze until running was an option, returning to our small home and our parents in the forest. A river would take care of her scent, but I was already planning on returning, maybe even bringing one or two of the younger pups with me.

Why should we struggle to hunt, when the humans were so easy?

Screams woke me, but I ignored them as I licked the double dew claws that had held her down and torn into her flesh. They were peculiar to our family but helped when we met others of our own kind. We always knew our relatives by them.

"La Bête! La Bête du Gévaudan! Il l'a tuée! A tué Janne Boulet et l'a mangée!" *The Beast! The Beast of Gévaudan! He has killed her! Killed Janne Boulet and eaten her!* I relished their screams, even as I nudged my brother to his feet and we retreated, leaving as silently as we had arrived. They didn't know that we were there, that we understood them.

That sometimes, we walked among them. Now my brother knew my longing, my obsession, I could relax. He would help me with future kills, I could see the hunger and desire for killing the humans warring with his fear of our parents. I didn't share that fear, even after the licking I'd taken last time they found out my obsession.

We would be the Beast of Gévaudan, and we would worship our own strength with blood. Let them try to stop us!

CLICHE STORY: In fiction, "cliche" is the last thing you want to hear about your writing. From the manic pixie dream girl to the hunky vampire with a soul to the nerdy forensic tech who specializes in all forms of evidence, cliches are tough to avoid. For this Event, cliches are exactly what your story needs! Write a story with as many cliches as possible in one cohesive tale.
Core Concept: narrative, tropes

A Common Bond
LS Fellows
First Place

Blood's thicker than water. That's what Mum said when she dropped the bombshell about my - I stress the word "my" - month-long visit to Great Aunt Lulu's cottage in the middle of nowhere. It was the summer of 1976, and already proving to be a scorcher. I had been quite happy to spend the holidays at home with Mum as we had always done, especially since I had my own plans at the library.. Then this promotion thingy came up, and, like a bolt from the blue, my suitcase and I were bound for the countryside.

It had been just the two of us since Dad died in a traffic accident two years earlier. He'd gone to fetch his parents from the airport - they'd flown over from Italy to spend Christmas with us. All three were killed when a lorry jack-knifed on the motorway. As a result, Mum and I were extremely close. Two's company, she would say. And it was. But I was almost ten when the time came for her to return to work full-time.

'Beggars can't be choosers, Janie. You know I'd let you stay here if I could, but this promotion will help us both in the long term.' She had tears in her eyes when she told me, but I sensed her excitement too. She loved her job working two days a week at the travel agency on the High Street. On those days, I would go to the library after school and wait for Mum to fetch me. She wouldn't let me go home alone. To be honest, I was more than happy to have a few hours to myself, reading my favourite books, discovering new worlds and having the sort of adventures in my head that other kids couldn't even imagine. It was harder during the school holidays, but not impossible. I had volunteered to help the assistant librarian teach some younger kids to read, and I was looking forward to being the "teacher".

When Mum first told me about the promotion, I was happy for her. I had my "job"; she had hers. It promised to be a great summer. Then she said she had to go away on a series of training courses. For a month. Twenty days, plus weekends.

'They won't let you home at the weekend, Mum?' Her story - for that's what it felt like - was as clear as mud to me.

'Of course I can come home. It's just not practical. All the travelling, and the cost on top. We'd barely get a few hours together and I'd have to leave again. No, Janie, it's better this way.'

'But Great Aunt Lulu? I've never heard of her until now. How can she be so great if I don't even know who she is?' That was my ace card, and as soon as I said it out loud I knew it was the wrong thing to say. Instead of feeling as pleased as punch, I wanted to eat my words. Mum's face twitched from teary to disappointed in the blink of an eye.

'Janie, please, I'm trying so hard to do what's best for you. Aunt Lulu was wonderful to me when I was young. You'll love her cottage. It has a stream, and apple trees, and she keeps chickens. She used to have goats too.'

Yeah, but how long ago was that? I knew I'd be bored to tears. A month without the library, I bet she didn't have TV either.

'Okay, Mum. I'll give it a go. It's only a few weeks after all.'

'Thanks, love. I'm sure you'll come to love Lulu in no time. She's a real character, as sharp as a tack, and calls a spade a spade. You'll get on like a house on fire, you mark my words.' She ruffled my hair and drew me into a hug, almost squeezing the life out of me. Mum was on cloud nine, I could at least give Great Aunt Lulu the benefit of the doubt. This could be the best summer of my life. Then again ...

As luck would have it, the journey from the Midlands to the Yorkshire Dales was trouble-free for the most part. Changing trains and running across from one platform to another, however, was by no means easy. The further North we went, the slower - and smaller - the trains became, as city smoke gave way to fields, and fields, and more fields.

On arrival at the nearest station to Great Aunt Lulu's village, after six hours travelling, Mum turned to me while we sat on a bench waiting for a taxi. 'Right, Janie, now don't go expecting the red carpet treatment, Lulu's bark is worse than her bite. She means well, but she doesn't suffer fools gladly. Keep your chin up and knuckle down if she asks you to help out. I'm sure you'll grow to love the outdoors lifestyle. Not everything can be found in a book, you know.'

'Don't worry, Mum. I'll be as good as gold. Great Aunt Lulu won't even know I'm there. I'll do my chores and I promise not to get under her feet.' Needless to say, I had every intention of burying my nose in a book whenever possible. If that meant doing a few jobs around the cottage to keep the peace, then it was a small price to pay. Wasn't it?

The taxi driver took my suitcase from the boot and plonked it at my feet, stirring up a cloud of dust that made me cough. He mumbled something to Mum and got back into his car, pulling out a flask and a newspaper.

'He's going to wait for me, then take me to the airport. I can't stay too long, else I'll miss my flight.' She picked up my case and headed towards the only - I repeat, "only" - building on the horizon. Well, as far as I could see through the heat haze anyway.

The dirt path was set at a slight incline, but every step felt like we were mountaineers. The sun was still high in the sky, and pounding down on us like we were objects to be destroyed, burnt to a cinder. Sweat trickled down my back, and Mum stopped walking, rummaged in her bag for a hanky to mop her own brow. She passed the damp cloth to me, but I declined politely.

As we neared the stone cottage, I saw a trough full of apples balancing on higgledy-piggledy bricks under one window, several buckets of water under the shade of a tattered, striped canopy, and a lot of brown feathers underfoot. Mum rapped on the solid wooden door. In my head, I began the countdown - 5 - 4 - 3 - 2 - 1. Nothing. No answer. Mum was right, definitely no red carpet treatment here.

'Maybe she forgot we were coming.' I could hope, couldn't I? Although I had no idea what would happen if I were proved right.

'She's probably in one of the outhouses. Run round the back.' Mum sounded ready to press the panic button, her voice pitched up a thousand decibels.

I sped off and took the corner wide, running slap-bang into a solid mass of a woman, as wide as she was tall.

'Oof!' she said, holding out her arms to steady herself.

I grabbed her thick wrists so that she didn't fall.

In the nick of time she regained her balance. 'Child! Did your mother never tell you not to run like that?'

Words escaped me, and I could only stare at the head-scarved woman, sleeves rolled up to the elbow, with a nasty reddish stain on her otherwise white blouse. It turned out to be beetroot, nothing sinister, but first impressions left me uneasy.

'What's up,' she barked, 'cat got yer tongue?' Beady eyes pierced every fibre of my being. This was it. My fate for the next four weeks was signed, sealed and delivered. Child slavery it would be.

Mum caught up with us. 'Aunt Lulu, this is Janie.' She leaned in to kiss the woman's ruddy cheeks.

'I'm no fool, Sandra. I guessed this delightful young thing belonged to you.' She looked me up and down, instantly taking a dislike to my salmon-pink hot-pants by the looks of the curl of her lip. Calling my mum by her full name - as opposed to Sandie - didn't bode well.

'Sorry, Lulu. Of course. How are you?' Mum's attempt to gloss over the atmosphere was commendable, albeit unsuccessful.

'Fine. All the better for seeing you.'

Well, if that wasn't a bare-faced lie, then Lulu deserved an award.

Mum laughed, at least I think she did, but it came out as a whimper. 'Say hello, Janie.'

Did I dare say exactly that? It was something I would usually do, but Mum's glare made me lose my nerve and instead I offered the expected greeting of 'Hello, Great Aunt Lulu. It's lovely to meet you.' When it comes to bare-faced liars, it takes one to know one.

'Lulu, forgive me, I have a taxi waiting. At least, I hope he's waiting, my suitcase is still in the back of his car.' Another attempt at levity from my mother. No one could say she didn't try.

'If Seth said he'll wait, then he'll wait. We're 'onest folk round these parts. None of yer fancy-talking Southern nonsense.'

I wanted to tell her we'd come from Coventry, not the South at all, but again I thought better to make the best of a bad situation than to make matters worse. I had the distinct impression that Mum's memories of Aunt Lulu were not all she'd made them out to be. By the looks of her face, Mum was coming to the self-same conclusion. It was time to put her out of her misery. 'Off you go, Mum. Great Aunt and I will be just fine. Can't have you missing your flight, can we?'

Relief flooded her body; I swear she sagged by at least three inches. She offered me the broadest smile she could muster and tugged me out of Lulu's way.

'See you in a month, Sandra. No more. No less.' Lulu shifted forward and stared at me.

What was I supposed to do? Mum rescued me by placing her hands on my shoulders and whispered in my ear. 'This hurts me more than it hurts you, Janie. Please be good, and try to have fun.'

As she released me, I nodded. 'I'll be fine, Mum. Love you.'

She stepped away. 'I love you, too.' She made another attempt to kiss Lulu's cheek, only for the older woman to anticipate - and dodge - her move.

'Enough fuss, Sandra. You're not going to the moon.'

'Thank you so much, Lulu. I wouldn't be doing this at all without your help.' She looked at me. 'I'll phone you.'

'No phone mast,' said Lulu.
'I'll write then.'
'Postal strike. Don't you listen to the wireless?'
I'd never seen Mum look so down in the dumps. 'Write anyway, Mum. It might be over soon,' I said. Lulu tutted and walked past me, towards the house.
Mum grinned, hugged the life out of me and then turned back down the dirt track. 'Be good, Janie. It'll fly by.' Then her voice, choked with tears, vanished into the heat haze with her.

And so it was that I began my four-week sentence courtesy of the "hostess with the mostest" - I knew she'd not have a TV! That night, we ate in something akin to silence, apart from the clucking of the hens and the bleating goats, all of whom I met the next morning (if you call 5AM morning, that is).
'Up you get, child. There's work to be done. Put on some proper clothes, not them short things, you'll get scratched and pecked to smithereens in them.'
Of course, the immersion heater only went on at night when Lulu took her bath, so it was cold water or nothing. After a lick of the flannel over my face, I met my Aunt outside in the dark - she had a torch in one hand, a bucket in the other - and told me to "fall in behind her" and not make a sound. She opened the gate to the chicken enclosure and shooed me inside, thrusting the bucket in my hand. 'Let 'em out, feed 'em in the yard, then 'mind yer 'ead,' she said, pointing to the door to the coop. 'Gather up the eggs inside there and put 'em in yer empty bucket. We can clean the coop out after breakfast.'
Without saying a word, I did as I was told. No guts, no glory, and definitely no sense in ruffling any feathers - hers or the chickens - if I could help it. The eggs were still warm, but the stench made me retch. It was a baptism by fire, and for the first week breakfast was always preceded by me throwing up. However, it was worth all the pain and suffering, because Aunt Lulu's eggstravaganza breakfasts were to die for - metaphorically speaking.
That same day, after the best meal of my life, Lulu introduced me to Gruff, the goat. Gruff by name, and gruff by nature, he was as blind as a bat and as cute as a button ...from a distance. His lady friends were much calmer, but Aunt Lulu set me the task of distracting Gruff while she herded the goats in for milking. Well, come hell or high water, he wasn't having any of it, and despite his lack of vision he could smell a fox in the hen house from fifty paces -

I didn't stand a chance. As it happens, that was a test. To see if I had any mettle. After the dust settled, I realised Aunt Lulu had tricked me, hook, line and sinker. She milked those goats by herself every day of the week. She didn't need anyone to distract the old billy-goat. Clearly the image of me running around with Gruff on my heels amused her, because I heard a lot of snorting. Goats don't snort!

Still, when we sat outside on the deck that afternoon, she treated me to some goats' cheese, with a dollop of home-made apple sauce and some made-that-morning wholemeal bread. I melted like a snowman in Hell. Whatever she asked of me, I would be her compliant servant. Food like that was worth its weight in gold, silver, lead, tin, and more besides.

From then on, Aunt Lulu's kitchen became my favourite place in the house, where I would sit to my heart's content at the huge oak table with a cherished book at hand and a feast of delectable food. What Aunt Lulu lacked in conversation, she more than made up for in food. And, boy, did my appetite increase with all the physical activity. Once I grew accustomed to the law of the land - to do whatever Aunt Lulu said - then we rubbed along nicely. It goes without saying, everything came at a price but I was a fast learner, and a willing one. Mum had described Aunt Lulu before we arrived as being nobody's fool, and in that respect we were like peas in a pod.

Even Gruff came round to my way of thinking; all it took was a bribe of rhubarb leaves and I was in. Milking his harem was easier said than done, and Aunt Lulu watched me like a hawk, grunting and sighing at my uselessness. Until, one day, the penny dropped and I got into my stride. This time, Aunt Lulu was as quiet as a dormouse, which I took to be a good sign. After three successful days of milking, she no longer supervised me. Returning to the kitchen with a full bucket of warm milk, I picked up a feather and wove it into my plaited hair. Aunt Lulu noticed, but as was her way she said nothing. So, as was my way, I filled the void. 'I don't have a cap to wear, so consider this a feather in my plait instead.'

Her lips twitched. 'Fishing for compliments, are you, child?'

'No, Aunt, just blowing my own trumpet.' Before she could answer, I went outside and headed to the vegetable patch, pulled up a few carrots, picked some green beans, and dug up two decent-sized potatoes. All without being asked. Not that it was a chore anymore. Okay, so my blisters had blisters at first, but in no time at all the hard work became less exhausting, and the great food we ate was reward enough.

It was midway through week three before she called me by my own name, usually she just barked out orders, or added on what was for her a term of endearment - child, do this, or girl, fetch that. When it came, I almost missed it.

'Janie, child, are you deaf?' She yelled at me one hot Thursday morning. The postman had just been; I'd zoned out as they chatted on the doorstep. Aunt Lulu had caught me red-handed, eavesdropping on her neighbourly chats once before. I knew better than to get caught again.

'Sorry, Aunt Lulu. How may I help?' I'd been savouring some hot toast, butter dripped down my chin as I spoke.

'I don't need your help, child.' I sensed a softening of attitude, and so many words that early in the day constituted the longest conversation we'd had to date. 'There's a parcel and stuff from your mother. You might want to wipe your hands and face first.'

I unwrapped the parcel to find a new book. I flipped the pages. 'Mmm,' I mumbled, breathing in that new-book smell I loved so much. A sudden yearning to be back in the library overwhelmed me. There were ten days to go before Mum would come to fetch me, so I checked the number of pages, divided it by ten and swore to ration myself and make the book last.

'You like to read, don't you?' Aunt Lulu hovered nearby, drying the breakfast dishes.

'Yes.'

'I noticed.'

Well, it wasn't difficult, I wanted to say, considering I sat at her table every day with a book.

'You going to read those letters then?'

And we were back to square one.

Or so I thought.

In the afternoon, when I planned to start my new book, I took my usual seat and waited for Aunt Lulu to leave me a glass of milk, and something to nibble. But this time, there was no glass. No snack. Instead, she pulled up a chair next to me.

'Everything alright with your mum?'

I nodded.

'Good. I'm sure you don't want to be here a moment longer than necessary, do you?'

Her tone was cautious, her stare intense. I fidgeted under her watchful gaze, wary of saying the wrong thing. Walking the tightrope might have been easier. How was I supposed to reply without offending her?

'It's not so bad.' I didn't dare look up.

'That's good to hear. You're not what I expected either.'

I detected a softening in her voice when next she spoke a few moments later, breaking the awkward silence between us. 'Janie, I have a surprise for you. Follow me.' She stood and walked over to the pantry, but rather than fetch food, she pulled a key from her apron and unlocked a side door, covered until now with a full-length curtain. 'Come on.'

Being a curious child, I jumped up and gasped as she opened the door to reveal a room filled to the rafters with bookcases. One after the other, after the other. Each one brimming with books.

'In you go.'

Hang on, would she lock me in? The thought vanished in a jiffy when I realised I didn't care if she did. There were books inside that room.

She pulled back the wooden shutters, and sunlight bounced off the glass cases. I raced to the first one, wiping away my breath on the misted glass to see books by Charles Dickens, Jane Austen, the Brontës, Lewis Carroll, and my current favourite from the library, Mark Twain.

I clapped my hands together, squealing, and bouncing on my toes as though I'd found the Holy Grail.

'I thought, maybe you'd like to read one to me later.' Aunt Lulu spoke in a whisper.

'Me? Really?'

She bowed her head.

'Oh, would I? You bet I would.' But I had one burning question that I needed an answer to first. 'Why now?'

'I saw how you almost ate that new book earlier, sniffing the pages and breathing in that musty book smell. And, you've been doing your chores without being asked. You deserve a treat.'

I wrapped my arms around her waist, tears of happiness running down my face. 'Thank you, thank you, Aunt Lulu. I'll read whatever you'd like.' I loosened my grip, a little shocked that she hadn't backed away, and wiped my face. 'Do you have any preference?'

'No, Janie, you can choose. I'll leave it to you.'

'I have a higher than average reading age, you know. Eleanor, the librarian, lets me read almost anything. How about that one?' I pointed to The Secret Garden by Frances Hodgson Burnett, and saw Aunt Lulu smile for the first time. Really smile, I mean, not just a curl of the mouth or a twitch of the lips. She looked so much younger.

'One of my favourites, too.' She slid back the glass and motioned for me to take the book out.

I wiped my palms on my trousers then reached up and teased the book from the shelf. I hugged it close to my chest. 'Shall we start now?' It was true, good things did come to those who wait.

'Why not. But not in here. This room needs a good airing. Maybe we can work on that tomorrow?'

In the kitchen, I took my place at the table, at Aunt Lulu brought out two glasses of milk and a plate of fig rolls. We sat for an hour, as I read the first chapter, stopping for sips of milk and a biscuit now and then.

That evening we made plans to clean out the book room, and Aunt Lulu explained why it had been shut up for so long. As it turned out, she had been an avid reader too. As a young girl, she had read to her father. She had wanted to be a librarian, but opportunity never knocked on her door. When her mum died, she had to take over the running of the cottage. Her older sister, my mum's mother had already married by then, so the responsibility fell on Lulu's shoulders.

It all began to make sense: why Mum used to spend the holidays here, why Aunt Lulu lived alone after her father passed, and why she locked the room up for so many years because it reminded her of happier times. She confessed to preferring the company of animals to children. 'Animals never bite the hand that feeds them, and they don't answer back,' she said with a chuckle. A chuckle!

The next day, after milking, we cleaned the room until it was spick-and-span. Every now and then, I got distracted by a book title, the sunlight glistened on the gold lettering of the books' spines.

At 4PM we stopped, downed our tools and headed into the kitchen for the next chapter. It was to be our last afternoon there, since the following day the book room became our storytelling sanctuary.

It was there, that on day twenty-eight, Mum found us both holed up, chatting away and discussing the next book to read. We were as thick as thieves, caught up in our very own world of make-believe.

'Hello there. What is this room? Aunt Lulu, I've never seen this before.'

'Oh, look what the cat's dragged in,' Aunt Lulu said, giggling behind a hand.

''Charming,' said Mum, but her smile was as wide as the horizon. 'Look at you, Janie. Lulu what have you done to my daughter? I've never seen her look so healthy.' It was true; her pale-faced kid had rosy cheeks, sparkling eyes, and muscles when there had been none before.

But it was time to go home, and neither of us were ready to say goodbye. Aunt Luu told me to pick my favourite book for the journey home, but only if I promised to return it.

Without a moment's hesitation, I chose the first book we had read together. Her eyes glistened with approval. She waved us off after handing Mum a package of treats for the train ride home. It had been the best summer of my life, and in later years she admitted to feeling the same way..

I went to Lulu's every year for the summer after that. As an adult, I spent my annual leave there, and as a teacher that gave me and Aunt Lulu more precious time to get through her book collection. We didn't quite make it, but we gave it our best shot.
Now it's my home too. Lulu died peacefully in her sleep ten years ago, and bequeathed her house to me. I've just retired, and live there permanently.

At the end of the day, Lulu was truly deserving of the Great Aunt name-tag. If fact, I'd go as far to say she was the greatest Aunt ever. It just goes to show, you can't judge a book by its cover.

Dressed to Kill
CE Snow
Second Place

All the offices in the world, and she had to walk into mine. I knew the minute I saw that dame, she was going to bring nothing but trouble. Trouble with a capital T. Dressed to the nines, she sported a neat, expensive suit, every detail perfect down to the ruler straight seams on her hose, pristine white gloves, and a black velvet hat perched – just so – on her fiery red curls. The mesh half-veil obscured her eyes, and I wondered if they were blue or green. She was one put together doll, the stuff dreams are made of.

Then she took a step and shattered the illusion. As if unused to wearing heels, she wobbled like a day-old colt. I shot around the desk in a flash. For the first time in ages, I appreciated all those high school football medals tucked away in my old steamer trunk. Not for nothing, had I been an all-star running back.

I made it just in the nick of time.

She pitched backward and collapsed into my waiting arms. Deer in headlights, she stared up at me, and I got my first look at her face. A smattering of freckles kissed the bridge of her nose. She'd tried to powder over them, but to no avail. A button nose and naturally rosy cheeks that had no need for rogue, gave her a doll-like appearance. Long lashes fluttering, she blinked her eyes at me.

For the record, they were green.

"Whoa there, easy does it."

I eased her into my rickety visitor's chair, wincing as her silk stockings snagged on the uneven rungs. It had always served me well to keep my clients unbalanced, on the edge of their seat. It made it easier to coax out the truth. Folks tended to forget that they were airing their dirty laundry to a stranger, when they were worried that the chair beneath them was a heartbeat from collapsing. But my clientele weren't usually this kind of high society broad.

As I sank down into the leather desk chair that I should have offered her, I rubbed my stubbled chin. Not a proper beard, but more than a 5 o'clock shadow. How long had it been since I'd had a shave? I dropped my hand and swept the near empty, illicit bourbon bottle off my desk. There was a mouthful or two left, so I quickly stashed it in a drawer. In these times of prohibition, it was waste not want not, and I fought a guilty urge to straighten my collar. Instead, I looked up at the bombshell across from me.

"Madam, to what do I owe this pleasure?" Inwardly, I groaned. That sounded pompous. I wasn't the type to put on airs, but those emerald eyes had my knickers in a bunch.

"Eloise. Eloise MacArthur." Her voice was satin smooth and carefully cultured.

I clamped my teeth together to keep my jaw from dropping. I knew the name, how could I not? It had been in all the local rags when millionaire playboy, turned nightclub mogul, Dean MacArthur had married a common wash-girl last month. The blue bloods had thought it was all quite the scandal. My own dear departed mother, may she rest in peace, had been a laundress, so I'd applauded Miss Eloise's ambition. Score one for the home team. Now that I'd met the dame for myself, I could see what all the fuss was about.

"What can I do for you, Mrs. MacArthur?"

She sniffed. "Eloise, if you please, Mr. Kelley."

"Anthony. Some folks call me 'Ace.'"

She gave me a dubious look and shifted in her seat. The traitorous chair creaked.

"Or Tony. Tony's fine too."

"Tony." She favored me with the ghost of a smile. "Perhaps you've heard of my husband, Dean MacArthur?"

Her silken voice hitched a little on the word 'husband' and a warning bell sounded in my head. I had a bad feeling that all wasn't well in paradise. Her next revelation confirmed my suspicions.

"Dean's…oh God, he's dead!" She buried her face in her hands.

I reached in my pocket and handed her my handkerchief, wrinkled but clean. My mother, bless her soul, had been a force to be reckoned with and her lessons were ingrained – cleanliness was next to godliness, she'd liked to say. Ironing, well that was another matter altogether.

Eloise took the rumpled cotton square and dabbed at her eyes. While she composed herself, I chewed on what she'd just told me. Dean MacArthur, dead. That was a shock to beat the band. I glanced at the day-old paper on my desk. There hadn't been a whisper in its pages and those newsroom vultures would've had a hay day with this juicy bit of gossip if they'd known. Either MacArthur's untimely demise was fairly recent, or someone was keeping it hush-hush.

"Mrs. MacArthur…Eloise. My sympathies for your loss." I gathered myself, hesitant to press her. Or to disappoint. "I'm unsure why you're here. Have you been to the police?"

"The police think I did it!" Her eyes snapped, and her voice lost its genteel smoothness. "A gold-digging washer woman who murdered her playboy husband for his money. That's what they're all thinking!" She drooped abruptly, like a limp dishrag. "I know what the gossip columns say, but it's not like that. Dean gave up carousing when we married. He said he only had eyes for me."

Indignant on her behalf, or perhaps bewitched by her dimpled smile, I was already mentally on the case. I reached across the desk and awkwardly patted her hand. Smooth operator I was not.

"Why don't you just tell me what happened?"

"I'd been at Saks Fifth Avenue yesterday afternoon. Dean had told me to get myself something special for his new club opening tomorrow night." She paused, swallowing hard.

So, the death was fresh. I expected the papers would be splashed with ugly headlines in the morning.

"And did you purchase anything?"

"You'll laugh." The tips of her ears flamed red, matching her hair.

"Madam, everything you tell me is confidential. On my honor."

I placed my hand on my heart and schooled my features into a tried and true image of honesty. It was a well-practiced look, honed by hours in front of the mirror.

Eloise took a shaky breath and carried on, "Everything was so beautiful, but expensive." She shook her head. "I know Dean can – could – afford it. But it seemed so frivolous. I left without buying anything. Embarrassed by my silliness, I dismissed the driver, figuring I'd walk home through the park."

"And he just left you, alone in the middle of Manhattan?" I frowned.

"The staff is used to my...*oddities* by now. I didn't grow up with a silver spoon in my mouth. All the fuss and attention makes me uncomfortable. Besides, my own two feet have always been good enough to get me where I'm going." She flashed me her dimples. "A least when I'm not wearing heels."

This broad was one diamond in the rough. I wondered if MacArthur had known what a treasure he had married.

"What happened when you arrived home?"

"It was about an hour before dinner. I wasn't expecting Dean to be there. He'd been so preoccupied with the new club opening that some evenings he didn't arrive until the plates hit the table. He was burning the candles at both ends, but he was as happy as a kid in a candy store. So excited about the project."

Eloise paused when I cleared my throat.

"I thought I'd read in the 'Inquirer' that Mr. MacArthur was a silent partner in the night clubs? That he just fronted the money and his partner – what's his name, Frankie Rizzoli – really ran the show."

Eloise shivered when I mentioned Frankie's name and I made a mental note. No surprise though, Frankie was a snake in the grass – sneaky, poisonous, and quick to strike. Everyone knew that Frankie's 'nightclubs' were really fronts for speakeasies, but MacArthur's name added legitimacy. That, and his money kept the police out of the clubs. In an official capacity, anyways. I, myself, had been known to raise a glass or four of smoky, amber spirits in the duo's fine establishments, seated next to the Chief of Police and his off-duty lackeys.

"My husband learned a lot about running the clubs from Frankie." Her nose wrinkled when she said Frankie's name. "So much so, that Dean thought he might try the next one on his own."

I bet Frankie was thrilled by that thought. I redirected her to the matter at hand.

"So, when you arrived home?"

"The house was quiet, the staff busy preparing the evening meal. It was the butler's day off, so I hung up my coat and headed to the front parlor. It's way at the front of the house, you see, far from the hustle and bustle of the kitchen. I thought I'd have a quiet moment alone before Dean came home for dinner."

Eloise hesitated, and I nodded encouragingly.

"The parlor door was closed, which I thought odd at the time. When I went inside…"

She hid her face in my handkerchief, shoulders shaking. I could barely make out the mumbled words – *strangled* and *scarf* and *horrified*.

"Madam, please dry your eyes. It's always darkest before dawn, but I'll find out who did this to your husband or die trying."

I only hoped that the last part wasn't prophecy. I hated to toot my own horn, but as private eyes went, I was good at what I did. But petty theft and dockworker's disputes were small potatoes compared to a high society murder. Had I bitten off more than I could chew?

The next morning at the MacArthur residence, I elbowed my way past reporters circling like sharks in blood infested waters. A young officer, still wet behind the ears, stood at attention by the door. I whipped out my credentials, flashing them too fast for him to see.

"Private Detective Kelley, here at the request of Mrs. MacArthur."

"Detective, eh?" The voice behind me dripped sarcasm. "That's what yer calling yerself these days?"

I glanced over my shoulder into the doughy face of Captain Cross of the Manhattan precinct of the NYPD. I nodded.

"Captain."

"Ace."

He narrowed his beady eyes at me, then glanced to the officer at the door.

"Let him through, kid. There ain't nothin' he's gonna turn up that we ain't already seen. The *lady* of the house requested him personal like." He drawled out 'lady' as if it were a dirty word.

Eloise had been right, New York City's finest had already made up their minds about her. Their constant assumptions and bungled cases were why I'd left the force in the first place. I balled my fists at my sides. It took all my willpower not to clock him one, right in the kisser, but it wouldn't do to get on Cross's bad side. He still owed me a favor, after I broke that smuggling case wide open for him last spring. No reason to give him an axe to grind and forget what side his bread was buttered on. Then where would I be? Up a creek without a paddle, that's where.

Cross showed me through into the foyer, down the hall, and into the parlor. He folded his arms over his chest, his belly straining the buttons of his uniform shirt. I shook my head, noting a greasy smudge on his sleeve.

"Listen Ace, there ain't nothin' to see. MacArthur was found in that fancy armchair over there. Strangled by a lady's scarf. The Missus already confirmed it belongs to her." His face split into a disgusting leer. "Them redheads have tempers, eh?"

"Really, Cross? And pray tell, how would a delicate young flower like Mrs. MacArthur have the strength to overpower a large man like her husband."

"Drunk as a skunk. We found an empty glass beside him." The Captain puffed up like a balloon. "Sherry. I *sniffed* it." Cross seemed proud as a peacock with his stellar detective work.

I, on the other hand, was less than impressed. Drunk? In the middle of the afternoon? Wantonness and extravagance were much flaunted in the face of prohibition, but I had a hard time believing a businessman and gentlemen like MacArthur would be befuddled before the dinner hour.

Scuff marks in the carpet in front of the armchair caught my eye. I leaned over to inspect them more closely. Definitely a sign of a struggle; MacArthur hadn't gone quietly into the void. I stood and rubbed my temples, a headache coming on. It throbbed like a bass drum behind my eyes.

"Do me a favor Cross and don't arrest Eloise just yet."

"Eloise? So that's how it is?"

He was beyond the pale. Once again, I fought down the urge to pop him in the mouth and wipe that stupid smirk off his face. God, I needed a drink.

"Your case against *Mrs. MacArthur* is circumstantial at best." I raised my eyebrows and shot him a pointed look. "You owe me. Just give me until tonight and I'll give you the real killer, wrapped up in a tidy bow."

There was no way, Eloise had done this. I was beginning to have my suspicions about who and why. I was going to have to bite the bullet and go see Frankie Rizzoli.

After making arrangements to cash in that aforementioned favor, I headed out to the grand opening of Dean and Frankie's new nightclub, The Pink Pearl. The siren song of cool jazz wafted out of the smoke-filled room, almost making me forget why I was there. I handed my hat to the coat-check girl and made my way across the room to settle at an empty table. Back to the wall, I ensured that I had a clear view of the room.

"What can I get ya, boss?" The serving girl wore a scandalously short skirt and her dark hair, black as coal, was held back by a wide headband. A cheeky feather attached at the side waved like a flag at full mast.

"Whiskey. Neat." I held up my hand before the waitress could turn away. "Make that a double." I tried not to stare at the swishing fringe on her skirt as she waltzed away.

While I waited for my drink, I let the music creep into my soul. The rhythmic plunking of the bass, the brokenhearted wail of the sax, the brassy lament of the cornet, all blended together in an age-old tale of love lost. The song was familiar, and I wracked my brain trying to remember the title. It was on the tip of my tongue when the glass of smoky ambrosia arrived.

I tossed the serving girl a dime, my good deed for the day. We paid to see the show, but the spirits were complimentary.

MacArthur had thought of that, a loophole in the law, allowing them to operate openly, unlike a normal speakeasy – if push came to shove, he couldn't be booked for selling alcohol when he was giving it away for free. Clever boy. I took a sip and let the glorious, peaty burn run down my throat. It seared away my headache and left me sharp as a tack, crystal clear.

I surveyed the room. Frankie had yet to show his face but unsurprisingly, the club was chockablock full of a boisterous opening night crowd. I nodded to a familiar face at a table near the band. Patrons had come out in droves, once they learned that one of the owners had been found murdered. The whole sordid affair was front page news and every daily rag in the county was fighting to one up their competition with sensational headlines.

Playboy Heir to the MacArthur Fortune Found Strangled in Parlor

Dean MacArthur Gone Too Soon, Who'll Be Next

Murder in Manhattan: Even the Wealthy Aren't Safe

And the least savory of the lot –

Gold Digging Wife Primary Suspect in Nightclub Owner's Gruesome Death

Eloise had rung in a tizzy when she'd read that last one. It took several long minutes, and the gentle reminder that I was on a party line, before she calmed down. Or perhaps it was the surreptitious cough in the background that talked her off the ledge. You never knew who was listening in, most likely my landlady – a hatchet-faced woman whose bark was worse than her bite.

Once Eloise had composed herself, I had told her to stick close to home. I was getting close to finding out who the real killer was. The closer I got the more danger she was in. I promised, with the luck of the Irish, her name would be clear by morning. It may have been a fool's promise, but I couldn't help myself.

I took another sip of whiskey and continued my surveillance on the room. Speak of the devil, and there she was. So much for sticking close to home. Eloise looked a vision, her long, fitted dress a riot of sparkling sequins. It flared at the knees and left her creamy shoulders exposed. Her bright russet waves were offset by black elbow gloves and a velvet choker around her elegant throat.

She greeted the patrons like a queen receiving court. There was something to be said about her poise, nature versus nurture, or some such tired proverb. I doubted she had learned that grace from her husband's blue-blood kin. It was born, not learned. She caught my eye and had the good sense to blush. Stubborn woman.

Across the room, Frankie Rizzoli finally graced us with his presence, stepping out from behind a door marked 'Private.' My stomach clenched as he noticed Eloise and a dark cloud crossed his swarthy face. He stalked towards her and I leapt to my feet, pushing through the crowd.

Desperate to reach Eloise first, I plowed across the dancefloor, shouting apologies over my shoulder. I clipped a laughing young woman, her drink clattering to the floor. Her date roared and took a swing, but against all odds, I managed to duck the blow. I spiraled through the dancers, as if clutching a touchdown pass, evading the hefty linebackers looking to tackle me to the ground.

As I burst through the throng, I caught a glimpse of Frankie clamping his hand like a vise around Eloise's arm. Quick as a wink, he hustled her through the storeroom door. Heart in my throat and breathing hard, I followed. I rued the fact that I wasn't quite as spry as I was in high school, my old knee injury singing.

I crashed through the door and skittered to a halt. Frankie had a Colt .45 pressed against Eloise's fair head.

"Close the door."

With a click, the jazz dampened, still audible through the closed door, if subdued. I took a step around a crate of whiskey bottles, mind whirling, abandoning plan after plan on how to get out of this pickle.

"That's close enough, Ace."

I raised an eyebrow.

"Oh yeah, I know who you are. Goddamned meddlesome, washed up, ex-copper, that's who."

I measured the distance between us.

"Come now, Frankie, you don't have to do this. Why don't you hand me the gun and just walk out that back door, free as a jaybird?"

He laughed and cocked the pistol. Eloise whimpered, and I froze.

"Or how about I kill you both? Self-defense, you know? She killed her husband, then she came after me."

I shook my head. "But you and I both know Miss Eloise didn't kill anyone."

"Tell that to the jury."

"Why Frankie?" Eloise pleaded, voice shaking. "You and Dean were friends. We were all as thick as thieves."

"Don't pretend you ever liked me, doll. I've got your number." Frankie snorted. "And Dean was no friend of mine. He was pushing me out, so he had to go. Nothin' personal chickadee, but I had to set you up. With Dean-o dead and you in jail, full ownership of the nightclubs reverts to me. All of them."

Gotcha.

"I think we've heard quite enough, don't you Captain Cross?"

Behind me, the door shot open and two plain clothes officers crowded in. Cross hovered in the doorway, his police issued Smith & Wesson .38 special trained on Frankie. To his credit, despite being stuffed into a too-small smoking jacket like a sausage in a casing, he didn't waver.

"Drop it, Rizzoli. Or not. I've been looking fer a reason to put you down fer years."

Quick as lightning, Frankie pushed Eloise at me and dove for the door. Cross squeezed off a round, bullet ripping through the horsehair plaster. Frankie pointed the Colt over his shoulder and fired without aiming.

Time slowed. I sprang forward, bum knee protesting. I ignored the pain. The only thing that mattered was Eloise. I pushed her out of the way and fire exploded in my shoulder. The roar of gunfire sounded muffled, as if my ears were stuffed with cotton. Then the world went dark.

I came to with Eloise patting my cheek, tears streaming down her face. Behind her, the bullet laden corpse of Frankie Rizzoli lay sprawled, a crimson pool of blood staining the hardwood. Guess he never made it to the door.

"Hey now doll-face. Don't cry for me; I'm right as rain." I struggled to sit upright. Agony lanced through me and I flopped back down, gasping like a fish out of water.

"Naw, don't get up Ace." Captain Cross's broad face swam above me. "Yer gonna get a ride in the NYPD ambulance." He grinned but all I could see through my pain-blurred vision were his crooked teeth. "It's the first of its kind you know. Police transport only, but fer you we'll make an exception."

Eloise gripped my hand and I stared up, losing myself in her angelic eyes. I had known, the minute she had walked into my office, that dame would cause me no end of trouble. I hated always being right.

Corrine Ji's Story
EB Stark
Third Place

    For Corrine Ji, life had always been more dark-and-stormy-night than once-upon-a-time. She stood in front of her vanity pulling a brush through long, limp tresses that had about as much vitality as her social life. She turned this way and that, scrutinizing her not-quite-Lucy-Liu frame—boobs too small, waist not small enough; not to mention the pimples that dotted her non-descript face. *Screw it,* she thought. Jacques had chosen her. That had to mean something, right?

    Jacques Hooza douche—the dreamy French guy who had taken their baseball team all the way to nationals—had asked *her* to help him in trigonometry. He could have chosen anyone in the entire school, and oh-my-god-are-you-serious, he chose her. So there was a chance after all—one last chance to get someone to fall for her before prom.

    She pushed tortoiseshell frames up the bridge of her nose and took one last look in the mirror. *What am I missing*? She grabbed a tube of Lipsmackers and glossed those heart-shaped lips—with strawberry flavor, of course—in case he wanted to kiss her. Then she bounded down the stairs, past her passed-out uncle (same ole, same ole), and out the front door.

    And there Loy waited—as if he lived his life just to be there when she needed him.

    She slid into the passenger side of his baby-poop-yellow Chevette and pulled on a worn loop of leather. "Your dad still hasn't gotten you a door panel?"

    "Not in the budget," Loy said, cranking the volume knob down a couple of notches.

    "Wow. I can almost hear myself think now."

    He cranked it down a couple more notches. "At your service, madame," he said with an exaggerated flourish and put the car in reverse.

    Corrine flipped down the visor mirror and studied her features some more. Loy thumped the steering wheel while the Fine Young Cannibals testified about chicks driving them crazy.

    Though everyone who was anyone at Justin Aver Ridge High School thought they were too cool to hang out with the shy-and-tragically-orphaned-Asian-girl, Loy L. Bessdi had always acted like there was no one on the planet he'd rather spend his hours with than her. And that's why she loved the kid—in the most platonic way possible, of course.

Loy snuck a glance at Corrine. Then another. He belted out the chorus—as loud and off key as he could manage—until she acknowledged him.

"Could you be any more annoying?" she gaped at him.

"Sure, I could," he said. "But then you probably wouldn't tell me."

"Tell you what?"

"Why you agreed to tutor the biggest jerk in the school."

Corrine rolled her eyes. "You wouldn't understand."

"Really?" he said. "Thought you said I knew you better than anyone on the planet."

"So?"

"*So*," he said, "how many times have we watched the guy push underclassmen into lockers? Knock stacks of books out of the Chess Club's members' hands? Grope cheerleaders' butts?"

Corrine stared out the passenger-side window, refusing to look at him.

"We even saw the prick cheat on his girlfriend," Loy said, his voice rising.

"They're not together anymore," Corrine said, and took a deep breath. "He likes me now."

"What?" Loy gawped.

"Think about it." Corrine turned to face him. "Why didn't he choose any of the Honors or AP kids?"

"Because they're not Asian," Loy said.

Corrine drew in a sharp breath. She was so tired of people's ignorant assumptions. "Wrong." She looked back out the window. "I know he likes me. And the feeling's mutual."

Loy yanked his FYC cassette out of the player and shoved a new one in. Richard Marx's crooning voice glided through the speakers assuring her that no matter what it took—or how deeply his heart might break—he'd still be there, waiting for her.

All Corrine could think was, *since when do you listen to Richard Marx?*

Corrine walked into the Starbucks on Main, and it was already teeming with teenagers. She found Jacques and met him at the back of the line. "How are we going to study in all of this?"

He gave her a blank look and said, "Were you going to order anything? I've only got eight bucks."

Corrine was too ashamed to admit she had no money, so she just shrugged. "Can't stand coffee, actually." That was lie number one—she lived for coffee. *Not starting this relationship out very well*, she thought.

"Perfect," he said and folded his wallet.

She must have been seeing things, because it sure looked like a fat stack of bills pushed in there, all willy-nilly. And wasn't that Andrew Jackson's white swoop poking out?

"What can I get you, sweetie?" the barista said when it was their turn.

"Yeah, Caramel Macchiato, venti, coconut milk, extra shot, extra hot, with extra whipped cream. Oh, and make it skinny."

The lady whose nametag read "Mamie" repeated all ninety-seven instructions with a smile, but Corrine could read the disdain hiding behind her plump, dimpled cheeks. If disdain was all she'd felt at that point, though, they could all have gotten away unscathed. Unfortunately, that's not the way the stars had written it to go down.

Mamie called him once she'd finished his drink—well, the brash American pronunciation of his name, anyway. And that's what got the whole thing started.

"*Jock*? Was that supposed to be a cheap shot, lady?" he goaded her.

Her mouth opened as though to respond, but nothing came out.

"Let me guess; grew up the token fat girl, right?"

"No, I—" Mamie's eyes had more liquid pooling in them than the Colorado River. Corrine wanted to disappear.

Got your ass razed daily by the jocks, huh?"

The barista's lip trembled and the straw she held bounced like a Mexican Jumping Bean.

Corrine reached out for Jacques' arm. "Hey, she didn't mean—"

He turned to look at Corrine, but continued his assault. "Same gluttonous, pathetic loser." He snatched his drink and stalked off.

Corrine looked at Mamie and wanted to cry, herself. *He had still been talking to Mamie, though, right? Even though he was looking at her?* Corrine mouthed an apology and ran after Jacques.

She found him glowering at a table in the middle and took a seat across from him.

"I'm not in the mood to study, anymore," he gruffed at her.

"Okay," Corrine said in a voice as tiny as she felt at that moment. "Are you going to take me home?"

"You didn't drive?"

"Yeah—no, I have a ride. It's not a problem." Her face and ears burned. She turned to leave.

"Wait. One thing." His voice has softened a note or two.

"Yeah?"

"Are you, uh—" Jacques twirled the steaming paper cup in his palms. She heard a snicker coming from the group of guys in the booth across from them.

The silence filled the space between them, and Corrine felt as though it sucked all the air out of the room. She just needed to get out of there. She turned again, toward the exit.

"Would you go to prom with me," he said in a sprint, squishing every word on top of the one before it, so that she couldn't be certain what he'd said.

She stood frozen for what seemed like forever, until finally she mouthed the one all-important word. "Prom?"

"Yeah," he said, looking at the surface of the table.

"Oh, my god, *yes*," she almost squealed, and then fought the urge to run and hug him.

And then the booth across from them erupted—guffaws, hoots, and high-fives all around. And then—the unmistakable cackle of the school's Queen Bee—Eve Vilbitch herself. She pranced toward them like the Christ Himself, her seven disciples at her heels, each clamoring to see who could lick Eve's ass the quickest and best. And she couldn't seem to stop laughing.

"My god, you did it," she gushed, and planted a huge, sloppy kiss on Jacques' mouth right in front of everyone. "Okay, you win my forgiveness."

Jacques' face slid into an oily grin and Corrine felt the bile moving up her throat.

"So yes, my love," she said, and looked straight at Corrine. "Yes, I *will* go to prom with you. Because you fucking *earned it*."

Loy was still outside in the parking lot when she burst through the exit doors, tears and snot and mascara running rivers down her cheeks—and he jumped out and scooped her up in his arms and told her Jacques was the stupidest guy on the whole planet.

"Who *wouldn't* want to take you to prom?" he said, smoothing her hair after the tears had spilled and the snot had dried on his favorite t-shirt.

And all of a sudden Corrine understood his sudden interest in Richard Marx and his newest hit single. *Right here waiting.*

Mom Life
Katie Evans
Fourth Place

"Can you *please* put your shoes on Jeremy!" I yell for the fifteenth time while holding a bobby pin between my teeth. I pin the purple bow into Mia's hair, because, of course, the pink bow I had pinned in there earlier wasn't acceptable with her glittery puppy shirt and she's already had a meltdown.

I barely have time to add more coffee into my travel mug as I push the kids out the door, into our shiny SUV at the end of the driveway. They strap their seatbelts on and both pull out electronics for their morning screen time. I know I should stop them, that we should talk or sing songs or something, but I'm so frazzled at this point in the day, that I don't care.

And that's the worst of it – when did I get to the point where getting two kids to school frazzles me? I gave up my career to be a stay-at-home mom. I was in sales, I had plenty of clients who threw temper tantrums and I had plenty of deadlines. I navigated that just fine.

I realize I've left my phone, so I yell to the kids that I'll be right back. They barely look up. I take a deep, calming breath as I walk back in the house. It's a beautiful home, with a welcoming entryway where our shoes and coats often wait for us. The refrigerator is covered in Mia's drawings, Jeremy's good grades, pictures, and new baby announcements. I have one of those "Live, Laugh, Love" scripts on the hallway wall. There's an honest-to-goodness white picket fence in the front yard.

On the drive to their prestigious private school, I relax. My morning ritual awaits. I pull into a parking space and help the kids out of the car. With kisses, hugs and loving words, I send them off to their classes and stroll over to my usual crowd. A circle of moms wait for me and welcome me into their tribe. Most of these women grew up here too.

"Good morning Rachel!," they greet me as a chorus. I smile in return.

"Crazy morning," I say. "Rebecca, I just don't know how you do it with three!"

And so begins our usual banter, until Leah's dad walks by. That's when conversation ceases, and our eyes tell the whole story. The handsome, recently-widowed lawyer walks hand-in-hand with his lovely daughter to the playground every morning. Our daily eye candy: James Westfield.

"He even brought her to school before his wife died," says Tiffany. "I don't think Ken has even done it once."

Her grimace changed to a bright smile when her eyes met mine.

"At least Chris does it sometimes, right Rachel? But, of course, Chris Green would!"

Everyone in town knows Chris, well both of us really. We grew up here together. High school sweethearts. We were the captains of the football team and cheer squad, then prom king and queen. We'd gone off to college together and come back to our home town to start our family. In addition to owning a local business, Chris was the president of the Chamber of Commerce. It was fair for Tiffany to assume the best, because she was right. Chris is the best.

James walks by again and gives us a wave.

"So Rachel," Rebecca asks. "What are you bringing to the PTA meeting tonight? I hope it's those chocolate chips cookies everyone loves!"

Panic. I totally forgot. Now I have to bake cookies today.

"Of course!"

"Great! We have a lot to talk about with our big fundraisers coming up!"

I smile and excuse myself. Now I need to get to grocery shopping and make sure Chris will be home on time.

I climb into the car and use my Bluetooth to call him as I rush to the store.

"I completely forgot about this meeting. Can you please be home by 5:30 tonight to take care of the kids?"

"I'm sorry babe!" he says. She can hear his keyboard clicking the background. "I can't. I already have an important meeting scheduled tonight, didn't I tell you this morning?"

Honestly, he might have. The mornings are a blur.

"Okay, I'll call a sitter. No problem."

"Thanks. Hey, I have to go, a client is calling on the other line. Have a good day, love you!"

I reach to hang up the phone but drop it between the seats. I think I hear a click before I hear Chris again.

"Oh Sarah. I can't wait to get my hands on you tonight. I've been thinking about your body all morning."

Time stops. Thankfully I'm at a red light. I stop breathing.

"Sarah?"

I swallow hard.

"No, Chris. It's still me."

Six months later, I push my shopping cart slowly through the store. I glance down – Uncrustables, chips, and wine. Lots and lots of wine. I also catch a glimpse of a stain on my yoga pants. I am not sure of the last time I washed these.

"What did I need again?" I mumble to myself. My messy hair hasn't been washed in a few days. I can feel tendrils of it falling from the bun onto my neck and face.

"Rachel?" I look up to see Rebecca standing right in front of me. Her cart is full of produce. She's in yoga pants too – clean LuLu Lemon yoga pants with a perfectly coordinated top. Her sleek dark hair is cropped at her chin and styled perfectly. "I'm so glad to see you. I've been calling. Um…are you okay? Are you feeling sick?"

"Oh…um…no I'm fine. Just doing a little shopping. I…um…I just left the gym actually," I lie and try to smooth my hair back.

The look on her face tells me she doesn't buy it for a second.

"Look Rachel, I know that you're having a hard time with the divorce," she took a small step toward me. "This is a probably a bad place to have this conversation, but you haven't returned any of my texts and I am worried about you."

"Oh, no. I'm fine. I've just been really busy lately."

Rebecca presses her lips together and gives me a sympathetic look.

"Okay Rachel," she says. "Take care."

She walks away. For a moment, I'm tempted to yell for her – to tell her I'm not okay and to come back. That I need a hug and a shoulder to cry on. That trying to make this as easy as I can on the kids has forced me to hide my pain away and suffer alone in my room all night, every night. That I need a friend.

But I let her walk away.

When I get home, I carry in my groceries and see myself in the entryway mirror. I have bags under my eyes and they're are red from crying this morning. My clothes are dirty. My roots are grown out and about half of my fingernails are covered in chipped pink polish.

I grab the mail I'd previously tossed on the counter to distract myself. Bill, bill, junk mail, something from the lawyers, and…an invitation. It is time for our high school reunion. It is addressed to Chris and I together; apparently the reunion committee isn't up on the latest gossip. I flip it over in my hands. The event is going to be

Great Gatsby themed and held at a new swanky restaurant. I wonder if Chris knows. I wonder if he will take Sara with him and introduce her to everyone – all the people who voted us "Cutest couple" in the yearbook. I can't bear the thought of it.

I've met Sara few times now, when I drop off the kids to visit their dad. She is beautiful, of course. She's an athletic blonde, about five years younger than I am. She has perfect boobs, because she's never had children. And she's always so composed, so well-put together. I guess that's how I probably was before kids too, but it's hard to remember.

I am sure if Chris wanted to go to his reunion, she'd be thrilled. She'd dress up and look stunning, she'd laugh at all the right jokes, she'd tell engaging stories. I guess I used to do that too.

I throw the invitation away and I grab the keys off the counter. Time to pick up the kids. On the way to the front door, I pass a photo from a girls' night out. It feels like it was a million years ago, but really it wasn't long at all. I am laughing with my girlfriends. We all look wonderful. Rebecca has her arm around me and all seem to be having the time of our lives. Chris isn't in this photo because he wasn't there, of course. And look at what a good time I'm having without Chris.

I realize in that momentthat I've let Chris control my happiness for a long time. Even now. He's not even my husband anymore, but I've let him be the deciding factor in so many things that I do.

I set down the photo, walk back into the kitchen and pull the invitation of the trash. We'll see about this.

At school, I park my car and walk over to my mom friends. I smile. I talk. I tell them I'm sorry for being so distant. They hug me and encourage me and forgive me – just like good friends would.

With both kids buckled in, I climb into my front seat. I grip the wheel and take a deep breath. I feel good, really good. Determined.

When we get home, I feed them a snack and set up to do their homework. Then I go upstairs, I shower and (finally) shave my legs. I put on lotion. I even blow dry my hair.

I text Rebecca and ask her to coffee tomorrow, where I will apologize to her more than I was able at the school.

I spent the rest of a happy afternoon playing with the kids, and I go to bed feeling satisfied and grateful...and eager for the tomorrow.

Once the kids are at school, I pull out my phone and do something I should have done a long time ago: I shoot an email to my old boss asking for a meeting. She responds right away.

"Rachel! It is so good to see you," I stand to greet Rebecca and give her a huge hug. She gives me big, genuine smile. "You look great."

"I owe you an apology." She tries to wave me off. "No. I do. You've always been a good friend and I've been terrible lately."

"I understand. You've been through a lot."

"But I should have looked to you for support instead of pushing you away. You were very kind and patient."

Relief floods my whole body and I feel my shoulders relax. We fall into comfortable conversation for awhile – what antics have the kids taken up now? Must we really participate in that bake sale? Can you believe what Tanya said about Lisa?

"I might have some news," I confess. Rebecca raises her eyebrows and sips her coffee. "I have a meeting with Angela this afternoon. I'm thinking of going back to work, just part time, but I think it would really be good for me."

"That's a great idea! You were always so good at your job and you seemed to really love it."

"I did really love it. I mean, I love taking care of the kids too, but I miss my job. Chris really wanted to me stay home, but I'm not sure that's what I really wanted."

Rebecca nods at me.

"I got an invitation to the high school reunion yesterday," I continue. "I'm going."

"Really? What about Chris? Is he going?"

"I don't know and, honestly, I don't care. But I'm going. I'm not going to let Chris control my life anymore."

"You're like a new woman this morning!"

Two weeks later, I am wearing a gorgeous green cocktail dress – Chris hates green on me. My hair is styled in Gatsby-era waves, and I even have on fake eyelashes. My heels are sky high. The sitter is already playing a game with the kids when I step out the door. Rebecca and her husband, Steve, are picking me up.

Steve wolf whistles at me as I step to the car.

"You look great!" Rebecca adds. "Green is your color!"

As soon as we step into the restaurant, a server offers us champagne. I take a flute. The bubbles tickle my tongue.

I lift my head high, smile and start to mingle. It's so nice to see everyone! I can't believe I almost missed out on this. I get to catch up with people who moved away and friends I never see anymore. We snack on passed hor d'oeuvres. I sip more and more champagne. A group of us hit the photo booth, making goofy faces and wearing silly props.

I step out of the photo booth, still laughing, and come face to face with Chris. I stand up straight and give him and Sara a polite smile.

Chris shakes his head a bit and looks me up and down. "Rachel?"

"Hi Chris. Hello Sara."

"Wow. You look…uh," he glances at Sara and composes himself. "You look very nice. It is nice to see you."

"Thanks! Try the scallops! They're delicious!" I turn on my heel and saunter away towards Rebecca, who is smiling wickedly.

I pick up another glass of champagne and clink it with hers.

"That. Was. Awesome." She replies.

We pass around the aspirin the next morning at the school drop off, but we are still in good spirits. The reunion was a lot of fun and has left us with a lot of "Can you believe *he* became a doctor…"-type stories. I am so glad I went. I feel better than I have in years – even with a hangover.

James Westfield walks by and we all pause to look. He kisses Leah goodbye and she runs off, backpack bouncing behind her. I smile at him and he gives me a small wave. Rebecca elbows me in the ribs.

"Go talk to him."

I smile and take the first step.

Reflections
Dominique Goodall
Fifth Place

　　　I glared at the mirror in mute hatred. I couldn't see my reflection, but I knew what it would show. Long, black hair, black eyes, skin so white I made milk look yellow. Teeth that peeked from below my lips, sharpened like those of a cat. I was every Hollywood vampire and worse. I was haunted by the people I killed and yet, when hunger called me, – I had to answer. And she was a mistress so bloody that death was what she demanded from me.
　　　I knew his touch before he spoke in my ear, lips so close to my throat that I shuddered with a fearful kind of ecstasy.
　　　"You look gorgeous as always. You'll hunt well this evening, even though you left it late." The scolding was mild, and I smiled at my master over my shoulder, peering up at him from beneath demure eyelashes, lowered protectively across my dark eyes.
　　　"Of course I will. I've never let you down, have I?" I spoke even as he swept himself away from me, two words echoing around my room, coffin opened and ready for bed.
　　　"Feed. Now!"
　　　And the demand was again so loud that I had to leave the darkness of my castle room to hunt for food. My stomach gurgled as I moved through the night, head lifted proudly. I knew that I had powers no human could match. I left the Kiss behind me, knowing that they could sense my growing hunger and the urges that I refused to ignore. Blood, death – they all equalled power that my Master offered to me. I knew he took a portion of it for himself, but there was a reason for me to be the strongest of the Kiss.
　　　I stalked the streets, delicate heels drumming on the cobblestones. I clutched my shawl close around my shoulders, carefully curled hair tumbling around my shoulders. I looked like a prostitute – an upper-class one, but a prostitute, it was true. I deliberately cultivated the look with darkened cosmetics around my eyes, until the black was bottomless. I stretched myself against a damp wall, writhing slowly against it as I sensed the warmth of potential victims coming close.
　　　"Anyone looking for some company?" I purred the words out, keeping my teeth hidden behind pouting lips. I could have bespelled the lot of them with ease, but the less power I expended now, the

more I could keep. I could smell the alcohol in their blood, see it in the way most of them struggled to stand upright. Bravado seemed to be stronger in men that were in groups *and* drunk.

"Pretty sure we're out of money, love. Move on to the next group. There's a good lass." The only person who didn't smell of alcohol made me narrow my eyes. He was the one I wanted most, simply because he was the one who'd offer me the biggest challenge. Running my tongue across my lips, I dragged myself off the wall, sauntering closer and stroking a razor-sharp nail along the shoulders of my targets.

I didn't bleed them *yet* as I approached him, smirking as he stood his ground. He wouldn't admit to fear, not even when I heard his pulse rocketing. He might not have understood it consciously, but his body knew he was prey, and that I would happily drink him down to nothing. Bracing my hands on his chest, I stood on tiptoes despite my heels. Lips pressed to his ear, brushing sensually against it as I whispered into his ear.

"Them, I'd charge. You… I wouldn't. Why would I charge someone who takes such care of his body?" I ran my fingers down his chest, lingering on his stomach as I backed off a little, peering at him from under my eyelashes.

"Get in there, Joel!"

"She wants a piece of you!"

"Let ya hair down for once, ya fool!"

I let his friends taunt him as I cocked a hip. I knew somewhere deep inside, I felt guilt and remorse. But I knew just how to seduce a man, especially one being catcalled by his friends.

"Maybe you wouldn't know what to do with me, hmmm Joel?" I let the tease and challenge fill the air between us, dark eyes gleaming as his green ones met mine. I didn't play with the powers that offered me strength. I let everything that made me a vampire speak for me. I was slender, but curvaceous, with an alluring way about me… with confidence. Most men didn't like the shy, quiet women of the Kiss. They preferred my arrogance.

"I can't leave you guys behind. Who'll drive you home?" He was making excuses now, jade eyes looking at me with longing more than anything else. I knew he'd never had a woman like me before. I also knew he wouldn't truly have me, but they didn't need to know that. My stomach growled, and I peered quickly at the sky. I'd spent hours raging in front of a mirror. How close to dawn was it?

I had time. I had to have time. I saw no shadows, so I should be okay for now. In my worry, I'd missed the conversation between the men, and my target, my victim, stood in front of me, suddenly seeming shy. Smiling up at him, I slipped my arm through his, patting his hand with my own.

"Don't worry, we won't go too far, Joel. Just somewhere to… get to know each other better." I spoke softly, letting him lean over me to hear my voice. A voice that I allowed to gain some power now, so he couldn't resist. We walked off, ignoring the comments and somewhat crude suggestions of his drunkard friends.

"You're cold…" I peered at his unfocused green eyes and smiled, feigning a shiver.

"I've been outside for hours. A gentleman would at least put his arm around me." I teased him, even though the faintest tendrils of my strength held his disbelief and misgivings at bay. He put his arm over my shoulder and I cuddled into his chest as we made our way into an alleyway. I may not have believed my own charade, but sometimes it was nice to pretend I wasn't undead and seeking to drink someone's blood.

He took charge when we were in the darker shadows of the alley. One hand slid from my shoulder to push me against a wall, and if my heart still pumped, it would have skipped beats. The other cupped my jaw, sliding into my hair seconds later as he leaned himself against me. I shuddered then, bloodlust kicking in as his movements forced my head against his shoulder.

"I see girls like you, all the time. So fun and easy… happy to be whatever their newest boytoy wants them to be, as long as he's paying for it." He growled, even as I swooned under the heat of his body. My hands rose of their own accord, clinging to his shoulders with feigned, feeble strength as he stroked one hand down my side, groping for my skirt.

"I didn't make you pay money for me, did I?" I whispered, even as I felt his rough fingers touch skin, the dip of his shoulder helping to put me in striking range. I was like a snake, eyeing my distance easily as I darted forward, sharp teeth splitting the skin of his throat, puncturing his jugular.

I didn't intend to let him leave.,

He sagged against me, groaning weakly and jerking to my lapping, swallowing motions. My hold lightened and he struggled as he dropped. I was glutted by then, stomach aching – and yet, his death was needed. That was the rush I needed to finish my meal. My stomach snarled for it, as his final tremors knocked us both to the ground.

"Ooops! Wrong place!" I ignored the voice as I straddled my victim, knowing just how it would look to the interloper. I just needed the final flailing he made to fill my stomach, able to sense my master's eagerness as he shared in my desire and my need. He was all I needed. Humans served only one function – they warmed my body and gave me strength.

My victim's final breaths came in a panicked gasp, his heels drumming his body into the ground. I rode him as easily as though he were a pony, or a docile old horse.. In truth, that's how I saw him. His blood had been clean, untouched by alcohol. He'd given his life to preserve mine.

When he was finally still, the thundering of his heart was no more than an echo to linger in my own – his death a reflection of my own, though weaker and, paler, as he wouldn't be reborn as I had been. Licking the blood from my fingers, I nudged his corpse closer to a wall, knowing that rats would soon clean up my meal for me. He'd been a good meal, strong and full of vital strength that was now wholly mine and my master's.

The lightening of the sky when I left the alleyway sent a frisson of panic through me. Pulling my bloodied shawl over my head, I ran, fleet of foot and more agile than any mountain goat. My coffin and and my master awaited, as dawn sapped my strength away. I had to survive long enough to get to the place of safety everyone in our Kiss had.

The sun was on my heels as I passed the castle entrance. I panted, even though I didn't need to. Even though I'd been dead for more than three centuries, the panic was real as I collapsed into my silk-lined coffin and knew no more.

Event 4

CAMPFIRE: Oral storytelling has been part of our tradition since humans developed language. For this Event, write a story to be told around the campfire.
Core Concept: description, narrative, rhythm

The Stained Glass River
Javeria Kausar
First Place

That was a spooky story, Jeffery, and you know spooky stories give me the chills.
No, don't say anything. I understand that camping stories are usually horrifying; but I, Michael Wulfed, am a nervous old grandpa... Well, I do realise that you're a grandpa too, but—
Well, anyway, it's my turn to tell a story. First of all, I'd like to say that I'm glad that I came to this reunion camping trip with you all. It's great to have someone to get together with even at such an old age. It's especially great to spend time with people my age.
So, today, I'd like to tell a story that is a bit, um, different from the usual campfire stories. But I'll have you know that this is a story close to my heart. So here I begin:
"Okay, I'm ready," a man whispered to himself. But a second later, he said uncertainly, "At least I think I am."
Shaking his head as vigorously as he could manage without causing a sprain in his aged neck, the man in the loose nightdress gripped with all his might the railing of the bridge he was standing upon, "There's no time for thinking. I know I'm ready. I have to be ready. There's no other way. I can't keep on living like this."
He stood silent for a moment and then bent over the railing of the old stone bridge. The water had seemed warm and inviting to him every afternoon during his daily walk, but now, in the quiet of the cool summer night—a night much like this one—the river lay before him like an abysmal abyss. He shivered, "No, I can't do this." He looked up a few seconds later, "Can I?"
Soft grey clouds swam in the dark night sky, competing with each other to reach the moon. All the stars had already drowned, but the solitary glowing disc refused to give in, as though it still had some hope within.
He sighed and looked off into the distance. His eyes seemed to penetrate deep into the town that lay shimmering in the quiet night. He was sure he saw his family through the stained glass windows of his old Victorian-style villa. He had spent all his youth building that villa, and his wife had added the colourful stained windows a year after their wedding. Those reminded him of her every single day; so much so, that whenever he felt lonely, he would go talk to one of the windows. He did not know whether the

deceased could see or hear anything of this world, but he strongly hoped they could. His wife always listened to him, and he wasn't keen on giving up that now rare pleasure and comfort of being listened to, even though his wife had passed away seven months ago.

"Oh Anna, if only you were here," he found himself at a stained glass window every morning after getting out of bed, and every night before going to bed; not that he could remember the last time he actually slept at night. Being old and alone was hard as it was, but being cursed with extra time, an entire night that too, to brood over his life and circumstances was more than his exhausted mind could handle.

Still gazing at the town of his birth, he felt that he could see his family members having the time of their lives at the party in his villa. His children and teenage grandchildren had been planning for weeks, and now they must surely be dancing the night away, probably blissfully unaware of his absence. Those kids were as good as strangers when they had parties or guests anyway, so he wasn't surprised. But still, but still... how could they forget their own father?

A painful thought crossed his mind, *'What if they didn't forget? What if they noticed I was gone and just said 'Good riddance'?*

That was possible. But, but how could they? Had he not looked after them through long days and longer nights? Had he not been overjoyed at every minor achievement of his kids and depressed at every little sorrow life threw their way? Had he not rushed to wipe off their tears, even though he had to stumble over rocky terrains himself? Had he not given up the only job he ever loved so that his kids wouldn't have to be left alone at a day-care centre? And now, they were planning to send their father to an old-age home? He knew because he had overheard his eldest son asking someone, undoubtedly someone from an old-age home, to give him a bit of discount on the fee, because he was 'pitiably going mad' and speaking to stained glass windows; and also because they couldn't afford a place for him in the asylum!

That good-for-nothing eldest son of the man had always been a miser. But that was not the issue now. If his family didn't want him, was there still any reason left to live? For as long as he could remember, he had lived for them, and now that he was so insignificant that he wasn't even worth having at home, why should he still live through the endless nightmare that life had become?

I'm sorry. I get a bit emotional whenever this incident, um, story comes to my mind. No, Janet, I don't need a tissue, thank you. I just need a moment to collect my thoughts...

Yes, so where was I?

Yes.

So the old man made up his mind. Two wrinkled hands clutched the railing tight as a worn leg slowly went over it. He soon found himself sitting on the railing as though he was on horseback. Just as he was about to bring his other leg to the outside of the railing, his phone hummed a familiar tune, indicating that his youngest daughter was calling.

He had set different ringtones for all his children so that he would never miss their calls, however intermittent they were.

A fresh surge of energy seemed to flood his body. He leapt back onto the safety of the bridge, almost tumbling on the stones that had turned smooth due to always being trod upon. His entire being shook with excitement and joy. With some difficulty, his quivering fingers managed to finally press the answer button.

"Daddy," the sugary voice instantly filled the old man with regret. He felt so angry at himself to have even thought of leaving his family, especially his youngest daughter, forever. He chided himself mentally, *'So they did remember me! Of course no one would be able to forget their own father, or live without him.'*

The daughter interrupted his thoughts, "Daddy? Are you there?"

"Ye-yes, yes, yes, yes, sweetie. I'm here," the man excitedly replied.

"Where are you?"

Before the grateful and happy man could answer, the daughter said, "Where in the world are you? We have been looking for you for two hours!"

Goosebumps enshrouded him as he smiled to himself. *'What in the world was I thinking! Of course they still want me. There's no way I can leave my kids while they still want me.'*

He answered with renewed energy, "I'm here. I'm not far from home... I'll be back soon, my dear Julia. I-"

"You better be," the sugary voice turned as bitter as burnt caramel, "You better be here in ten minutes, old man."

"Julia! Honey, why are you speaking like that?" The old man asked, surprised.

"How else do you want me to speak? Do you want me to serenade you for your senseless actions?" she rattled on in an annoyed voice, "I'm tired of your antics, dad. You just give me and my brothers a hard time. Why can't you act normal and stay put for one single day? Even today you had to run off by yourself, even though you knew we had a party at our place. Because of you, the guests were all worried and they left early. You just enjoy getting all the attention, don't you?"

"Julia, listen to me-" the old man said, helplessly, but the daughter cut him off, "No, dad, you listen to me. I have heard that old people become like children and I was ready to bear that, but you are going overboard now. I know you miss mom, but you have got to get over that. That happened like a year ago. You-"

Before the daughter could complete her rant, the man said in a wheezy voice, "Seven months."

The annoyed daughter nastily said, "What?"

"I said that it has been seven months since your mother passed away," he nearly screamed.

Julia, the daughter seemed to be taken aback at the mild show of hostility, but she recovered quickly, "Well, whatever, just get back here, okay? And don't be melodramatic and cry all the way home. There are still a few guests here, so you better behave."

Before her old father could answer, she disconnected the call; and the man just had one thought hammering his brain: Was it really his daughter? His sweet Julia?

His head became heavy as he admitted to himself that he was being treated exactly the same by all his children; only Julia had never spoken to him that way before. Now he could cross that off his mental list of things that could potentially kill him- drinking, smoking, poison, losing Julia's love, the river...

The river.

The list was meant to be a list of things he had to avoid at all costs, and yet, there he was—almost ready to leap into the silently churning abyss below.

He quickly took his horseback position over the railing again. He stared at the dark river below and felt drawn to it. He wondered if the unshed tears that hid in the bags under his eyes had anything to do with it. They undoubtedly wanted release without being judged or called fake—which was easily possible underwater.

He forcefully shifted his gaze from the water to the direction of his home. He kept gazing in that direction until he was sure that he could see the stained glass windows of his villa.

"Anna," he took a deep breath and whispered, "Oh Anna, I come here every noon, and I go back home afraid. The river scares me. It's like a deadly, watery gorge. I've never had the confidence to even touch that water... but today, I think I do."

He peeled his eyes away from the direction of his villa. He felt ready, and as soon as his eyes met the river, his heart skipped a beat. The river had suddenly turned into a stained glass window. It seemed to him a welcoming sight. He stared at the stained glass river without a word.

"Anna," he said to the river, "I know that taking my life is a sin, but I can't keep living like this. I'm sure you want me to think it through. But—"

He squeezed the railing as his bloodshot eyes opened wide upon a sudden realisation, "Oh no, Anna! What am I doing? If I kill myself, won't the kids be in more trouble?"

He kept gazing at the stained glass river, waiting for a response, just as he gazed at the windows at his villa. His grip loosened, "But if I kill myself now, Anna, the kids will not have to deal with me every day," a chill ran down his bent spine and a tear ran down his sagging cheeks as he said, "They seem to hate me. I, I annoy them."

His grip tightened with rage, "But I was never annoyed at the little annoying things they did as kids, was I, Anna?" he said through gritted teeth and then paused. After thinking for a second he said, "Well, at least I didn't show it."

His grip relaxed again, "But they are my kids...

"And I'm their father. I deserve some respect.

"But I'm sure they mean well whenever they yell at me.

"Oh, who am I kidding? They clearly can't stand me any longer. I should just go away.

"But how can I leave them alone? They are still my kids. I have to stay.

"But... but I bother them, and give them a lot of trouble. I never wanted to, I never tried to; but they say I do, Anna. It's better that I go."

After his conflicting monologue, he gazed hopefully at the stained glass river, "Oh Anna, I want to come to you... But I don't know what to do," he burst into uncontrollable tears. "I suffer every single day, and think of death every single night. I see no other way to put an end to my misery. But still... I cannot put my kids into misery either."

He then sat silent upon the railing. He had finally expressed his feelings, his hopes, his fears, and his long-due tears. He had always thought that being able to give vent to his inner turmoil would somehow heal him and allow him to see things more clearly. But the storm of despair within him raged greater than ever before. He was pining for a true end to his pain, for true relief. He straightened his back with resolve, "Tonight... tonight I will decide- once and for all," he tightened his grip over the railing and shut his eyes tight, "Whether I choose to live or die, I'll do it on the count of three."

He tightened his grip and said with determination, "On the count of three, I will jump either this way, onto the bridge, or that way, into the stained glass. This way, I'll stay with my kids; that way, I'll come to you, Anna."

He took a deep breath and swayed a bit to the right, towards the inviting stained glass river,

"One."

Taking another deep breath, he swayed slightly to the left, "Two."

Janet, why are you crying? Oh, yes, you hate sad endings, right? But the fact is that happy endings are rare.

Why're you getting up, Nancy? Don't you want to hear the rest? No? You don't like sad endings either?

You don't either, Jeff?

Well, why don't you listen to the rest of my story? I assure you that the ending is not as you expect.

C'mon! I listened to all your stories... please listen to mine. I have... I have been wanting to share it with someone... and I'd be glad to share it with you.

Thank you.

So, so where was I? Yes. So the man took a deep breath and counted, "Two."

He then opened his fatigued eyes and dropped both his hands to the side. A couple of seconds passed before he gripped the railing again. He looked at the stained glass river which seemed to shine brilliantly. There was not a cloud visible to his eyes in the river that reflected the sky. His mind was made up. He let go of the railing again, shut his eyes tight, and whispered,

"Thr—"

Before he could complete his count, a voice boomed from behind him, "Hey! Is that you, Mike?"

The old man, Mike, opened his eyes, confused at the strangely familiar voice. Who could it be? Who remembered old Mike?

The booming voice drew closer with each syllable, "Is that really you, Mike Wulfed?"

Mike could hear excited footsteps almost running up to him. The prospect of seeing someone who actually remembered him thrilled him. He forgot everything and almost jumped back onto the bridge. Before him stood a well-dressed man, about the same age as him, with a shining bald head and an equally brilliant smile.

"I knew it was you," the man exclaimed and hugged Mike with incredible energy and warmth, "I'd know that face anywhere!"

Mike could not recognise who the person was, but he felt immensely happy. He thought that the person had mistaken him for some friend of his who was also named Mike Wulfed. He was grateful for the happy mistake which allowed him to experience the joy of being wanted by someone once again.

The person released Mike, "Mike Wulfed! So, how are you?"

Mike Wulfed just smiled with plain confusion written upon his face. The man understood the expression and asked with genuine care, "Don't you remember me, Mike?"

Mike was embarrassed. He lowered his gaze and said regretfully, "I'm sorry. Maybe you've got the wrong Mike."

"No way! There's no way I'd forget that face. Mike, I'm Jeff. Don't you remember? We were in culinary school together back in '86."

Mike's eyes widened, "Jeff? Jeff, the chef?"

Jeff guffawed, "Ah! So you finally remember!"

"How can I not remember? How can I not remember the top student in class! Your food always turned out better than the instructor's," he laughed, "I always thought you'd become a great chef one day and give the instructor a run for his money."

Jeff grinned, "Well, I wouldn't call myself a great chef, but I did work at a Michelin star restaurant for over twenty years."

"That's amazing, Jeff. That's really great!" Mike said.

"What about you? You loved cooking too. Where did you end up working?" Jeff asked eagerly.

Mike's excitement seemed to wane as he remembered the past. A pained smile spread across his face, "I did get a good job, but I gave it up to look after my children."

Jeff sensed a tinge of sadness and tried to change the subject, "Well, what are you doing these days?"

"N-nothing much," Mike replied and looked at the stone railing and the stained glass river waiting beyond.

"Anyway," Jeff said enthusiastically, "We've got a lot to catch up on! I just retired from my job and came back to my hometown.

I've been roaming the entire evening in search of a friendly face. I'm glad I met you."

My eyes widened and my voice quivered, "You're glad to have met me?"

"Of course! Aren't you glad to see this old friend of yours?"

I broke into a smile, "I am. I'm really glad."

"Great! I can't wait to spend more time with you. Let's hit all the old restaurants in town, like we used to in culinary school. Then, it was for research, now it'll be to relive our memories. What do you say?"

For the first time in many months, I felt genuinely elated, and I instantly agreed to accompany Jeff.

"Great! How does tomorrow morning sound?"

"Sounds wonderful!" I told him.

"Then it's fixed- breakfast at Pappy's Diner at eight tomorrow morning. I can't wait to have those loaded chocolate chip pancakes again."

"Me too! Those were my favourite too," I flushed with vigour.

"Then see you there, old friend," Jeff howled as he left, "Pun intended! You are an old friend but you are old too!"

You all know how bad Jeff's jokes are.

My happy gaze followed Jeff until he disappeared. For the first time in seven months I felt overwhelmingly optimistic. Finally, I had something to look forward to. Finally, I was wanted.

I, Mike Wulfed, was wanted!

So I mentally started preparing for my breakfast with Jeff immediately. I planned to wear my green t-shirt and the matching running shoes. I also decided to wear that beret I used to wear back in the day. Oh! And I thought of taking my walking stick, just in case we decided to walk around town. And if we were going to walk and talk a lot, I reasoned that I'd better have a good night's sleep.

So, I... so Mike Wulfed hurried back home with a long-lost skip in his step. And behind him, the stained glass river once again churned back into an uninviting abyss.

...I'll have that tissue now, Janet.

Stay Close to the Fire
Danielle Kiowski
Second Place

Do you hear that? There's a rustling in the forest. No, I don't think it's a bear. And I don't think you'll see it with that phone flashlight. I think it's much too smart for that. What do I mean?

Put that log in the fire and take a seat here next to me. Let's cook up these sausages and I'll tell you. It's a true story, as sure as I sit here — one that happened in these very woods.
I was a boy at the time, not much older than you are now. My daddy took me out here to go fishing. That's your great-grandaddy. No, you didn't ever meet him. He died the year before you were born. That's where you get your middle name from. Yes, his name was Roger. I know you don't like that name too much, I see your nose wrinkling. But you may change your mind yet. Let me tell you what he done that day.

We'd been fishing all afternoon, just like me and you today, but that day we hauled in more than empty lines. Yessir, we had quite the catch. It was sizzling over the fire, skin blistering in the heat, juices bubbling. It was a long day on the lake and I was hungry as anything, so I was sitting there watching it cook. Pa was tending the fire.

My mama was the best cook I ever saw. She had these legendary Sunday suppers. Pot roast and mashed taters. Mm! I remember the carrots that would get stuck at the bottom of the pot and get this crust on them, just pure flavor from that roast. And her pies, I tell you what, they were something else. I never had a pie half as good as her lemon meringue. But I never tasted anything, not anything, as good as a fish that my daddy roasted over a fire after a day out on the lake.

So I was sitting there waiting when we heard a crack in the woods like a shot. Pa jumped to his feet.

"Get close to the fire," he said, and I scooted in as close as I could stand it and I don't mind telling you I was trembling. Pa picked up a branch from the pile of wood that we had for the fire and dipped it in the flames to make a torch. I had never seen him look so fierce, with a blazing branch in one hand and a gutting knife in the other. He was ready, knees half-bent, eyes straining, walking slow around the edge of the clearing and peering into the shadows of the woods beyond our camp.

Well, then the leaves took to rustling something fierce. Pa crouched down and raised that knife up and waited. I wanted to cower down but it was scarier to not see what was coming, so I sat with my eyes fixed on the forest.

And out of the woods, just over there, stepped—

Turn your skewer over, son, see where the sausage is starting to smoke? Don't let it burn. Yeah, I used to say I liked them that way too, back when I was too young to wait for it to cook right. Try it my way and you'll see that patience is worth it. Where was I?

Oh yes. The leaves were rustling. I thought sure it was a bear come to get our fish, and can't blame him either, as good as it was. Pa thought so too, I think, and there he was, ready to face down a bear with nought but a fish knife.

What came out of the woods weren't no bear, though, I'll tell you that. What was it? Well, I thought at first it was a grizzly standing there on its hind legs. Pa had his back to me, standing between me and it, and he stood stock still, just frozen, looking at it. Then it took a step forward and I could see its face in the light from the fire.

It was a man, must have been eight feet tall. He was covered with brownish red hair like the fur on a bear. That's why I mistook him for one at first. But he was a man alright, come straight out of the forest that night. He wasn't wearing a stitch of clothes, but that hair was everywhere on him except for on his face and the palms of his hands.

Don't give me that look. I know how it sounds, an old man telling a tale of a bigfoot in the woods. But I know what I saw. He stood right there, plain as day in the firelight. No use looking it up. You won't find it in a book or nothing like that. There are things out there that you can only find in the woods, and then only if you happen upon them or they happen upon you.

Well, he happened upon us, and he stood there just staring back at Pa, and Pa staring at him. Then he pulled his lips back and bared his teeth. They were big, blunt gnashers, gleaming white. My, but he looked fierce with that snarl on his face. I thought sure he was about to attack.

Pa waved the torch to scare him off. His eyes widened a little. He didn't run off though, just let out a growl from deep in his throat, sounded like a wild beast. Then he swung one of those huge hands and batted the torch out of Pa's hands like it was a matchstick. It tumbled through the air spitting sparks, and before it could land Pa lunged at him.

The man was stunned at first but he reached out by reflex and grabbed Pa's arm. He took him to the ground. They was wrassling, but Pa wasn't making no headway, not against the strength that man had in him.

Pinned to the ground, Pa twisted his neck around to look at me.

"Run," he called out. I scrambled to my feet and made to take off but I stopped dead in my tracks when the big man looked over at me. I don't think he'd noticed me crouched down over by the fire. He looked right into my eyes, and I saw something in those eyes. That's when I knew for sure, and I stand by it today, that he was a man. No beast has eyes like that, with that much intelligence and maybe even compassion, looking at a little kid scared for his daddy.

He sprung up onto his feet and hauled Pa up off the ground. He lifted him up by the front of his shirt and stared right into his face. Pa's hands were free, and I saw him raise the hand holding the gutting knife. I reckon the man didn't know what a knife was, living out here in the woods the way he did, so he didn't even notice that Pa had it in his hand. The blade glinted in the light of the campfire but the man didn't notice, he was so intent on Pa's face.

Pa was looking back at him, right back into that searching stare. Their eyes were locked together, and Pa was inching that knife closer to his throat. That's as scared as I've ever been in my life.

Then Pa stopped and lowered the knife. He just hung there, staring into those eyes. He saw something too, same as I had—something human looking back at him.
The big man set him down and lumbered backward into the forest, keeping his eyes on us. Then I saw the light reflecting off a set of eyes hiding in the branches. There was another one sitting there, one about half his size. The little one looked near as scared as I was. The man reached out his hand and he set off with his son. They just vanished into those trees.

Pa and I packed up right quick after that and headed home. Mama was surprised to see us home so soon, but Pa told her the weather had turned and there weren't no fish biting anyhow. Good thing, too, or she'd have never let us come out here again. We did, though, every year, but Pa started bringing the hunting rifle with us. We never saw the man again.

My Pa would have died to save me that day, but we lived because he was different than most men. He looked into a stranger's eyes and saw himself. And that's something you can be proud of.

    Well, now, these sausages are just about ready to eat. Will you take a look at that. Perfect, ain't it? Look at that color on there. That'll be just bursting with the flavor of the fire. Just like I told you, well worth the wait. Yeah, all right, you've been patient enough. Let's dig in. Here, take a bun. You want some ketchup, mustard? Mmhmm, that looks good. All set. I tell you what, though, why don't you scoot up a little closer to the fire?

The Virgin Stretch
Irina Tyunina
Third Place

I just can't imagine why this story has come to my mind now like a sudden memory flash. Probably stories know their ways much better than we do.

At that time we, a group of students, were backpacking at the Altai Mountains, eager to reach the high altitude lakes. (This is the place where the rapid Kumir River heads down to the valley: first, being the tiny rivulet of Kizilgaya, later changing its name as it gains power.) We were walking along the unscalable Korgon Ridge – up and up again. The early May hadn't even dressed the trees into the light green of newly-emerging leaves. The forest was bare but it didn't spoil the spring beauty. The turquoise flow filaments of clear water, reflecting sunlight, were like the eyes of a sweetheart; they were interlacing as though a beautiful girl was braiding her shiny flaxen hair. The threatening rapids were thundering in the deep gorge. A proud eagle was circling above our heads as though it was patrolling the area.

It happened when Vova picked out his bow and arrows and decided to shoot at the bird. Back home he went to an archery club so he wanted to test his skills. We shouted to him not to do it, but he persisted. Standing at the edge of the rock with the bow-string stretched, he looked like Robin Hood, mighty and handsome. He knew that and was showing off for the girls. The bow-string strummed and the arrow went into the blue. We gasped. The eagle shrank back, frightened. The only feather, hit out of the wing, rolled like a roulette, slowly descending to the cliff. We were following it with our eyes. As soon as the feather touched the ground, we gave out a terrified cry.

The cliff, where the nebbish archer was standing, began to slide irresistibly bit by bit. Vova waved his hands clumsily in an attempt to stop his fall. He vanished behind the edge, rolling down to the rapids. We froze in terror, unable to do anything. Our mate's lonely cry was dying down into the gorge.

Having recovered, we rushed towards the cliff's edge. No dead body, left on the sharp rocks. No sign of our friend. Where was Vova? Suddenly we saw him, safe and sound, climbing up the winding path. He was accompanied by an old local wearing a strange, seemingly ancient garment. He had a shabby long jupe, knee-high leather boots and a triangular hat fringed with fur. The man was drawing on a snaggy stick while walking. Vova was out of breath, hardly keeping up with him, while the man didn't seem tired at all.

When they had finally reached us, the old man - he was really old, if not ancient! – bowed. His silver beard was about to touch the ground.

'Let health enter your home!' he said. We gave Vova a questioning glance.

Our mate got hasty to explain: 'This is Granpa. He saved me. I'd nearly…' he was out of breath. 'I broke the law…He said it was kind of punishment… But Grandpa helped…' Vova was too excited to continue.

'Hush, Young, hush!' the old man interrupted him. 'You're boiling soup in your head,' his voice was as deep and calm as a wooded valley. 'You wanted to kill the celestial servant. That was the instant karma sent by Ilanys,' he got breath. 'A hunter mustn't kill if he isn't hungry.'

'Ilanys?' I was degusting the unfamiliar name. 'Who's that? 'I've never heard of her before.

'She is the Keeper of the Sky in these parts,' the old man took in the surroundings.

'Thank you for our friend!' I bowed in response, feeling somewhat confused. 'Anyway, we have to continue our journey. We've lost so much time!' I suddenly recollected that I was being inconsiderate towards an elderly person; if that wasn't enough, he had rescued one of us. 'Would you like to join our company, Sir?'

'You'd better set camp right here! The sunset is behind that peak,' he waved towards the nearest mountain. 'There are no more convenient places for today.' I wanted to object, but he added: 'I'll join you with pleasure, Young Chief.'

Grandpa, as we called him, was ready to assist in everything - be it erecting tents, picking wood or setting fire. We felt uneasy watching our mysterious guest do all the evening duties alongside the members of the group. He seemed not to pay attention. Once he roused himself, when Vova took an ax to cut a young birch to hold a canvas-tilt over the fire: 'Don't do that!' he bellowed abruptly.

'What's wrong?' Vova smirked. 'Is it another case of 'instant karma'? I bet one more Keeper is ready to punish the culprit?'

'Absolutely right, Young!' Grandpa said. 'Tegerik would never let go of a ruined soul of a virgin!' Vova lowered the ax with his mouth open.

It happened that our camp was in one of the most picturesque spots of the Kumir, the rapid called the Virgin Stretch. Tall cliffs pressed the river in their palms, and it was violently rushing down into a beautiful slough. The place was so calm and peaceful that you'd never even guess what a roaring hell of water was ripping and tearing immediately behind your back.

Grandpa took a bucket and headed for the slough to fetch some water. I secretly followed him, hiding in the bushes. His footsteps were as light as the ones of an adolescent as though years weren't pressing on his shoulders. He approached the river bank, bent, doused his hand into the water and raised his hand to his forehead: 'Good whatever time of day it is, Toylu!'

Questions, so many questions were tingling in my mind like bubbles in a fizzy drink. Our strange guest had occupied all my thoughts.

Later, as our group was sitting round the campfire, I asked, burning with uncertainty: 'Who are these people, or goddesses you've mentioned?'

'No gods, spirits maybe, Young Chief,' he had a speculative look, staring off at a distance, as though something sacred revealed exclusively to him. Grandpa was wandering in a dream world. 'I'll tell you the story connected with this place,' he said. 'But it happened long, long ago.'

Meanwhile, night fell, and the only spot of light in this gloomy forest was our fire. It randomly caught one or the other face out of the darkness. We felt like the ancient humans, being one to one with the endless night.

'I know a legend related to this place!' chattered Vova joyfully. 'It was…'

'Hush, Young, hush!' Grandpa stopped him. 'Listen to the wolves howling!' Later, I found out that it was an Altai saying applied to those who are too chatty. But at that moment all of us suddenly went silent, sitting up and taking notice of the noises of burning wood, slight rustling, murmur of growing grass dying at a distance. We even seemed to hear far-off howling.

'Long ago it occurred,' Grandpa started. 'In one Altai settlement there lived a man, called Akchabai. He had three daughters. The eldest, named Tegerik, was nice and stout like the blessed land of the Altai. She helped her father look after the house, grow crops and pick fruits of the earth. The middle daughter, Ilanys, was as light and quick as a spring wind. She enjoyed running from peak to peak, speaking to birds and beasts. She knew all the paths in the mountains. The youngest and the most beloved daughter was Toylu. With her eyes as turquoise as the clear mountainous river, Akchabai called her the Child of Water. Since babyhood she liked playing beside the river. If she was hungry, a fish would jump right into her hands.

But happiness doesn't last forever. The violent Dzungar nomads invaded the peaceful land of the Altai. People were not ready for it. All they could use as weapons were sticks and stones, and some hunting things. Though, could hunting arrows and spears compare with the war tools?

In one battle Akchabai received a mortal wound. Crying were the sisters at his death-bed. 'You must leave the settlement, my daughters! Don't wait for the captors!' father demanded.

'I can't leave my land!' said Tegerik. 'I love it!'

'I know every path in my mountains,' said Ilanys. 'I'll have time to escape!'

'Promise me, Toylu, that you'll never deliver yourself up the enemy's hands!' said Akchabai.

'I can hear you, Father, and I promise.' said the youngest daughter.

They buried their parent at the foot of the mountain so that in his new life he could walk there and hunt. They would probably meet one day or one night when no enemy or any danger would disturb them.

Girls collected their things, mounted their horses and set off, leaving their settlement behind the back. They were nearing the range when Tegerik suddenly turned around, taking a hard look at the birthplace. She seemed to hear something. 'I'm coming back. I can't leave my land!' she said.

'But Father's will was to escape the enemy! The Dzungars will kill you!' cried the sisters.

'Warriors don't fight girls.' said Tegerik. 'I'll come back and stay on my land.'

'Then be ready to welcome the new dawn as slave!' answered Toylu in her eldest sister's back as Tegerik turned her horse to the settlement.

While she was nearing the place, the noise created by the cries of terror was growing till it deafened her. What she saw was horrifying! The settlement was burning with the streets covered with the bodies of defenders. The lone cries of girls were shaking the air here and there. The mad Dzungars were rushing across the settlement like a storm. And girls were falling under the swords of the enemy like young birches. In terror, Tegerik rushed towards them in an attempt to shield them. And fell Tegerik under the sword. And the irate land gaped to swallow the murderers.

On and on, the sisters continued their ride. And the Dzungar horses rushed towards them to stop.

'Let's fight!' cried Toylu to her middle sister.

'Let's get through, or die!' answered Ilanys.

The girls used their swords and arrows to ride through the group of Dzungars. And they did. The Dzungar chief was so impressed by their courage that he joined his warriors and ordered to catch the girls alive. The thud of hoofs and who-whoops were chasing the girls.

On and on, the girls rode. Ilanys's horse fell. 'Sit behind my back!' shouted Toylu. 'We'll go on mine!'

'I know the way,' said Ilanys. 'Follow this path. They won't catch us.'

Up and up the sharp ridge they went. The enemies followed them hard on heels.

'We need to top the ridge,' said Ilanys. 'Then, pass the gorge, and nobody will capture us!' Suddenly an arrow whistled in the air. Ilanys jolted and leaned against her sister's back.

'I hear and I follow.' said Toylu. When they topped the ridge, Ilanys fell. Toylu got off the horse. Nobody was seen around.

'Along this path, across the gorge,' her sister whispered the last words. Toylu buried her under the rocks as high as she could. Alone, she was now.

'Sleep, Sis. Sleep, Ilanys. You loved the sky, so keep it!' A wind got up to stop the pursuers. Some fell off the cliff. Others continued the chase.

Close to the gorge, they gained on a fugitive. Toylu was sitting on her horse, her back to the abyss. No way was left.

'Surrender and be the chief's concubine,' cried the warriors. The unbending decision to do or die flashed in the girl's eyes. She shook her head and turned her horse to the gorge. The chasers gasped as she flew down to the sharp, deathly stones at the bottom.

And raged the small rivulet, and turned into a mighty rapid river. The roaring waterfall grew in the gorge, reaching the top edge. And furious waters captured the most zealous pursuers. But after passing another inferior level the real disaster transformed into a quiet turquoise slough. There she was, Toylu – peaceful and free.

The celestial expanse of the slough was sparkling like the eyes of the proud girl, luring the intrepid warriors, and the Dzungar Chief couldn't resist it. He stepped towards the dream, towards his fate.'

Grandpa finished his story, but we were sitting silent for some time, enchanted, unable to speak. It was far past midnight, and everyone felt sleepy.

I was the only person, except Grandpa, staying at the campfire. I couldn't help thinking about all the events, which took place long ago where I was sitting now. 'How do you know this story in such details?' I dared ask, rubbing my eyes.

'It's getting cold, Young Chief,' he said, passing me my sleeping bag. 'Don't forget to cover your head.'

'You told us all that as if you were there,' I insisted.

'Sleep, Young Chief,' he said. 'My name is Akchabai.'

'But...' but I was sleeping. In my dream I could see tender, slim birches speaking to Tegirik. She was slowly walking through the grove. And light-footed Ilanys was running up the path to pick flowers, singing with birds. And enchanting, laughing eyes of Toylu were looking deep inside my soul, studying its shadows. She smiled at me and waved goodbye.

In the morning everything was covered with snow. It was quiet in the forest. I could hear only the distant voice of the Virgin Stretch. The old man had vanished, leaving no footprints on the primeval white of the snow bed-sheet.

The Penance
Srivalli Rekha
Fourth Place

A thunderbolt startled Jill from her slumber. She straightened in her chair and looked through the fogged window. The trees dangerously swayed, threatening to crash on their tiny one-room cabin. She knew it wouldn't happen. A deep sigh escaped her lips. Jack grumbled and continued to sleep. His head lolled to the side with his mouth hanging open.

Rain lashed at the windows threatening to break the glass. Jill turned to look at the destruction outside. Lightning flashed once, then twice. She understood it was time.

"Jack, wake up." Her melodious voice quivered a little as she shook him.

He blinked and stared at her in confusion.

Before he could respond, a brilliant flash of lightning illuminated their sparsely decorated cabin. The door opened with a crash. A young man tumbled in, red drops dripping from the curly mop on his head. His ivory shirt turned pale pink with rain and blood. He fell to the dusty floor with a groan. The door closed softly behind him.

"We have our 879th guest." Jack motioned for Jill to help him lift the man. They eased him onto a thin mattress that lay in a corner.

"He is severely injured. The wound is deep." Jack wiped the blood with a clean cloth. Jill removed his boots.

"He will catch a cold. I'll get the warm clothes." Jill went to a cupboard that stood in another corner of the cabin. She plucked out a thick sweater and woolen pants from the bare shelves.

"Tsk... He is hardly twenty-five years old." Jack said to himself as he applied lavender scented salve on the wound and bound it with a white cloth. He had the man's head cushioned on his lap. They stopped wondering about the wounds a long time ago. Jill rubbed heat into the man's hands and feet. "His hands are freezing, poor boy."

"When will he wake up?" Jill would have to cook a stew to feed him.

"In a few hours, if the bleeding stops. But..." Jack trailed off as the bandage was turning crimson. It was not a good sign. His fingertips turned red as he touched the bandage cloth.

"I'll make the Calendula paste. It'll heal faster." Jill reached the two flower pots that sat beside a single wooden stove.

She placed her hand into an empty pot. She found nothing. Frowning, she tried the other one and picked up two bright orange flowers.

She sat to crush the petals when Jack wrinkled his nose. "Add some Echinacea as well."

Jill sighed. "We don't get everything we ask. I'll try."
She went back to the pots and found nothing. She shook her head at Jack.

"Darn!" He spotted a piece of wood in the man's wound.

Gently he pried it out with his long fingernails. "This is the culprit." Throwing it away, he applied the Calendula paste and tied a new bandage.

Jill heaved a sigh of relief. The blood flow stopped. They sat in silence lost in their thoughts. The man reminded her of their younger days. Jack had a similar build with black curls that reached his neck. His hair now looked like snow and still curled around her fingers. Even after another half a century, things would remain the same. They still had more than a hundred guests to heal.

The storm unleashed its fury around the cabin. Jill knew the cabin would stay intact. It would not have a single scratch as proof of the years it survived. How old was it anyway? Jill thought hard. An image floated in her mind. It was of a lifeless body of a young girl. Jill shut her eyes. No, she would not think about it. It happened a lifetime ago.

"Let it go, Jill. We committed a crime. We are repenting for it." Jack's gentle voice made her want to cry. But she couldn't. It was a part of the punishment.

She looked at Jack who gave her a sad smile. The cabin was silent except for the faint heartbeat of the unconscious young man. That sound was music to their ears. Living in a confined space with eerie silence was worse than a nightmare. They got used to it though. Their existence itself was an illusion. They were neither alive nor dead.

Hours passed as the storm continued. The man's body began to twist in pain. Jill tried to brew a painkiller, but the pots gave her nothing.

"Please! It's for him, not us." Jill pleaded without luck.

"Maybe he has to suffer. Come, sit with us, Jill." Jack gestured to the place beside him.

Jill slumped onto the mattress. She held the man's hand trying to soothe him. He was burning with fever. "What did he do to deserve this?" Jill touched his face.

"We do not know. Better now than later." Jack's voice was thick with regret. Jill nodded. The heavy rain continued throughout the night.

Only a faint change in light indicated that the morning had arrived. The dark clouds still loomed above. The wind picked up after a brief lull. The cabin looked the same as ever- bare and devoid of life.

"His fever has gone down. He is out of danger." Jack informed his wife. She was staring through the morning mist into the unknown.

"I'll make some stew. He needs food in his stomach." Jill hoped her request would be accepted. To her relief, she found the required ingredients in the pots.

Sitting near the stove, she began to slice the vegetables and boil them. The smell made them hungry. But they could not eat. They had to endure the torture.

"We have to suffer." Jack murmured echoing her thoughts.

The young man coughed as she fed him the stew. "It's okay. You'll be fine." Her musical voice gradually eased the tension from his limbs. He swallowed a few mouthfuls of the hot liquid and drifted into a peaceful sleep.

"He'll be good by the time he wakes up. The wound is healing faster now." Jack showed Jill the gash on the man's forehead. It was clean. The edges began to pucker.

"Why do I still feel a knife twisting in my heart? Will it ever go away?" Jill's anguish choked her. She was helpless to do anything.

All they made was one mistake. It transformed their lives forever. The cabin became their prison. The walls that surrounded them held them captive in their past.

For more than a century, Jack and Jill tried to heal their guests. "We should be glad that no one died after the penance began." Jack reminded her.

Jill shook her head. "Saving a thousand lives will not bring back the one life we took away in greed. No punishment will be enough. Oh, Jack! What did we do?"

"Shh… Jill, calm down. You'll scare the young man. See, he is starting to wake up." Jack reminded her about the pact. No guest was allowed to know their true story.

The young man groaned as he tried to open his eyes. His head hurt. His lids felt heavy. A soft hand touched his face. He smelled roses. The fragrance soothed him. Bit by bit he forced his eyes open.

Gold and silver hair fell in wayward tendrils around her round face. Her deep blue eyes reminded him of the ocean. Wrinkles made her look gracious as she smiled at him.

"Granny!" He croaked.

"Boy, you scared us." Her voice was magical. He gave her a weak smile and tried to sit.

Jack helped him. "Careful, kid. Your wound is tender."

The young man looked around the tiny cabin. Nothing registered in his mind. He had no idea where he was. The place was dark. He wasn't sure if it was day or night.

"There is a storm outside though it's middle of the day. You will get back your memory as you heal. You hurt your head." Jack explained.

The man tried to nod and winced. The old couple looked friendly. They saved his life. But why was he there? Who was he?

"I… my name…" He trailed off frowning.

"Don't fret, boy. You are still too weak to be thinking. Why don't you relax? I'll make some stew for you." Jill's sweet smile made him feel a lot better. She must be his grandma. But he did not remember.

Jack sat with him to change the bandage again. He applied the salve when the man protested. "It's rotten."

"Yes, Calendula smells bad. But it heals faster. I used some of the lavender to mask the smell." Jack placed a flat cushion between the man's head and the wall for support.

Jill fed him the stew when his hands trembled. Tears streaked down his face at the tenderness in her eyes.

"You are angels." He whispered.

"It's okay. Why don't you take a nap?" Jack spoke.

The young man moaned. "I don't feel like it. Why can't I remember anything? What if I don't get back my memory? I don't even know my name."

Jack calmed him. "Getting agitated will only hurt you more. Trust me, boy. I've healed a few head wounds before. You will get back your memory very soon. That's a promise."

The young man looked doubtful but nodded. He would trust them. After all, the old were more experienced in such matters.

Exhausted, he dozed off. The more he slept, the faster he would heal. He heard them murmuring about something. Their presence was like a balm to his mind. He felt protected and secure.

Jill wished for the millionth time that she could cry. The words stabbed her heart with renewed force. They were not angels. She wanted to yell, but she could not.

Jack stood behind his wife as she touched her forehead to the cold glass of the window. He knew she was thinking about the fateful day. The scene played in his mind, the vivid details making him shudder.

It was a stormy day; similar to the one they were witnessing now. Jill sat weaving baskets from dried leaves while he sharpened his knives. The cabin was cold. The embers from the stove gave them no warmth. But they were used to it. Money was limited. They had to be careful. A sudden knock on the door surprised them.

People rarely ventured deep into the forest. To have a visitor during a thunderstorm was strange. Jack opened the door. A girl tripped into his arms. He caught her by instinct. She had cuts on her arms and a deep wound on her shoulder. Blood drenched her dress. Her platinum blond hair stuck to her smudged face.

"Oh dear! What happened?" Jill rushed to her. They helped her onto the same old tattered mattress. Jill pressed a clean cloth against the wound while Jack began to heat some water.

The girl was delirious. She thrashed on the bed.

"Don't move," Jill ordered.

The girl's eyes were wild. She clawed at her clothes and gave a silk pouch to Jill. "Keep it safe. For granny..." She gasped and fell unconscious.

Jack took the pouch and dumped the contents onto his hands. Gold!" He exclaimed in wonder.

Jill stared, her eyes widening at the nuggets of gold in his hands. Lightning flashed outside. The gold sparkled, transforming the dull cabin a deep shade of yellow. Never before in their lives did they see such wealth.

They looked at the girl. She lost a lot of blood. The mattress soaked up the liquid. But with the gold, they could buy a new one. They would become rich.

Before they could rethink, Jack pressed a cushion on the girl's face. Jill held her legs as she twisted. In less than a minute, it was over. Her body lay lifeless on the bloody mattress. The gold belonged to them.

The cabin shook. The walls cracked. The door was smashed open. Jill shrieked. Jack moved to stand in front of her. Flames danced around them. They were trapped. Only a thunderbolt could start a fire during the storms.

The girl stood in front of them. Her dress was neat, her hair piled on top of her head. She had not a single wound on her body. She looked more like a nymph than a human they killed a minute ago.

"How?" Jack stuttered. His mind reeled.

The girl's laugh echoed in the cabin.

"What did you think? That you could kill me and take away my gold. I am the child of the forest. Her power flows in my veins. You failed in the test to prove yourselves worthy of living on a sacred land like this." The girl snapped her fingers. The flames rose higher.

"Jack!" Jill yelled and jumped.

"Please spare us." Jack whimpered.

"You greedy fools! You destroyed my body by forcing life out of it. I cannot go back to being a human again. You took my life and separated me from my old grandmother. Who will take care of her? I will take lives, but not completely. You will be suspended in time. You will only feel pain, hunger, and regret. But you cannot cry or eat. No one will see you. You will cease to exist in the world." She pronounced the curse. Her eyes spat fire.

"NO! Please, forgive us. I will care for her." Jill pleaded. She was terrified.

"Please, child. We made a mistake." Jack begged. He looked confused and scared.

"Mistake? You committed a crime. There is no forgiveness. I will not let either of you get anywhere near her." The girl shot back.

"Don't, please. We never harmed a soul before. We were out of our mind. Show mercy, please." Jill got down to her knees and pulled Jack with her. They begged and groveled. The flames inched closer to them.

At last, she relented. "A curse cannot be taken back. But I will give you a chance. Save the lives of a thousand people and the curse will break. Until then, you cannot leave the cabin. The wounded people will come to you."

Jill nodded. "We will save everyone."

"It will not be easy. You are not allowed to tell them the truth. The door will open when the person is ready to go back. He or she will forget everything once they step out of the cabin. But if you tell them the truth, they will remember it all. You will lose your chance to break the curse." She warned.

Jack agreed. "We will be careful."

The girl added. "You will be supplied with the items you need to save them. But if by any chance one of them dies, the count will start from the beginning."

"We will not let anybody die. I swear. Please, can you not let us outside?" Jill implored.

The girl shook her head. "I've given you far more than you deserve. Now rot in here. This is your personal hell. I have a parting gift for you."

She vanished. Jack stared as the picture of their wedding, the clothes in the cupboard, the vases and the little food disappeared along with her. The two barren flowerpots, the wooden stove, an empty cupboard, a broken table with two chairs, and the ruined mattress remained.

Jill's scream of horror echoed in the cabin. "Jack! You... No!" She examined her hands to find the smooth skin wrinkled.

Jack felt the energy drain from his body. His fingers cramped and knees turned weak. "She made us old."

Jill dumbly nodded. She cried, but not a single tear fell from her eyes. "Just like her granny. What will we do, Jack? We don't even have a child. And we will never have one."

"I don't know. We have to wait to complete the penance. The gold vanished with her." Jack sat on the chair.

"Good that she took it away. We were happy with the little money we had. What use is gold when we are not even alive?" Jill hit the table with her fist. They made a terrible mistake.

Jack assumed it wouldn't be long before they healed a thousand people. He was wrong. The first man came staggering after a decade of the wait. They were clumsy and made mistakes.

He hovered on the edge of life for a week before he began to recover.

Jill observed that the guests appeared only during a thunderstorm. It lasted until the person was fit to go back. The door would open to the sun shining brightly. Once the person stepped out, it would close until another arrived.

Initially, they saved people only with the intention of not wanting to start from the first. But, saving lives changed them. The true repentance began. They treated the people as their children; the ones they could never have.

Together they watched the years pass. Trees grew old and fell to the ground. New life sprouted to become strong. The summer sun, the autumn leaves, the rains were always out of reach. Nothing reached the inside of the cabin, except for the lightning. It announced the arrival of a guest.

A groan from across the room brought them back to reality. The young man was waking up. He sat on his own before Jack could reach to help him.

"I am better now. I think it's the stew. There's magic in your hands." He smiled at Jill. She forced herself to return the smile. She did not deserve the affection.

"Jill is an excellent cook." Jack agreed.

"Did you guys eat? I haven't asked before." The young man blushed.

Jack patted his shoulder. "Don't worry. We are taking care of you. It's not the other way round. We had our supper while you were asleep."

"You look fine. Another round of the salve and you'll be good by tomorrow morning." Jill announced. The storm turned into a shower. She knew the signs.

"Oh, that's good. But where will I go? I don't remember anything." The man asked. He touched the bandage and winced. The pain was mild, but it still hurt.

"It will come back to you," Jack assured him.

He held his nose as Jack changed the bandage. The questions started next. A century of practice helped them evade most of the difficult questions. Jill force fed him another bowl of stew. He fell asleep soon after. Breathing a sigh of relief, they waited for the sun to shine. Hours passed in silence loaded with regret, concern, and acceptance.

Finally, the clouds cleared. Golden rays passed through the window to touch the young man. He slowly woke up. Rubbing his eyes, he blinked at the golden rays brightening the cabin.

"Oh! The sun is out. I love sunshine." He told them with a smile.

Jill gave him the food she found in one of the pots. Jack gave the young man his clothes. After changing, he stood uncertainly.

"What is it, boy?" Jill pushed the curls away from his handsome face. A stubble grew on his cheeks making him look rugged and cute at the same time. He would break hearts with his looks. She smiled.

"I don't know where to go." He murmured taking her soft hand in his.

"Sometimes, all it takes is to step into the sunlight. Try it." Jack encouraged him just as the door opened. Light flooded into the cabin making it cheerful. Jill knew it wouldn't last long.

"I think you are right. Thank you very much for taking care of me. I will never forget you both." He hugged them and went to the door.

Jill exchanged a sad look with her husband. The man was on the threshold. One step outside, he would not remember a single thing. It was better that way.

"Goodbye, son." They whispered.

The moment he went outside the door closed. The cabin was dark again. They knew he would have gone back.

"Oh, Jack! I can't bear this anymore." Jill wailed.

"You know we have no choice, Jill. We survived this long, what are another few decades." Jack squeezed her hand and went to his seat.

Jill sat on the other chair at the broken table. Time stood still in the soundless cabin as the world moved on outside the window.

Plain Jane
Oonagh McBride
Fourth Place

Thanks, guys, your stories were all fantastic. Creepy stories are the only thing that could improve a night drinking cocktails on a tropical beach with a roaring fire. No, I won't tell a story. I'm no good at making up stories. I guess I don't have a lot of imagination. The only good story I know is entirely true, but it's a bit gruesome. Are you sure you want to hear it? Ok. Well, you asked for it.

My story is about two girls who had been friends since they were very young. They met on their first day of school. Let's call the first girl Plain Jane as even at the age of five, there was nothing particularly cute or appealing about her. Now, you should know that she wasn't ugly or grotesque; she was just decidedly ordinary with thin, mousy hair which wasn't quite curly, pale lips and washed out blue eyes. When Jane first saw Francesca, she thought that this was possibly the most beautiful girl she had ever seen, and it made her sad to see her standing alone in the playground crying. Tears tumbled out of her deep brown eyes onto her milky skin. Of course, she didn't suffer from the swollen eyes, red nose and accumulation of snot that afflicted Jane when she cried. Jane tried not to cry because her mother had told her that it made her ugly, and even at that young age, she realised that she had to keep her mother's revulsion at bay. She wondered how anyone with such beautiful, shiny dark brown hair could be so unhappy and decided she had to help.

"Hello, what's wrong?" she said. She really wanted to touch Francesca, so she tentatively tugged on her hand.

"I left my dolly at home," said Francesca grasping Jane's hand dramatically.

"Oh." Jane felt tears pricking her eyes, but she tried to fight it as she didn't want to look ugly in front of this beautiful princess. "You can borrow my dolly," she said and handed over her favourite doll. It actually looked a bit like Francesca.

Francesca smiled at Jane, and this made her feel wonderful. She never returned the doll, but she sometimes let Jane play with her. Jane didn't care as long as she could be Francesca's friend.

They were friends all through school and even went to the same university. People said they were inseparable. That first meeting set the tone for their friendship in that Jane did a lot of giving, and Francesca did a lot of taking. As you might expect, Francesca blossomed into an extremely attractive young woman. Poor Jane was still decidedly plain and quite accustomed to her role in the background of Francesca's dazzling achievements. But, is anyone really satisfied to be the supporting actor in someone else's drama?

Jane decided to forge out on her own in the summer break after their second year at university. She'd got a taste of being Jane Green, instead of Francesca's friend with her fellow students on her physics course. Obviously, Francesca had more glamorous and exciting new friends from her film studies course, but Jane didn't mind if her new friends weren't cool. That summer, Jane got a job in a hostel in the Scottish Highlands where she could indulge her love of hiking in the mountains. This wasn't a love that was shared by Francesca, and as a result, the adolescent Jane had found this interest embarrassing. Now, at the age of 19, she was starting to learn that she could have passions that were not centred on the lovely Francesca.

Although she was enjoying her independence, she was still excited when Francesca came to visit her for the weekend. It was only natural that she missed her best friend, and it was also natural that she wanted to show Francesca what was so special about the new life she had forged without her. So, Jane planned a weekend camping and hiking trip into the remote Scottish countryside. She knew that it wasn't really Francesca's kind of thing, but you never know, maybe she would like it. If anyone but Jasper had asked to join them, she would have dismissed it out of hand, but she really liked Jasper. Jane had never had a boyfriend. It was tough to get noticed when your constant companion was the most gorgeous woman in the world. However, in her new solo life, she'd grown close to Jasper over the summer and was starting to hope that he saw her as more than just a friend. She liked his ready smile and enjoyed their easy banter.

So, Jasper brought his friend Bob, and they drove to their starting point in an old van borrowed from the hostel. En route, Bob repeatedly called Jasper by the name Casper. Each time he did this Jasper looked irritated. Eventually, and with great relish, Bob told them that everyone in school called him Casper after he claimed, in tears, to have seen a ghost in the school library.

"You should have seen him. 13 years old and snivelling like a baby in front of the whole class. Even the teachers called him Casper."

Only Bob laughed, and Jane noticed in the rear view mirror that Jasper's face was bright red with embarrassment.

The sun was setting as they arrived and they didn't walk far from the car before choosing a spot to make camp. Jane put up the girls' tent up single-handedly, while the boys pitched nearby. She could hear them bickering. Once the tents were ready, they got out the disposable barbeques, cracked open their first beers and started to cook. Nothing fancy, just burgers and sausages. Jasper smiled at Jane as she handed him a burger which made her feel insanely happy. She hoped that Francesca and Bob would hit it off, although Bob seemed like a bit of a dick. She was sure that Bob would like Francesca, who wouldn't, but she was pretty fussy when it came to men. Having said that, Bob was ridiculously handsome and looked like he spent half his life in the gym, so perhaps it would work.

After dinner, they opened more beers and started to plan out the weekend hike. Jasper and Jane laughed when they both pulled out copies of the same guidebook.

"Great minds think alike," said Jane.

"I've had this for ages," said Jasper. Jane was pleased to see that his Munro book, like her copy, was well-thumbed with notes in the margins.

"Have you done this mountain before?" she asked.

"No," said Jasper.

"It's beautiful," said Jane." You're in for a treat. I used to climb this with my Dad when I was young."

"Cool. It will be one more Munro ticked off the list for me," said Jasper with a smile.

Jane imagined travelling all over the country with Jasper and ticking off their Munro list together. She really had it bad. Francesca, who, as you can probably imagine, wasn't accustomed to staying in the background, asked, "I don't get it, what's the big deal about a Munro?"

Jasper laughed, and Jane tried to ignore the sinking feeling she felt in her stomach.

"All mountains in Scotland over 3,000 feet are called Munros. Look at my tick list. I'm working my way through them."

She looked at his list, tossed her silky hair and said, "Cool."

Poor Jane tried not to worry. After all, if she was going to get together with Jasper, it was important that he got on with her best friend.

The rest of the night passed pleasantly, and Jane found herself alone with Jasper when the others had gone to bed.

"Jane, can I ask you something?" asked Jasper in a quiet voice

"Of course," said Jane. She thought that he was going to ask if he could kiss her. She actually shut her eyes in preparation.

"Is Francesca seeing anyone?"

For a second, Jane had a crazy hope that he was asking on behalf of Bob, but she soon realised that he liked Francesca. Of course, he did. Why would anyone like Plain Jane? She'd lived this same scene countless times since Francesca intervened in her first crush on Peter Bradford when she was fourteen.

"Yes, she has a boyfriend," Jane lied.

"Oh," he said crestfallen. "She probably wouldn't be interested in someone like me anyway."

"No. She certainly wouldn't be interested in you." Jane followed this statement with a cruel and mocking laugh. You can't really blame her. Jasper shook his head in confusion.

Jane made her way to her tent, burrowed into her sleeping bag and allowed herself to wallow in misery. She cried quietly to avoid waking Francesca, and being Plain Jane, her eyes became swollen, and her nose was red. She could imagine her mother looking at her with disgust.

Jane woke early the next morning with a heavy ache in her head from the tears she had shed the night before. She shuffled out of the tent and into the cold morning air which was wet with dew. There was nobody around, but she saw a note under a rock next to the campfire. It read,

Gone for a swim, Jasper and Bob.

There was a cute little map of how to find them. Jane scrunched the note up in disgust as Francesca emerged from the tent. How could anyone look so fantastic at 6 am following an uncomfortable night on a thin sleeping mat? What Jane did next wasn't planned. It just happened.

"Jasper and Bob have disappeared." She said this in a breathless panicked voice. "I heard something drag them away. They were struggling." Francesca looked at Jane with wide, panicked eyes and this encouraged Jane to elaborate. "One of them started to scream help, but they didn't manage to finish the word."

"Oh, shit," said Francesca grabbing her phone out of her pocket. "It's dead," she held up her phone,

"Mine too," lied Jane.

"Jane, what if it comes back?" she whimpered.

"C'mon," said Jane. "Let's run to the car."

Jane led the way, and they started to run. But, Jane didn't lead her towards the car, Oh No. She led her into the forest and further from civilisation and safety. She just wanted to make her suffer a bit. Perhaps, punish her slightly for being so perfect. It was just a joke. Francesca didn't doubt Jane. She trusted her. Why wouldn't she? Jane had been there sacrificing her needs and wants to Francesca's since they were five-years-old.

They ran through the forest, and Jane enjoyed Francesca's growing panic. She had put Francesca in the middle of a real live horror film. They reached a clearing and stopped at the edge of a small lake. Francesca was breathless from both exercise and fear as she said, "Oh God, Jane, what are we going to do?" Jane showed some pity and suggested that they stop and rest for a bit.

"We can't stop. If we stop whatever got Jasper and Bob will get us," panted Francesca.

"Not if we're quiet." Jane was making up the logic for her horror film as she went.

"Maybe we should go back to the camp. The guys might have left a cell phone with some battery life?" whispered Francesca.

"Which way is camp?" Jane asked as if she didn't know.

The funny thing was that if this were a horror film, Francesca would be the one to survive. The monster, or bear, or madman, or whatever would kill everyone else, but she would persevere and triumph. The final shot would be Francesca, slightly dishevelled, but, of course, still stunningly beautiful as she flagged down a car. Plain Jane, however, would have been dramatically killed in an early scene. Collateral damage, like all unattractive friends.

Jane considered her options. Perhaps it was time lead her back to camp and find the note. However, before she could act on her generous impulse, Jasper arrived in the clearing with his hair still wet from his morning swim.

Francesca ran over to him and threw her arms around his neck. "Oh, Jasper. You're safe, you're safe."

"Typical" thought Jane. She hardly knew Jasper, but she needed to be the centre of any drama.

"Well, *I'm* safe," he said and hugged her back tight. Jane noticed the emphasis on the word I'm, but Francesca was oblivious in her relief.

He looked deliberately into Jane's eyes as he continued to hug her friend.

"Where's Bob?" asked Francesca.

"Ohhhh, I'm afraid the monster got him." He raised his eyebrows at Jane, and she realised that he must have been following them and eavesdropping on her bullshit.

Francesca started to sob with her face buried in Jasper's shoulder.

Jane didn't know why he was acting so weird, but she was shocked to find herself more attracted to him now that his mouth formed a mocking sneer and his eyes were cold.

"Yeah, Jane. The monster is real," he laughed then his face became serious. "The monster killed Bob." Francesca started to struggle, but Jasper held her face tight against his shoulder. "Long story, but you know that some friends are toxic, right, Jane?"

Francesca made a high pitched 'Mmmmmm' noise as her struggles become ever more frantic. "So Jane, are you going to save the lovely Francesca?"

Jane felt hypnotised by his eyes which held her gaze as he suppressed Francesca's frantic attempts at movement. She did nothing. She said nothing.

"I thought not," he said in a soothing tone. "I know what you are Jane."

Jane felt a desire for Jasper that she'd never felt for anyone before in her life.

"Are you going to help me?" he said.

Jasper put a hand around Francesca's neck and pushed her head into the loch. She fought desperately and managed to break the surface to take a painful breath, but Jane's hand pushed her head back into the muddy water. Jasper and Jane looked into one another's eyes as they crouched on the bank and worked together to keep Francesca submerged. At last, she stopped struggling, They dragged her to the centre of the loch and allowed her to sink down to join Bob among the reeds.

Oh sorry, I got quite carried away there. I can see I've shocked you all a bit. Don't worry, there is kind of a happy ending. Jasper and Jane fall in love and eventually get married. They go on a beautiful tropical honeymoon to celebrate their love. Oh, I can see my husband coming. I'm still getting used to saying the word husband. See you all tomorrow at breakfast.

Loving You Best of All
Pamela Wagner
Fifth Place

Whose turn is it to tell a story?
Mine!
Oh no. Really? You always wimp out. Can you make it scary this time?
Oh yes.
Really scary?
Really really scary.
Okay. Then do your best.

Not in my time, not in your time, but in someone's time, there was a little girl whose parents died when she was very young. Her aunt rejected her; her uncle denied her; her grandparents maternal and paternal believed that she died when her parents died.

It was a dark time for orphans in those days, my friends. No one cared enough to look after her so she left her home and walked deep into the darkest part of the forest.

She walked for days. For days, she walked. She ate berries off bushes, she drank water from creeks, she slept on the ground, on the soft pine needles which became her mattress on the forest floor. She wasn't afraid. She was too young to fear the animals who stalked their prey in the day, the owls and small rodents that stayed up all night. She felt comforted by their sounds. She felt protected by their presence. She was alone, and not alone. She was an orphan and yet felt held by the love of the forest creatures. In fact, one day a lone red fox cub pitta patted pitta patted pitta pitted up to her as she slept and curled up against her all night, keeping her warm and toasty and secure. And then the night after, and the night after that. They were companions during the day and warm blankets for one another at night.

Over time, the little girl and the fox became each other's family. And so they named one another. She was Mädchen and the fox was Fuchs. Simple names. Simple friends. Simple life. They did not speak the same language but it did not matter. They helped one another, they cared for one another, and they thrived in their mutual care.

As Mädchen grew, the clothes she wore on the day she walked into the forest no longer fit. She was resourceful. She had to be and so she used what she could: pieces of bark off trees, and once a hoodie she found at an abandoned camping area.

Over time, Mädchen forgot how to speak words, and Fuchs forgot how to bark. But that doesn't mean they didn't talk to one another. Their communication mimicked one another's and their language became an amalgam of sounds they remembered from their babyhood and childhood. They yipped, they spoke bits of words. Their unique shared language meant they understood one another completely. They survived. They thrived. They lived, and they loved one another. No two creatures ever got along so well.

Until….

The day Mädchen turned thirteen, she was washing in the brook near their home when she heard human voices. She didn't know. How could she? The memory of voices was long gone, but her curiousity got the better of her and so she quickly dressed, and went to find their origin. Fuchs was hunting and so Mädchen was all alone.

She hid behind her favourite oak tree which she had given a name I cannot say, and watched the three boys in the clearing for the amount of time it might take to stalk a rabbit, but for the boys was an hour. They were drinking something and they were talking loudly and they were sharing burning sticks. Their hair was long and they smelled putrid. Mädchen's sense of smell was very good, but theirs was not. She was confused about them. Who were they? Why couldn't they sense her presence? What game were they playing?

By the time Fuchs returned, Mädchen had tiptoe tiptoe tiptoed out from behind the tree getting silently closer and closer until she was right beside them, sitting on her haunches and gazing at them with open-eyed and unabashed curiosity. Fuchs was protective but nervous. Their scent disturbed him, their wild-eyed abandoned confused him, and so he too stood behind the tree, tail twitching, ears back, snarling silently.

At that moment, the boys noticed Mädchen and Mädchen stood up in her glory. They had never seen anyone so beautiful. Her long raven black hair flowed to her waist, her clear blue eyes looked directly into their own, and they all fell in love. No doubt, they all fell in love. Maybe even Mädchen a little bit. But they could not speak. She knew nothing of their language and they of course knew none of hers. They tried, and Fuchs watched, but finally the boys gave up and left. One of them, Gerhard, kept looking back as they left. He fell the deepest that day. Mädchen stood still as a statue, watching them leave. Fuchs had come up beside her and he leaned up against her, her dearest and until-then only friend. She idly rubbed his fur, keeping her eyes on Gerhard until the very last.

The boys told no one of her presence, and she could not speak of it even to Fuchs who became inexplicably protective and refused to leave her side. Mädchen returned again and again to the clearing, trying to lose Fuchs in her routes, but knowing that the fox would always be able to find her. Again and again, she returned, and sometimes Gerhard was there and sometimes he was not. Mädchen could not understand his routine; Mädchen and Fuchs had a life that was filled with adventure but also rote tasks, and their days were predictable, although their movements were not. There were dangers in the forest, and they were always aware of them. Fuchs now added Gerhard to his dangers because every time Mädchen and Gerhard met, they spoke some words Fuchs could not understand. At first, just a few: *Hello, How are you? My name is...* And then over the years, Mädchen came to understand the language of people, and she learned more of her past from Gerhard who had heard her story from the villagers: the once upon story of a wee girl who disappeared one day into the forest. Mädchen made him promise never to tell anyone of her presence, and he agreed, as long as she would meet him, and talk to him, and sometimes kiss him. She agreed. She liked the kissing. And he brought her gifts too: dresses which amused her, shoes which confused, and boots which gave her traction for tracking and hunting. She began to love Gerhard.

But not Fuchs. Fuchs hated Gerhard and Gerhard hated Fuchs. The years increased their hatred, but Fuchs knew he could not act like he hated Gerhard. One time, he had growled at Gerhard when he touched Mädchen, and she threw a stone at him to send him away. He never wanted that to happen again and so he tolerated Gerhard. Gerhard likewise tolerated Fuchs because he saw the love they shared and he knew that separating them—now—would only make Mädchen despise him.

The years flew by. Mädchen and Gerhard grew stronger in their secret love, and Fuchs grew stronger in his hatred. Fuchs was emboldened by his rage and began to wander away from Mädchen in the night. Sometimes, when his warmth was gone from her side, the cold woke her, and she sat up listening to the sounds of the animals around, and waited for his return. She would ask him in their special language where he had gone, but he would not say; he could not say.

For Fuchs had followed Gerhard to his village and watched him go to his home, where the door closed behind him, and Fuchs' hatred grew.

Mädchen loved everything about Gerhard. She loved his voice, his words, the language he taught her, the clothes he brought, the snacks they shared, the love that flowed between them. She felt only good things about him, and thought that Fuchs did too. How could he not? He was her family, and she shared her life with him. He must love what she loved. As she would love what he loved.

But Fuchs could not understand Gerhard. Fuchs did not like Gerhard. And Fuchs wanted him gone.

By now, Mädchen was eighteen years old, and a young woman. She was smart, beautiful, and an amazing hunter. But she could not read. She could not write. She could not live among people. But every day, as she learned more of Gerhard and his language, and heard of his stories, the more she wanted to be with him. At night, she found herself weeping into Fuchs fur. Fuchs did not know tears. Fuchs did not know longing. Fuchs did not know hurt. But he knew that Gerhard was taking Mädchen away from him, and he planned to stop it. Every moment Mädchen and Gerhard spent together was another moment that ripped Fuchs heart apart. Even though Fuchs did not know how to cry, what it meant to long for something or the feeling of pain, he began to feel something that he had never felt before. He howled for his loss, he wanted to be the reason Mädchen laughed and smiled. Without knowing what it meant, he was hurt by her distance, and he was afraid. Afraid of losing her even more.

Fear does terrible things to us.

Fear makes us think terrible things of others.

Fear takes us to our basest instincts.

Fuchs continued to watch Gerhard at night go into his house, and come out in the morning, and every day he stood beside Mädchen hoping that her eyes would light up for him, and her petting would no longer be a distraction as she sat and waited for Gerhard to come to see her. For all she thought about was Gerhard. All she talked about was Gerhard. And she started using the words Gerhard used. And Fuchs was enraged.

Seriously, when are you going to get to the end of this story? Chris has a really great tale to tell.

Shh. Wait. I'm getting to it.

Fuchs was enraged.

Before bed one night, Mädchen twirled around and around in the new blue dress Gerhard had brought to her that day. A present for their fifth anniversary of love. As she twirled around, the ruffles fluttered in the breeze and the stars sparkled on the skirt, and she laughed with love and happiness. Fuchs looked on. And Fuchs' anger grew.

That night, once Mädchen was fast asleep, Fuchs pitta patted pitta patted pitta patted out to Gerhard's house, and he saw something that he did not understand. Gerhard was kissing another woman outside his house. Gerhard was laughing with her. Gerhard was looking at her in the way he looked at Mädchen. Fuchs did not want Gerhard to be with Mädchen but somehow this made him madder.

He paced and paced up and down and down and up outside the house and growled and snarled and waited.

Did he have a choice? We always have a choice. Even foxes in love with young girls. We all have choices.

Is it done?

Whisper it with me:
Pitta patta
Pitta patta
Pitta patta

Back to the clearing where Mädchen was still asleep, the blood rushed to Fuchs' head, and his heart pounded and his head pounded...

...and he snarled
...and he growled
...and he LEAPT

When they found Mädchen naked at the edge of forest near the village, the coroner said that she had been killed by an animal. But no one ever knew who she was. There were no missing girls in their town.

"An animal? Are you sure?" asked the police officer.

"Well, it could be animal, or someone who wants us to think it's an animal," said the coroner.

That same night, a shadow passed by Gerhard's bedroom window, and he thought he saw Fuchs but believed he was mistaken. And so he fell back asleep. The sleep of the innocents.

The next morning, a bloodied dress—Mädchen's bloodied dress—was lain out in the bed beside him, placed beside him in the night while he lay sleeping. When his mother came to wake him in the morning, she saw the dress, and she saw the look in her son's eyes, and she screamed.

The police came to take him that morning and he was hung in the village square after a trial that lasted only one day. And Fuchs watched. Fuchs heart broke. But Fuchs watched, and then ran away never to be seen anywhere again.

So, if you ever see a fox in the woods…a wolf in the woods…a bear in the woods... Be wary. Be safe. Because you never know. You never know what they might be doing…

Where they might be going…

What they might have planned…

Pitta patta
Pitta patta
Pitta patta

BOO!

That was okay.
Okay but I didn't get scared.
I just heard a fox in the forest.
Can you come to my tent with me? Pleaaase.
Ma, how is this scary? The fox just loved her sooooo much.
My darling, anytime someone loves you sooooo much that they hate the other people you love, that they kill for it, then that's the thing to be the most scared about.
Ma, I'm scared.
My darling I will make sure nothing ever happens to you.

How can that really ever be true?
Oh, you know it's not. And that's the real BOO!

Stuck Like Glue: Sometimes, taking a different perspective can reveal a lot about a story that would otherwise go untold. For this Event, write from the perspective of an inanimate object.
Core concept: pacing, point of view.

Sins of the Father
CE Snow
First Place

    Pop. Flick. Snap. Pop. Flick. Snap. PopFlickSnap. Over and over in maddening repetition. Justin never runs his thumb over my wheel to spark the flame. He just pops my silver lid, then flicks his wrist and snaps it closed again as he stares at his father, Alexander, laid out, cold and stiff, on the dining room table. I'd rather be in Alex's hands. He knew how to have fun.

    It was sweaty in Alex's clenched fist. Not nerves, but excitement. In glorious paradox, I felt both the hot thrum of his pulse though his palm and the icy nip of night air between the gaps in his fingers. He scurried amid the shadows, avoiding a sliver of moonlight that illuminated the broken sidewalk. Grass grew between the cracks, but didn't dare to thrive. Parched, it turned brown and brittle. A little thrill ran through me, oh how it would burn, but Alex didn't stop.

    He glanced around, then darted around the back of an old, deserted house. The windows were boarded over, the siding peeling, a shutter hung askew. The back door sagged, one of its hinges rusted away, and Alex toed it open. The container in his other hand sloshed and the perfume of gasoline sang to me. Soon.

    Inside, Alex splashed the gas onto a mouldering, flower-patterned couch, across the shaggy carpet, up the age-yellowed lace curtains. The boards that had once covered the living room window, had been pried up, and the glass shattered. Desiccated leaves littered the floor, taking false refuge from the bitter autumn winds. They would burn without the accelerant's encouragement – edges curling, blistering, charring black. I nearly vibrated with impatience.

    Alex set the empty jerrycan down and admired his handiwork. I felt the tension running through him, a buzz of manic energy that shivered down his spine, rippled along his arm, and shocked me through his fingertips. His thumb rubbed over my casing, caressing the twisted vine engravings. He popped open my lid and spun the flint wheel. Once. Twice. Spark! My flame wavered then grew, blue at the base then rising to a pointed cone of softly glowing white.

    Anticipation blazed through me, mine or his, it was immaterial; our need to burn was identical. Alex grabbed a gas soaked rag and touched it to my flame. It caught and for a moment he held it, the fabric alight, heat curling the hairs on the back of his hand. The light glinted off his white teeth, mouth stretched in a wide grin, as he reveled in the almost-pain. Flame reached for him, but wise to its twickster ways, he tossed the burning rag onto the sodden couch cushions.

For a split-second eternity nothing happened. Then with a whump the sofa exploded into dancing light. I wanted to shout – burn! – but the fire didn't need my urging as it raced across the cushions, gobbling up the upholstered violets and tea roses. It leapt. The lace curtains singed; a forked tongue of red and yellow tasted the delicate fabric, before devouring it whole.

Balanced on Alex's palm, my small flame flickered in mirror image to the inferno that now raced up the curled wallpaper. Heat washed over us. Alex's hair lifted in the backdraft to encircle his head like a dark halo. He staggered back, cackling. The snap and pop of the fire echoed his laughter.

With a practiced flip of the wrist, Alex snapped my lid closed. My flame went out, but the house fire burned on with uncontrolled, infectious glee. Black smoke rolled towards us and Alex closed his fist around me, then threw his arm over his mouth and nose. We fled.

A few blocks away, Alex sat in the cab of his pickup. He turned me over in his hands, fingers idly tracing the loops and swirls of the vines embossed on my still warm casing. His touch both intimate and habitual. The faint bouquet of smoke scented the air, growing closer.

When the alarm came across the radio, Alex counted to one hundred, slow and steady.

"One Mississippi. Two Mississippi..."

When he got all the Mississippi's out of the way, he took a deep breath before reaching with trembling fingers to thumb the call button.

"Twelve fifteen, responding. ETA about five minutes."

"Roger that, Alex." The radio crackled with static. "Looks like another one of those abandoned house fires. Engine two is enroute."

"Copy that, dispatch." Alex checked his watch.

Five minutes later, he stuffed me into his jacket pocket. The truck's engine roared to life and the rotating flash of the emergency lights seeped through the fibers of my fabric nest. I snuggled into *the cozy warmth. The night would hold more excitement for Alex, but my part was over. Until the next time.*

Pop. Flick. Snap. Justin's hands are cool, in contrast to the familiar warmth that I remember in his father's. That heat's faded, Alex's fire snuffed out by lung cancer. It rankles that he went that way. He should have gone out in a blaze of glory, not a coughing, wheezing skeleton shackled to a wheelchair. They wouldn't even let my old friend hold me – too close to the oxygen tank, they said. It didn't matter that he'd promised not to strike my flame. Perhaps they knew he would have had little will to resist me.

Pop. Flick. Snap. Rain hammers on the window panes, as Justin digs a flask from his pocket and takes a sip. The flammable scent of whiskey entices, but he screws the cap back on and leaves me disgruntled. Stretched on the dining room table, Alex's stiff frown seems disappointed as well. So disparate, this father and son.

Pop. A small loaf of bread rests on Alex's unmoving chest and a cross splits the top of its golden crust. Justin frowns at the sight. From a straight-backed chair in the corner, a small bird of a woman sniffs, a pale drab finch that has lost its song, and Justin schools his features. He stalls the wrist flick and eases my lid back down with a gentle click. The bird-woman nods and smooths the brittle crepe of her black funeral gown.

Lightning flashes an instant of daylight. Justin counts under his breath, and for a moment I see his father in him.

"One Mississippi. Two Mississippi. Three–"

Thunder rattles the tea cups in their saucers, arranged in a precise semicircle atop the sideboard lowboy. The good blue willow china that the bird-woman only brings out for guests. Guests who politely sip and hide their grimaces when her back is turned, for serving visitors bitter and over-brewed tea in dainty porcelain cups is a formality of yesteryear.

"What did you say, dear?" The bird-woman's voice is brittle, her words clipped as if she has a finite amount of vowels and is using them sparingly.

"He's not coming." Justin points to the window. "The storm…"

"He'll come."

"People don't do this anymore, Nana. It's an archaic ritual. Weird even." Pop. "They take their loved ones to funeral homes." Flick. "They don't lay them out with a loaf of bread on their chest, right on the dining room table. And they definitely don't hire some old creep to come and *eat* their sins." The snap of my lid punctuates Justin's words.

The bird-woman purses her lips but doesn't reply. They've had this argument before and she always wins. For a dried up finch, she has a fire in her, and now I know where Alex got it.

Another shock of momentary daylight brightens the room, then in the thunderous aftermath vision succumbs to shadow. The lights give a halfhearted sputter and die. Startled, Justin jerks. I slip through his fingers to clatter across the hardwood, free of his cool, fidgety grasp.

"Damnit."

"Language." Disembodied in the dark, the bird-woman's admonishment echoes off the walls, hollow and eerie like a specter in an ancient crypt.

Fingertips brush against my case, sending me spinning on the smooth planks before Justin snatches me up. He pops open my lid and for the first time, runs his thumb over the flint wheel. Elated, I spark and flame. Like a magician pulling a rabbit from his hat, the bird-woman fishes chunky tapers from inside the lowboy and passes them over one by one. Soon the room is awash with the soft glow of candlelight.

Distracted by a heavy knocking, Justin abandons me between the teacups and the candlesticks to stalk to the foyer and answer the front door. The wind screams and tries to claw its way into the room, making the candles jump and hop as Justin hustles a tall, thin figure inside.

From her corner, the bird-woman lets out a whispery sigh and crosses herself.

"Sin Eater." I'm uncertain if it's a greeting, supplication, or entreaty.

The Sin Eater is lanky, gaunt even. It surprises me, for I expected someone greedy and stout, stuffed full of bread and wine and the Seven Deadlies. His lined face is dour and his eyes have the pinched look of someone in chronic pain. Like my firebrand Alex's had, at the end. Perhaps the sins do not sit well, gnawing at the stomach, trying to find their way back into the world, looking for a new soul to tempt.

This whole bizarre affair was at the bird-woman's behest, and yet she sits motionless, her beady eyes wide and her twisted, arthritic claws clasped in her lap. She leaves Justin to show the Sin Eater in. I get a sense that she thinks, in some antiquated fashion, that this is a thing to be done among men. She shrinks back in her chair and becomes, like I am, a mere observer at this heathen sacrament of exculpation.

Justin moves to speak, but the Sin Eater holds up one hand to forestall him, as if to say the ritual is ingrained and instructions are unnecessary. To break the silence with mundane banalities would be sacrilege. The air presses on me, suddenly heavy. Despite my proximity to the seductive warmth of the candelabra, I feel a chill. Unseen rime creeps across my metal case. If the oblivious Justin deemed to notice me, grab me up, I somehow know his fingers would burn. Frozen, not charred.

I watch, fascinated, as the grim stranger crosses the room with a hitched, uneven gait, and stops before the table. He raises his scarecrow arms, joints creaking. His fingers are too long, even for a man of his height, and his knuckles create knobby protrusions along their length. The wavering candlelight casts odd shadows, stretching like black, wriggling snakes across Alex's rigid corpse.

The Sin Eater draws a shaky breath and his thin lips move in barely audible prayer. Latin, I think. Or German? A language faintly remembered, from the time before Alex's father had filched me from the pocket of a dead soldier. A macabre souvenir of war. The Sin Eater drones on. With every word the candles dim. They flare just as high as before, but their luminescence is siphoned off, bit by bit, until the glow of the flames is nothing more than illusion.

The desire to burn rises in me, to set fire to everything and bring back the light – the bleached-white tablecloth, the heavy billowing drapes, the stark fabric of the bird-woman's dress. Justin's cheap, polyester suit. To char and consume sweet flesh, ablaze like giant tallow candlesticks. The craving swells to need, until I am no longer metal case and flint and wick, but hunger incarnate. Insatiable.

That's when the Sin Eater begins to eat. With quiet deliberation, his long fingers pluck the small loaf of bread from Alex's chest and break off bite-size pieces. Each morsel travels an infinite expedition, hand to mouth, then sluggish chewing, before reluctantly swallowed down. It seems every successive mouthful becomes harder. The journey from loaf to stomach tries the Sin Eater's will. Doggedly, he perseveres.

If every bite is more difficult for the arcane mystic, the process marches in reverse for the bird-woman. Her load lightens and her internal spark grows, as the loaf disappears by bites. She glows as the burden of her son's guilt is slowly nibbled away. Justin, on the other hand, watches the rite, arms crossed over his chest in skeptical repugnance. I remember his lizard-cool fingers upon my case, and know that his fire is too dull to be touched by magic. I wonder how he lived with himself, eclipsed by the brilliance of his father's bonfire-soul.

The clatter of cup on saucer grabs my attention. The loaf is gone, and the bird-woman offers the Sin Eater tea. He accepts, and washes the bread – and the sins – down with one grateful gulp. Lightning flashes, unenthusiastic, and in its passage the Sin Eater shrinks. He no longer seems as tall, his shoulders hunch. Thunder rumbles in the distance, muted as the storm loses its fury. It is done.

The Sin Eater glances up. The face that was lined and wan before the eating, is now haggard and shadowed. His eyes dart around the room, searching. They sweep over the silent bird-woman and dismiss Justin, before alighting on me. In their dark depths a fire burns. It twists and leaps, the hungry turmoil of Alex's sins. My own fever burns in response, but tinged with regret. The Sin Eater shivers and turns away.

He shuffles toward the foyer, trailed by Justin and the bird-woman. She gives Justin a pointed look and with reluctance, he pulls out his wallet. A stab of hatred and disgust slashes through me. I loathe the thought of his hands upon me, revulsed to think of him tracing the age-worn engravings like an uninvited caress. I'm no trinket, to be passed from a father who loved me to son who doesn't. He could never replace Alex, for we were kindred spirits. I wallow in my grief.

The creak of floorboards interrupts my self-absorbed reverie. Justin's girl-child, clad in a wispy nightgown creeps into the room. With wary glances towards the foyer, she inches forward on stockinged feet. I expect fear or distaste, as she hovers alongside Alex's wooden remains. She reaches out, fingers steady, and strokes his cold cheek. Her eyes, red-rimmed and bloodshot, remain dry. They flicker and snap; black, like Alex's. Urgent need burns in me.

The child smooths down Alex's shirt, tiny hands skimming over his pockets. She frowns. She checks again, fingers darting from starched breast to pleated trousers in a desperate hunt. Voices waft from the front hall. I want to scream – over here! I push my hunger towards her.

I'm here!

Drawn by my silent plea, she glances up. An unseen tether connect us, and my desire kindles something deep inside her. On tiptoes, the girl brushes a soft kiss on Alex's waxy brow, then steps around the table. Captivated, she glides forward like a sleepwalker, her movements slow and dreamy. Dark eyes fix on me and her fire smolders, awaiting a spark, the trigger to set off the underlying wildfire.

The front door closes with a thump and the girl jumps. Her breath catches in her throat, neither gasp nor sob, but a marriage of both. She squares her shoulders and dashes toward the lowboy, feet swift and silent. In a blur she snatches me up and flees.

A name flares as skin meets metal.

Alexandria!

Encased in her small fist, excitement sings through me. Alexa's palm is warm.

Infinitely Practical
LS Fellows
Second Place

Practical, that's me. Well, there are worse things to be called. Although, reliable, solid and pragmatic sound grander, but such labels would suggest a need to be appreciated. Which, of course, for an insentient object is surely impossible. You must agree. Who in their right mind would propose such an argument?

Allow me to introduce myself - you can call me Rope, 'though cord is acceptable, if you must. However, nylon or polypropylene are complete misnomers. In my early days, a steel girder held me aloft, tightly coiled and free from the harm that a dirty floor might inflict upon my natural fibres. Hoisted high above the inferior quality products that shared the same aisle in the DIY superstore.

That was until Man acquired me, at which time he reduced me to a length of ten metres, and carried me away in his white van. A dark, gloomy vehicle unlike the bright store lights. At first, the darkness proved restful; gone was the steady flow of customers who passed me by on a daily basis. An odd sense of something strange gnawed at me, though such realisation did not become wholly apparent until much later on. Being so much shorter with two ends stunned me a little; the new end had no sense of self and hid itself away. Survival of the fittest, I suppose. It didn't stand a chance!

Man moved fast, the ride bumpy but promising of a great adventure for me as a first-time traveller.

The doors to the van opened, bringing bright light once more into my world. He reached inside and dragged me out, slinging me across his body, something I would later appreciate as strange smells and clouds of dust bombarded me from every which way. What was this hell?

'Who wants a swing then?' he yelled.

A smaller person bounded outside and grabbed his hand. 'Me, please, Daddy! I want to go high too. So I can see the whole world.'

Together they walked across a dusty path; I clenched my fibres so as not to slip from Man's loose grip. The store-man always advised customers not to get me "wet" - whatever that meant - or dirty, a word I understood having heard store-people bemoan the dirty floors at the end of each day, before the lights went out.

Man placed me on a bench, in a shady area. The little person sat beside me, her tiny fingers tickling my strands. Customers had often touched me, snapping me taut to test my strength. I never disappointed.

'This spot, Betsy? Are you sure?' Man asked.

'Yes, Daddy. Underneath the oak tree, like Grandpa says in his stories.'

Hm, so this was a tree then. The term was not unfamiliar, but the sight was. It reached high up, filling my vision in its entirety. Glimmers of light leaked through here and there, casting shadows across me. A rustling noise followed as the ventilation system kicked in.

'Are you sure it's not too windy here?'

'Nope, it's perfect, Daddy.'

'Righty-O. Now be a good girl, take that end and help me measure.'

The "girl" grabbed the quiet end, while he held me in his clammy, calloused hands. 'On the floor, Betsy.'

Oh, the indignity of it. Fortunately my humiliation was short-lived, as after marking certain points with a pencil, he gathered me up and placed me back on the bench.

'Okay, now stand back by the ladder while I throw the rope over the branch.'

As much as I was accustomed to heights, what followed rendered me a little giddy. Had I not been so well braided, I might well have come undone. A lesser quality product would never have survived the flight as he hurled one end into the air. He caught my loose end as it fell to the ground, and pulled on it, rubbing me against the tree and, in so doing, generating an unwelcome burning sensation. He tugged, wrapped one end over the other and pulled again.

'Good catch, Daddy!' Girl shrieked, clapping her hands.

'Stay back, though, I need to do it one more time.'

I braced myself, knowing what to expect as he took a couple of steps closer to the tree and hurled my other end over the same branch. Man then climbed a step ladder and threaded my second spare end through the loop, yanking it taut and inducing anew that burning sensation. He moved across to check the first knot was solid, stretching me firm before giving a satisfied grunt. Then he got down and collapsed the ladder. From the ground, he stood back, admiring me. Two almost equal lengths dangled from the branch, secured by two loops knotted some seventy centimetres apart.

'Not a bad job, if I say so myself. What do you think Betsy?'

Impressed he might well have been, but such was not my verdict of his endeavours, since both my ends lay coiled on the dirt.

'It's a bit long, Dad.' Clearly, she shared my concerns. I liked Girl.

He snorted with laughter. 'Don't worry; the seat will take up the slack, and what's left will be reverse-braided to make it stronger still.'

Girl wrapped her arms around his legs. 'Thanks, Dad. It's going to be wonderful. The best in England. Just like in Grandpa's stories. My very own rope swing.'

That strange sensation I experienced before returned to gnaw at me. Yet, I could no more define it then than earlier.

Later that afternoon, in the shady corner of Man's private garden, an area he'd fenced off from his small-holding, Girl launched herself high into the air, gripping me tightly in both hands as we soared, descended and soared again. 'I can see over the trees, Daddy! I can see the stream, and beyond that the village, even our church spire. Wow! Higher, please!' she squealed. 'Look, Dad, there are the chalk hills and the woods. I can see the whole world.'

To say such excitement was infectious would be an understatement. I had left behind a place of bright lights, of noisy customers, pulling and stretching me, for one where I took Girl to the place of her dreams. I had found a sense of ... belonging, that was the word I searched for. I, Rope, from batch number 375: Natural - Sisal, had a home.

Of course, you might dismiss this as me being impossibly sensitive. You could be right. But, imagine this, if you are surrounded by and contribute to the joy of another, are you not then entitled to appreciate that pleasure yourself? It's a thorny issue, I understand, but that afternoon - and for many more lazy, summer afternoons to come, my purpose extended from practical to joyful. Would that swing exist without me? Would Girl see the whole wide world without me? I think not. What say you?

Should you need further endorsement of my place in that home, on that smallholding in the southern Downs of England, permit me to share with you another experience. For, I am not just a swing. In fact, I am no longer a swing, haven't been so for many a year, but let me explain.

Years passed, and Girl grew. She used me less and less, although the shade of the tree saw her lay down a blanket and lose herself in her books, or chatting with friends. After one quiet year, it was time to retreat to the shed, as I had done every year since my first autumn with the family. This time, my memories were fewer and time spent in my box in the shed stretched out before me like an eternity. For the first time, I craved the regular contact of the customers back at the store. At least there I had some self-worth. This constant change made me question my value, even when I came to understand the cyclical nature of my new home. Life on a farm moved with the seasons. Yes - for me, too!

When Spring came, as I knew it would, Man freed me from my misery and took me back to the tree. Dreading another slow season, I waited to be hurled and knotted as before. But this time, Man began tying me in knots, more than ever before; he twisted and pulled, snapped and curled, weaving me this way and that, before attaching my upper half to a large structure perched within the tree.

On the ground, Girl cheered. 'Way to go, Dad!'

He waved to her, releasing my full load to the ground. I braced myself, expecting to hit the floor. Instead, I swayed, or maybe I staggered, but one thing I didn't do was get dirty. Way to go, Man.

'Try it for yourself,' he said.

She clambered up onto me. At first, I strained under her weight, unused to her feet stepping all over me. It was all over in a few seconds as she scrambled to the top and stepped inside. 'My very own tree house. Just like in Grandpa's stories. He would have loved to have seen this, Dad.' She walked around the space, around two metres square. 'Oh, this old photo of you and Mum is beautiful. Thank you.' She hugged him, no longer reaching only his legs.

Who was Mum? I knew Dad, Daddy, Betsy the girl and I'd heard lots about Grandpa, but there was someone else in our family. I waited to meet Mum, yet I never saw her.

Girl would visit the tree-house daily, after school, bringing her books with her, filling the place with cushions and blankets - every shade of purple from lilac to Byzantium, mauve to pansy. Man always knew where to find her, but there was never any sign of Mum.

When autumn came I was no longer taken down and sent to the box in the shed. Rather, I was hoisted into the tree house, and allowed to rest my weary strands on a beanbag, the very height of luxury, albeit chilly in winter ... and lonely.

Once the snows melted, Girl would come back, unroll me and those halcyon days were once more to be enjoyed. Now she brought friends with her, and while my rungs were tested, they never drooped or sagged. As always, my goal to protect those who had given me this chance never wavered. Girl and her friends would giggle and talk till late, eating picnics and reading out loud, debating and then ... crying.

What could I do? Girl's tears were the harshest sounds I'd ever heard, and I was helpless once more. I had come to assume I could protect my family, to take them only to happy places. But it was soon evident I was no such saviour.

Silence reigned in the tree-house as she hid herself away. I heard the scratching of pen on paper, but nothing more. Until she began to play the guitar up there too. Oh, what I would have given for that earlier silence. However, slowly the squeals grated less, the twanging of strings faded into melody and after countless hours, days and weeks, the reason behind Girl's tears took shape in the form of a song. Lyrics painted a haunting picture of her broken heart; the wrong-doer heralded sharp tones and even - to my horror - blasphemous outrage. Soon, she began to laugh again. Old friends returned. Chatter resumed, and happiness moved back in.

I hasten to say, though, this Mum from the old photo still stayed away.

The tree-house had a heart beat again, and I dangled in the breeze, content to allow free passage to those who brought joy to Girl's life. Until one day, when rather than being left to hang outside while Girl and friends chatted, I was hauled up into the tree-house.

Girl beamed as I lay coiled at the entrance. Her visitor was altogether different from her usual friends. More like her dad in appearance. He made Girl laugh with his stories. But he was no Grandpa either. They - he and Girl - were a match in age, he being slightly taller, broader and with limbs as loose and floppy as a handful of rubber bands.

'Remember that trip to Blackpool?' she said, her voice soft and giggly.

I began to wonder why they had pulled me up to listen to this. Rarely was I witness to the goings-on within the tree-house. She ran her fingers through his hair. He returned the gesture.

'Yes, indeed. And the weekend in Paris. That was something special—'

She signalled for him to keep quiet.

'Betsy, are you up there?' Man shouted.

'Yeah, Dad. Won't be long. Just finishing my paper for college.'

'Okay, love. Dinner will be ready in half an hour. I've got something to tell you.'

I noted a hitch in his voice as his footsteps faded away.

'You still think your dad will be mad you're seeing me?'

'For sure. He's not a big fan of your father's business. Says his development projects are eating up farmers like him and putting profit before quality.'

'I'm not him though.'

'I know that, and you know that. It's just Dad's worried about the farm, and he's old-fashioned. He brought me up on his own when Mum died, and doesn't want to admit his baby girl is all grown-up.'

Ah, the famous Mum. At last, something about her made sense.

'All grown-up is exactly my point, Betsy. Your dad is in denial about that.' He said, silencing her with his mouth on hers.

At this point, I wanted to throw myself over the edge. I really cannot tell you how uncomfortable it was ... definitely "Too Much Information", as Betsy and her friends would say! You really don't need to know what happened next, suffice it to say I welcomed the leather jacket he threw on top of me. If only it could have prevented the noises ...oh, and the rocking motion. Ugh!

Girl came by less often after that, and this time when autumn blew in, I found myself back in the shed. And no longer with my own accommodation. Man hung me from a hook on the back wall, unknotted and coiled. Boxes blocked my view of the shed door, and my only visitors were the spiders who came to weave magical webs in which to catch flies and other bugs. Days ran into weeks, weeks into months. Activity beyond the shed ground to a halt. Nothing moved. The big chill set in. When, finally, the birds returned to chirp and slivers of sunshine sent the dust motes into a merry dance, I awaited my temporary release.

I waited.

And waited.

The shed grew stuffy. More boxes arrived. Even the spiders moved on to pastures new, checking out the rusting shovels and spades, the soil-clodden shears and scythes, the dusty buckets and grain troughs. My ends frayed, mildew moved in and bugs travelled between my fibrous strands. Initially their lightness of touch reminded me of Girl's tiny fingers when first we used to swing up high. But, then they itched and irritated me, biting at me till I grew numb and passed out from boredom.

In my somnolent state, there was nothing to my existence beyond hope, which waned a tad more with each passing day. Until the shed door was flung open, grunts and groans echoed as boxes shifted. Spiders scurried into the darkest corners, and daylight brought excitement to the damp shadows as they morphed into new shapes, displaced by the brightness.

'There it is, on the back wall,' said a sombre voice as a hand reached through a gap and unhooked me, tugging me forward. I could take the pain, any amount of it if it led to my release. Snagging on sharp corners, squeezing through tight apertures which chafed at my deadened fibres, nothing mattered if it meant freedom. And it did. With a gruff jerk, my confinement was over.

Outside the vibrancy of day filled me with a renewed exuberance. It mattered not why I had been abandoned for so long, nor why I was now needed. All that mattered was that someone needed me. A weak sun somehow warmed the breeze that caressed my coiled form. The stiffness of neglect sagged as the owner of the voice unravelled me, placing me on the ground to straighten out the kinks. Stretched to my full length, I experienced an awakening, not even the dry dusty ground could take that from me.

'Not bad. Still useable,' said the voice.

I detected a familiar hitch. It was Man; it had to be. Though his fingertips now bore yet more callouses, his touch was firm, maybe the pull not as strong, but nor was it frail.

With a blade he skimmed off loose threads, scraped away the blight of mildew, and restored my faith that I would once more be a reliable ally in whatever project he had in mind. A swing, a ladder, a tow-rope, anything at all. I was open to anything and everything.

He wrapped me around his body, much like the very first day when he fetched me from the store, and together we followed the dirt track to the old oak tree. Bare of leaves, the tree looked fragile, its branches more spindly than I remembered. Man dropped me at the base of the tree where roots puckered the dry earth. From my vantage I reconnected with familiar sights. Except this was no longer the happy hunting ground I so fondly called to mind. Gone was the tree-house, and the farm building took on a ghostly form with roof tiles missing, windows boarded up and painted surfaces in dire need of a new coat of colour. A sign in the yard immediately in front of the main read REPO -SESS- ION in thick red letters. What on earth did that mean? It wasn't there last time, of that I was certain.

Man trudged back to the main house, his stoop pronounced, his hair thin on top and his clothes threadbare. My enforced imprisonment had not treated him well either. Was that why he needed me? To bring the joy back? That had to be the reason.

Clouds overhead raced across the sky, blocking out the fragile rays of sun. There was a chill in the air. Still, I was free. Outside. With Man. Ready and willing to be useful.

An engine rumbled in the distance and Man reappeared, atop his tractor, struggling to hold his head up. His appearance concerned me. But I would bring him cheer and lighten his mood. It's what I always did for him … and Girl.

He jumped down from the tractor and ran straight for me, spreading me out on the ground, running around me, shaping me this way and that.

Hmm, Man had learnt a new trick it seemed. It was exciting to see him work, as he formed an "S" with one half, compressing the three rows with only a slim gap in between. His chest heaved as he pinched the three lines together in the middle, and the ends fanned out to create a bow-tie effect. This wasn't the usual knot he made. Much more intricate. Pretty even. Maybe for Girl.

Deftly he wrapped the bow-tie from the right side to the left, poking one end through the other, pinching and looping with a ferocious tenacity until his creation was complete. Definitely something with a distinct purpose. If only I knew what. Nonetheless, I liked a surprise, and today had been full of them already.

He threw the spare end over the branch, and caught it as it dropped back to the ground. He tugged and tugged till he had enough of me to hurl in the air again. This time, when he caught me, he wrapped that same end loosely around the trunk of the tree. This was nothing like the swing, or the ladder. Definitely something new. Something special.

He set off back to the farmhouse, giving me time to assess how I would move if he applied any pressure to the looped end that remained on the ground. Whatever he had in mind, I realised needed a very tight and firm hold. It was beyond me what he was thinking of, but then again I had never imagined the swing or the ladder before. I needed to trust him more, believe that he knew exactly what he was doing. Which he always did. It was a game. Of course it was. Silly me for thinking the worst.

I lay there for a long time until dusk crept upon me. A half-light, neither bright nor dark.

And then, BOOM!

Man re-emerged carrying the stepladder as flames licked at the farmhouse. The heat emitted grew to intense levels and smoke battled against the dark clouds for room in the sky.

Man placed the ladder directly under the branch, and then picked up the spare end he had bound around the trunk, tying it now around the tow-bar, then he climbed aboard the tractor and drove away. The greater distance he put between us, the more friction he generated as my fibres scraped against the trunk. Bark fell to the ground, splinters embedded within my strands and the looped end rose from the floor.

Another voice came from the direction of the burning farmhouse. More frantic, screeching, the type of noise I recalled from the superstore when little people tried to climb on the girder and anxious bigger people yelled at them to stop.

Man sped from his tractor, the engine still running.

'No, Dad, please don't!' It was a woman's voice. Panicked and quivering with fear. Girl?

Man climbed the ladder, held my loop in his hands and pulled it wide, resting his chin on the curve of the loop.

This was no game. This was serious. This was deadly.

Don't use me like this, Man. I'll tighten around your neck. I can't stop that from happening. Don't let me kill you!

If only he could hear me. I'm forced to acknowledge my true place in his world. A mere object. Practical, reliable, strong and firm. I could kill him. He wants me to contribute to his death. To be part of his decision. I am unable to object. Who was I kidding? To think I had a more important place in his world, in his family.

Someone stop him, please! I wanted to yell at him. But it was not - nor had it ever been - within my power to do so.

Derrick! I screamed his name. How did I know that? Had my familiarity overstepped the mark? Regardless, it would make no difference.

Girl came nearer, her voice thick with emotion. 'Dad, I found your note and came straight over. Please don't leave me. Not now.Not like this. My baby needs a Grandpa. Don't deny us that. We need you. We love you!' She clutched at her enlarged stomach. The extra weight suited her.

Girl, stop him. Tell him to stop. Beg if you have to. Betsy, please. Don't let me kill him.

'Dad, we can fix this. You're not alone. You never have been. Just your stupid pride. What would Mum say? We both know the answer.' She paused, as did he.

Then, Man's fingers loosened on my loop.

That last comment from Betsy resonated with him. Oh, thank the Lord. Thank you, Mum - whoever you were.

He pushed me away and fell, sobbing, from the ladder to the ground. Betsy raced towards him, dropped to her knees and wrapped her arms around him, just as a tall, loose-limbed figure in a leather jacket sliced through my loop, rendering me unfit for the fatal purpose.

It was over. For me. But not for them.

I am an insentient object. Practical in many ways, but not complicit in Man's death.

I'm a rope. Or rather, I'm now two pieces of rope.

Twice as practical. Or am I?

Time in Place
Mia Neishy
Third Place

It's been a month since I've moved into my new home. It's a pretty little room. And I'm starting to get used to it.

At first, I missed my friends terribly. We had so much fun in the big baby store, chatting about all the soon-to-be parents who visit us. If only they could hear us bickering about which one of us was prettier, sturdier, or worth more for the price. It was always a lively atmosphere but it does get quite loud on big sales days. It was on such a day that Hannah and Brent came to the store. They spent two hours browsing before falling in love with me and taking me home with them.

My name is Lia. That's the name given to me and many others by the craftsmen who built us. We all looked the same except for our color. I have an espresso finish which I think makes me stand out more than those who are white or light brown in color. I have four sides and four corners. My back is a graceful arched silhouette. My sides have sweeping arms that meet a level front. Rails of the same color are perfectly spaced on all sides. I have bun feet on each corner, which the craftsmen have carved to look like bulbs of a flower. Other detailed carvings cover the four posts that hold me together. I have to say I'm a mighty good-looking and stylish baby crib.

The walls in my room are painted in light grey. I am positioned against one of the walls with a large bay window to my left. Long, flowy pink curtains are usually drawn so the sun doesn't shine in. I wish for the curtains to be open more often. I like looking out to the blue sky and white, puffy clouds floating by. On the other side of the window is a glider armchair upholstered in a baby pink fabric, with a thin, white border around the cushioned seat, back, and arms. It has a skirted bottom, making it look like a pretty lady in a dress. I have seen Hannah sit in it and swivel around, grinning like a little kid. A square, pink ottoman with the same white border sits in front of the glider.

Almost every day since I've moved in, Hannah and Brent have added pieces and parts to the room. First was the glider and the ottoman. Then, she bought a pretty white bedsheet with tiny pink flowers to clothe me in. She added the soft bumpers to protect baby from hitting the railings on my sides the same day and brought a pink rectangular rug to place before me the next day. Next, came a grey soft elephant, that was big enough for her to cuddle. It sits in the glider now. Along with the elephant, a myriad of soft toys -- including a teddy bear that would be too big to fit in me -- sit around. Today, Brent moves a baby changing station into the room and places it to my right. Same espresso color. It has a flat area on the top and many drawers below. Hannah starts to fill it with diapers, wipes, swaddlers, and other baby things.

Each day Hannah comes into the room, she seems a little chirpier. She sometimes sings as she places toys and such around the room. Sometimes she sits in the glider and reads a book, all the time smoothing the bump on her tummy. I must say that bump keeps getting bigger everyday. She keeps bringing in one item of baby clothing after another. Some onesies, shirts, pants, dresses, and a pink tutu. This baby is going to have so many clothes.

One day, Hannah comes into the room, lovingly hugging a soft, pink baby blanket to her chest. She drapes it gently over me, soothing over the embroidered words, "Sophie". That must be baby's name. Hannah rubs her tummy and whispers, "Mummy can't wait to see you, Sophie." Then, she picks out a book, "Guess How Much I Love You", sits down in the glider and reads the book to baby Sophie and the grey elephant she has perched on the armchair.

It's been a few days since I've seen Hannah. The longest she has ever not come into the room. Sometimes, I don't see her for three days and that's enough to make me antsy. This longer than usual absence is worrisome. I wish I could walk so I can get to the door, open it, and go find Hannah. Or if I could just have hands to sweep open the curtains so I can look outside to see if I could catch a glimpse of her or Brent. If I had a real heart, it would be pumping so hard that it would splinter all the railings around me. I look over at the glider and the changing table. I wish I spoke or understood their languages so I could ask them what they thought. Alas, different furnitures grow up learning different languages and I only know 'Crib'.

Finally, I hear footsteps outside the room. I can tell it's Hannah's. She has a softer, deliberate step compared to Brent's stronger, determined walk. The door opens slowly. Then, I see Hannah. My joy immediately turns to surprise. She is standing at the door. Her eyes are sad and her face looks gaunt. Her shoulders drooped and tears start to fill her pretty blue eyes. In seconds, the tears are streaming down her cheek and her shoulders are shaking. She starts to sob.

"Hannah! Hannah!!" Brent is calling for her. He soon finds her and quickly gathers her into his arms, hugging her tightly. "Sweetheart, why are you here?" His lips pursed, mouth shaking, holding back emotions. Tears start to glisten in his eyes too. They hug for a long time, with Hannah sobbing away. Brent finally shuts the door and I hear the footsteps leaving me.

"What happened?" I want to scream. Where is baby Sophie? Why are you crying? Please tell me.

The next few days drag on. I sometimes hear Hannah's footsteps outside. Sometimes Brent's, but they never come into the room. I get excited then disappointed each time. I miss them, especially Hannah and her voice as she sang and read to me.

A few weeks later, I hear Hannah outside the door again. My heart is beating, anticipating. The door knob turns and the door slowly opens. Hannah cautiously pushes the door wider. She is standing at the door for what seems like eternity. She looks more haggard than the last time. Her eyes are puffy. Her shoulders lifeless. She takes one step into the room and stops. Her eyes are fixated on me. She takes another step. I wish I could cheer her on. She takes slow, calculating steps towards me. With each step, her eyes get more glassy. By the time she gets to me, the tears that have been brimming pour down her cheeks. She clutches the pink blanket with her hands. "So..phie.." she manages before a sob escapes her. She brings the blanket to her chest and sobs uncontrollably. She sways and tries to catch herself against me but falls to a pile in front of me. Still clutching the blanket, she leans against me, crying torrents. I am weeping silently, without tears. I wish I had arms to embrace her, to comfort her. I wish I could call for Brent to come hold her. In my mind, I am screaming at the top of my lungs for him.

Brent comes running into the room seconds later. Perhaps he did hear my soundless scream, somehow. He scoops Hannah up, whispering to her that it's going to be okay and that he loves her. He takes her out of the room as she continues to cry into his shoulder.

Hannah comes to the room again the next few days and weeks. Each time, she would break down and cry. I hurt for her. But I could not do anything for her. It is excruciating to see her run her fingers over the clothes in the closet or hug me as she cries. Sometimes, she would pick up a few of the toys and hug them.

Sometimes, Brent would come and get her. Other times, she would leave on her own. It feels like the air is sucked out of the room each time the door closes behind them. It is so dreary and sad.

Hannah starts to come in random times during the day, sometimes in the middle of the night, and curl up in the glider. She holds the grey elephant in her arms and starts calling it Sophie, telling it stories and singing to it. Almost always, she would fall asleep in the glider. Brent would find her there and at first, he would try to wake her up. But he would always be greeted with an outburst, so he soon lets her be. He would sometimes sleep next to her, resting against the glider. As the weeks and months drag on, Brent seems to be more weary and eventually less forgiving of Hannah's routine. I see him less and less. Until one day, he storms into the room and tries to drag Hannah out of the room.

"C'mon, get up!" He tells her.

"Nooo!!" She screams.

"This has to stop. It's been eight months since Sophie's gone! How long are you planning to do this?"

Hannah frees her arm from Brent's grip. Tears are sliding down her cheeks, but her hollow eyes are defiant.

"We can try again… Have another baby."

"No!! I want my baby Sophie!"

"She's dead, Hannah!"

Hannah starts to wail.

Seeing her sobbing and crying must have soften Brent. "I'm sorry," and he tries to reach for her but she steps back. "We need to get you some help…" he mutters and tousles his hair before leaving the room.

The day Brent and Hannah had the confrontation in my room was the saddest day of my life. If I could cry, like Hannah, I am sure there would be buckets of tears. It feels like this room that used to be filled with happiness will never recover. And I fear I am right as I never saw Brent or Hannah again. I start to lose count of time. Days, weeks, months… It just goes on and on. The room starts to smell musty and it feels suffocating to be in here. I would be gasping for air if I had a pair of lungs and a mouth. Dust has settled on top of me. Everyday, I cringe as more and more of them land on me. It's probably a good thing I don't have a nose or I might sneeze unceasingly, shaking these poor floorboards beneath me. I miss Hannah and Brent. What has become of them? What will become of me?

One day, I hear the familiar footsteps. Then, the familiar voices. I perk up. It's been so long and I'm getting excited. "Please, please come in," I plead silently. Someone is twisting the door knob. The door swings wide open. It is them! It's Hannah and Brent! They don't look unhappy. But they are not smiling either.

"Are you sure you can do this?" Brent asks cautiously.

Hannah nods slowly. "I am going to be strong."

"I'll help."

Hannah does not answer. But they both walk into the room. They grab the canvas containers and start to put all the toys and stuffed animals in them. Then, the baby clothes in the closet. Next, Brent rolls up the pink rug while Hannah starts to strip me of my clothing and the bumper. I am getting scared. What is going on? She sneezes. "Wow, this room is dusty."

"No kidding!" I want to tell her.

"I'll go bring the duster." Brent offers. He rushes out of the room while Hannah continues to strip me. I don't like being naked like this. It makes me feel vulnerable.

When Brent comes back, he comes back with a big trash bag. "I figured we will need this." Hannah nods. Brent helps dust all the furniture, which makes me happy. Hannah stuffs a bunch of toys and clothes into the trash bag. Then, she picks up the pink baby blanket and the grey elephant slowly. She stares at them for a long moment. Brent sees her and goes over to give her a hug. As if that was the support she needed, she gently places them in the trash bag. She is throwing away the last reminder of Sophie. I feel my heart break. Hannah must feel worse.

When they were done cleaning up and taking out almost everything, Brent covers the changing table with a large blanket.

"Are you sure you want to get rid of it?" Brent asks.

"Yes," Hannah says weakly.

Brent lets out a soft sigh.

All I could think of then, "Is it me? You are getting rid of me?" It's a scary thought and with no way of pleading for my case, it gives me a horrible sinking feeling. As I am despairing about my situation, I feel a large cloak of grey sheet thrown over me. It envelops me all the way to my feet and suddenly, it is dark. I hear Brent and Hannah shuffling for a few moments longer. Then, the door closes and silence.

Silence and darkness. That will be my existence for months and months. Minus the one day I hear Brent and some other unknown footsteps come into the room. I hear them talking about moving the glider out and Brent's voice commenting, "It reminded my wife too much of the time she spent in it with the baby…" His voice trailing at the end.

The poor glider must have been so sad to leave. It was such a beautiful lady with her ruffled skirt and white borders on her pink dress. I will miss her. But I miss Hannah and Brent more. I also miss having light. It's so scary to be in the dark. I'm losing touch of time and perhaps, my sense of self. Not being able to see myself, I am starting to forget how I look. I feel lonely and abandoned. I pray everyday that I may see light again someday.

That someday finally arrives when I hear Brent's footsteps one day. I pray hard for him to open the door and he does. But he starts moving me! I start to freak out. Please don't get rid of me. I don't want to go. Where is my voice? I need a voice more than ever. My panic doesn't last as he stops suddenly. Then I hear him moving the changing table then stops. What is going on? My curiosity is heightened. And I am annoyed that the covers are still keeping me in the dark.

Brent comes back into the room often after that. I cannot see what he is doing. But I hear him shuffling around the room. I hear rustling of newspapers. Then a can being opened? I think it's a can. I start to hear something being moved across the floor periodically. After about a week, I hear Hannah outside the room.

"Wow, honey," she says.

"Yeah, I'm almost done. And then, you can do your handy-work."

Hannah laughs. It's so good to hear her laugh. "I don't know about that…"

Brent must be done with whatever he was doing since Hannah starts to spend more time in the room. She is in here often, sometimes humming to herself. I like when she does that. One of those days, I hear her pulling at the curtains. All of a sudden, I feel a change. It is not as dark anymore. It's as if someone has switched on a little night light under the covers. I still cannot see well. But I can at least make out a silhouette moving in the room. It's Hannah! She's folding something large and flowy. It has to be the curtains. I then see her silhouette climb something. It's a tall triangle. A ladder? And her hands are moving in strokes. On the wall? It has to be the wall. I can make out some shades on the wall but I cannot really tell the shapes or patterns. Just the mere fact that I could make out Hannah's silhouette makes me very happy.

A few days later, Hannah comes back with an armful of linen. She moves the ladder to the window and hangs up the curtains. Then, she goes back to painting the wall. I can't really tell what she's painting. I wish someone would pull this cover off me. Don't get me wrong. I am thankful that I can at least make out some outline of things, even though it is not all clear. It's better than nothing. I'm just getting more and more curious about Hannah's painting. She must have heard me whining everyday as she eventually unwraps the cover off me one afternoon. I cannot believe what I'm seeing. The room has been transformed!

The biggest change is the wall. The grey wall is gone. In its place is an incredible mural. Right next to the window, Hannah has painted a tree with branches and leaves stretching over the walls and touching the ceilings. One long branch arches over where I normally sit. On this long branch, a lion sleeps, an arm swung over another branch. He looks so peaceful. At the end of the long branch, a giraffe gracefully reaches for the leaves. Below the mama giraffe, a baby giraffe nuzzles close with green bushes around its legs. On the wall next to the window, where the pink glider used to sit, a branch hangs low and on it, a monkey relaxes as he chews on a young shoot. A hornbill perches on a smaller branch close to the lion. This bird does not seem quite complete. Hannah climbs up the ladder and starts coloring the beak of the hornbill a bright orange. She finishes the face with a bright blue and touches up the rest of the body. She smiles proudly after painting the last stroke.

The pink curtains have been replaced by tan ones. They happen to be drawn wide open today and I can see outside. There's actually a tree outside. It must have grown while I've been forced to hibernate. The changing table is still on the corner and Hannah has removed its cover too. I feel an awkward bond with this changing table. We seem to be the only ones that have survived these last few months and now years. It still looks good. The cover must have helped preserve it.

The next day, Brent moves me back towards the wall. It's a weird feeling to have giraffes looking over me and a lion sleeping above me. But I am liking the cheerful vibe in this room. After all the bleakness and darkness, it's a breath of fresh air to have these animals light up the room and the sun rays streaming in. In the next few weeks, the room gets filled again with new toys and stuffed animals. I am no longer naked. Little giraffes are printed all over my ivory colored sheets. A new bumper runs around me. A brightly colored musical mobile gets attached to my left flank a few days later. From it hangs vibrantly colored frogs, birds, monkeys, and parrots. Finally, Brent moves a new glider into the room. It's tan-colored and about the same size as the old one. Hannah places a cuddly orangutan on the glider. She pats its head, with a wide smile plastered on her face. It feels good to see her happy. She's singing again. And reading to the little bump in her belly. Her voice is strong and bubbly.

I am nervous again. I have not seen Hannah or Brent for a few days. So, when I hear their footsteps outside the door, I am holding my breath in anticipation. I can still remember the sad face that greeted me the last time they were away for this long while. But this time, they are both smiling and Hannah looks absolutely radiant. In her arms, a little bundle. They bring this little bundle to the changing station, cooing at it. Suddenly, a cry. Both Hannah and Brent try to sooth it as they talk to it. Then, Hannah picks the bundle up and sits down in the glider. It's a baby, just as I have guessed. Now that they are across from me, I can clearly see it's soft pink face and almost bald head. Brent tries to cover the head with a knitted beanie as Hannah tries to feed baby. "What is baby's name?" I want to pester them. They look so peaceful and content as a family. It makes my heart swell.

Soon baby is asleep. Hannah stands up with baby and brings him to me. I'm so excited I could dance. She places baby on my flat belly, pats baby while humming a lullaby.

"My baby, you are going to grow up strong and handsome like your daddy," she tells baby.

"He's going to be just as smart as his mummy," Brent adds softly.

"Can we name him Shane after my grandfather?" Hannah asks.

"Of course, I told you...you get to choose his name."

Hannah smiles and pats baby Shane some more.

"Why don't you get some rest. He's going to be okay. We'll turn on the baby monitor."

"I'm so glad Shane is healthy."

Brent squeezes her shoulders.

"Let's go. You need some rest." He guides Hannah out of the room.

I never knew what really happened to Sophie. I just know we lost her. And it made Hannah very, very sad. I am ecstatic that baby Shane is well and sleeping soundly on me. Even though he cannot hear me, I tell him, "Welcome to your room. Your mummy and daddy worked really hard to make this room beautiful for you. I hope you will have many happy days in this room...with me, of course."

    They better keep me around. I don't think I can survive if I have to move somewhere else. Besides, being a convertible crib should help my case. I can be Shane's bed for many years to come. I want to see this kid grow up. In this room. With this family. My family.

The Silent Watcher
Paul Webb
Fourth Place

It was a cold autumn morning, and the first light of the sun had barely crept above the horizon when I first looked out at the place I would watch over eternally. The large hole dug in the frosty earth lay gaping at my feet, waiting, still filled with shadows. All around me was silent, the world not yet awake, the stillness disturbed only by the soft breeze, stirring the fallen leaves on the pathways into motion. I watched them rise and spin, a cartwheel of golden browns, then drift back down to settle once more and stand out brightly on the white-frosted ground. Thin tendrils of mist had settled over the stream running through the heart of the cemetery and now coiled around the dark yew trees and the great oaks which were scattered through the grounds. Somewhere behind me the church bells chimed out the sixth hour, and then the world settled once more into waiting stillness.

Several hours passed before the anaemic sun at last rose above the tops of the trees and shone down upon me. There was precious little heat in it but it was enough to chase the mist back down the slopes, and to melt the frost into glistening droplets of dew. It was then that I saw the first of them. Alighting the sombre cars and clustering together without talking, as though afraid to disturb the peacefulness of the place or its residents. Slowly but steadily more cars arrived, and from each there appeared several more black-clad mourners. When the whole party had assembled they were led towards me by the solemn-faced minister, followed closely by four men who shouldered the heavy wooden coffin between them, their faces strained with emotion and effort.

They all gathered around as the coffin was lowered into its place deep in the earth, some looking down into the grave, others gazing at my shining black stone face. Wherever they looked, every eye brimmed with tears. Some people clung to each other tightly, arms around shoulders and waists for support; others hand in hand; some stood apart, enclosed in their own grief.

The minister then took his place beside me and began the service.

'Dearly beloved, we are gathered here today to lay to rest and celebrate the life of James Edward Dawson. Saying goodbye to someone we love is always painful, especially when they are taken from us too early. James was only forty-eight when he passed from the physical world into the spiritual, and he leaves behind a loving wife and young son. But we must have faith in God's purpose, and trust that he is now in a better place and that we shall be reunited one day in Heaven. Now, let us pray.'

    They all bowed their heads and joined him in the Lord's Prayer. I could not help but wonder just how many times those words had been spoken before in these grounds, and if they ever brought comfort to those that spoke them. As I looked around at each of them standing before me I hoped that they would, at least this time.

    After the prayer the minister spoke again, reading a tribute pieced together from the memories of friends and family. Occasional murmurs of melancholic laughter rippled through the assembly as the speech recounted the time he locked the family out of their cottage while on holiday in France, and the difficulty he had resolving this with the small handful of phrases he knew in that country's language. There were nods and smiles when he talked of James' passion for the outdoors, and how he had spent many happy hours with his family or his friends hiking and camping. Deathly silence returned, broken only by the sound of barely stifled tears, as he spoke of the illness which reduced the man to a shadow of his former self before finally claiming his life, and then even the minister fell silent for a moment with head bowed and eyes closed.

    'We therefore commit his body to the ground,' he said at last, returning his gaze to those before him. 'Earth to earth, ashes to ashes, dust to dust; in certain hope of the resurrection to eternal life through our Lord Jesus Christ.'

    'Amen,' followed the congregation as one through their tears.

    The minister cast a handful of earth into the grave beneath my feet and I watched it scatter over the coffin lid. A woman then stepped forward unsteadily, her makeup tear-streaked, her trembling lips pressed tightly together as if she could physically hold back her emotions. With a whimper of despair which only I was close enough to hear she added her own scattering of earth, then stood looking down at it.

    With that I watched them all drift away, one by one, back towards their parked cars, until only two remained with me. The woman still hadn't moved, though now the tears ran slowly down her cheeks now matter how hard she tried to stop them. She pressed a crumpled tissue over her nose and sniffed. A boy came up alongside her, his eyes wide and puffy, and slipped his hand into hers. He was still obviously in his teenage years, his movements awkward and his features not yet fully formed, but he already stood taller than the woman beside him. They stood there together in silence, the three of us looking down into the hole below where so much sorrow lay. A cold wind traced its way along the path, tugging at their black coats, and the boy looked down at the woman.

'Come on Mum,' he said softly, squeezing her hand. 'Let's go and join the others.'

They turned and walked slowly back the way they had come. I watched them go until they had disappeared from my sight. As soon as they had gone I felt something on my shoulder. The robin which had landed there hopped to the ground and along the graveside. It looked along where the woman and the boy had disappeared, then into the grave itself, then at me. I looked back. It cocked its head to one side, bounced a little nearer, then flew up into the grey sky in a tiny flurry of wings.

Later that day men came and filled the grave. I watched as the earth swallowed the coffin and the turf was laid on top so that, were I not standing here, there would be no marker of any kind for the life which had passed. I stood, a silent sentinel over him as the pale sun completed its low arc across the autumn sky. Great flocks of rooks flew in, their harsh calls filling the air, to settle down to roost in the tops of the oaks. Shadows wheeled and lengthened before fading with the gloaming; the first stars shining out as the world around me was lost to the night.

The mists and the frost crept in once more, muffling the noises in the dark; the snuffling of nocturnal beasts, or the shrill cry of an owl. Through it all I stood alone with my charge at my feet, surrounded by a sea of the dead.

I had only to stand alone with James for a couple of nights before I saw her again. Clouds had rolled in and the rain poured from the sky, whipped by the wind into great sheets that lashed through the cemetery. The trees heaved to and fro, the last of their dying leaves clinging vainly to the branches. I remained, unflinching, as the rain lashed against my side, running in rivulets down my face. It was the kind of day where people stayed inside. And yet here she was. I hadn't even noticed her approach, it was only when she stood at the end of the grave that I did. She was no longer dressed in black, but her face was pale and still ravaged with grief. Her umbrella and raincoat looked as though they had long since stopped providing any protection from the weather. Her long, dark hair was plastered slick to her head and hung dripping against the sides of her face. She walked towards me, skirting the edge of the slight mound, then sank to her knees in the puddled grass beside me.

'I miss you so much,' she said aloud, her hand on my shoulder, before her whole body was racked with sobs.

I don't know how long she stayed there, crying without caring about anything else as the weather crashed around her. She cried so long that it was impossible for me to tell where the tears ended and the rain began. I thought she might never stop and I knew that, had I a heart, it would have broken for her that day.

I think it was the cold that eventually brought her back to herself. At last the sobbing slowed and she got back to her feet, soaked from head to toe and shivering. She wiped her eyes with the backs of her hands and laughed briefly before looking down sadly.

'I'm sorry,' she said quietly. 'I know you never liked it when I cried. Look at me, I'm a mess. I'd better go. I'll see you again soon.'

She turned and hurried away, still clutching the umbrella over her head and avoiding the worst of the puddles despite the fact she was soaked to the skin. I watched her disappear into the rain and thought, not for the last time, how hard and unfair life could be.

It seemed to me that day that she had cried out the worst of her grief. She came back often, at least every other Sunday through the winter. She brought fresh flowers then stood or knelt beside me to talk. Usually she came alone, but sometimes she would be accompanied by the boy, and while she talked he would stand there self-consciously, with his hands buried deep in his pockets and his eyes on the ground. I always looked forward to her visits for, although the news she brought was intended for the dead man at my feet, she always talked to my face, despite what must have seemed my cold indifference.

So the winter passed. Snow fell and piled up against me in drifts and the whole world turned white as though newly made. Then the sun began to burn more brightly and rise higher in the sky; the snow melted away and was replaced by the first signs of spring. Snowdrops and crocuses then daffodils exploded into colour all around. The lines of sadness on the woman's face had begun to fade and she seemed to me less pale; it was around this time that I actually saw her smile for the first time and I felt a deep sense of relief for her. There had indeed been times when I never thought she would pull through and make it out of the other side of her grief. Had it not been for the boy I still do not know if she would have.

In the early heat of the summer she arrived with such a bustle of excitement that I knew she must have some important news, and I waited impatiently as she hurried along the path towards me with a barely contained grin.

'So, Olly got his results this morning,' she began teasingly. She had been fretting about the boy's exams on many of her previous visits, and despite the obvious good news I still found myself feeling nervous for her when she paused before continuing. 'He got all A's! Our little boy is going to Oxford. Can you believe it? After all he's been through this year as well. I know how proud you'd be. I can't stay, we're having a little party today to celebrate, I just wanted to come and let you know. I wish you could be there with us.'

The end of that summer was the only time that the boy, Olly, ever came to visit alone. It was one evening at the start of September and the air was still warm and full of the hum of insects when he walked towards me. He looked tanned and healthy with the glow of youth, but a sadness still lingered behind his eyes. He didn't say anything, just stood there in that awkward way of the teenage years, at the end of the grave. He stared at me silently for what seemed an age and I stared back. At last his mouth curled into a half-smile and he gave a nod and an embarrassed wave as he turned to leave. To me these seemed to say more than any uncomfortably difficult words could have done. I hoped his father had seen them too and thought the same.

Those long summer days when I could enjoy seeing the smile return to her face couldn't last though. As Olly left for his new life at university the nights began to draw in and the autumn chill returned. Before I even realized it I had been standing in place for a whole year and a little of the sadness had returned to the woman's face. She arrived that morning dressed up and with several bunches of flowers to lay at my feet. She greeted me with a smile, but I knew her well enough by now to know that there was little happiness in it.

'I can't believe it's been one year already,' she whispered as she stood in front of me. 'Sometimes it feels like only yesterday. But then other times it all feels like another life. I know you can't really hear me when I'm talking to you, but I guess it just makes me feel like you haven't completely left for some reason. Ridiculous really I know but…'

Her words trailed off and she seemed lost in thought for a few moments. A little distance away were other figures standing by other graves, some talking, others simply standing in contemplation, all searching for a connection with the past that they knew they had lost.

'The house is so lonely now,' she suddenly continued. 'I couldn't be happier for Olly but, well, I guess I just never expected to be rattling around it on my own. It doesn't really feel like home anymore.'

She stopped and looked back over her shoulder. I could see several other figures approaching and when they drew closer I knew that I recognized them from the funeral. They smiled warmly at the woman and all exchanged hugs and friendly greetings before walking away and taking her with them. I was pleased that she had friends to help her through this day, I knew it couldn't be easy for her, but how I envied that closeness.

I also knew, deep down, that once she made it through the first year her visits would become less frequent. It was only natural. All of the visitors I saw in the graveyard wanted to keep their precious memories alive, but none of them could live in the past forever and she was no different. And so it was that winter, as the cold and dark wrapped around me and my dead charge once more, and the icy rain fell in neverending torrents from the leaden skies, I saw her for only a few brief visits.

It was on one of those perfect, crisp, clear days that were so rare that winter that I discovered the reason she no longer clung so desperately to the past. The rain and sleet had fallen for weeks, and would continue to do so again in a few days time, but on that day like an oasis of cold sunlight in a desert of grey she came again. Her cheeks were full of colour and her smile lit up her eyes, though there was a certain hesitance about her that I had never seen before. She knelt on the frost hardened grass beside me and sighed.

'Sorry I haven't been to see you much for a while,' she began, her brow wrinkling. 'It's just, well, things have been kind of busy recently, and that has to be a good thing right? I mean, I'm not just sitting in the house on my own anymore so you can stop worrying about that. But it's more than that. You remember when you were in the hospital near the end, and you told me you didn't want me to be alone for the rest of my life? Well, I thought you should know that I've met someone. I really hope you don't mind, and you know I will always love you, but you were right, and I'm going to try to move on with my life. I'll never forget you obviously, but I might not be able to get here so much now. He doesn't really like that I still visit you so often. I will still come and see you though, but goodbye for now.'

She placed a kiss against the coldness of my face before standing and I watched her walk away, heartened that she had found some new happiness but at the same time already dreading that I might never see her again.

After that she did indeed come less often. The flowers she had once replaced with such care and devotion were now left to fade and wither and die for many months at a time. Sometimes a whole year would pass, though she would always appear on the anniversary of the funeral. In between I would settle in to my lonely vigil, watching over the dead man at my feet but often thinking about the woman. When she did come in these years she no longer talked so much and, as much as I tried to pretend otherwise, I could see that unhappiness had crept back into her life though I knew not why.

I can never quite remember how long passed in that way but I do know it was another anniversary of the funeral when she stood before me nursing a painful looking bruise around her eye. She had tried to conceal it with makeup, and no doubt had succeeded in making it look less obvious, but she couldn't hide it completely. She stood before me, scared but defiant. Before she could say a word though a man approached that I felt sure I recognized. He had reached her before I could place the teenage boy I once knew. There was no awkwardness now; he was tall and strong, and his features had grown to fit his face well, with more than a hint of his mother in there. I don't think he even glanced over at me though.

'What happened Mum?' Olly asked as soon as he reached the woman. He didn't wait for an answer. 'He did it didn't he?'

'Olly, please,' she said shaking her head and gripping his shoulders.

'Where is he? He's not getting away with this again.'

'No, you'll only make things worse,' she said, wincing as her eyes welled with tears. 'Just leave it, he didn't mean it.'

'You can't keep making excuses for him Mum,' Olly said, pulling away from her. 'I'm serious, you have to leave him.'

'It's not that easy,' she replied.

'Yes it is,' he shot back. 'You should have gone to the police the first time. Give me one good reason why I shouldn't go to them now.'

'Because it's my life Olly, mine. I know you mean well but you're too young to understand.'

'Well explain it to me then Mum! Because I can't keep doing this. I can't keep seeing you and wondering where the bruises are going to be next time.'

'Don't exaggerate, it's only been a couple of times, and he's going through a stressful time at work, he's not himself at the moment.'

'Oh well that makes it alright then, doesn't it,' Olly snapped at her.

'Look, he helped me through a tough time,' she said with a sigh. 'After your Dad died and you left home I really struggled. He was there for me.'

'So it's my fault for leaving is it?' Olly replied.

'No, that's not what I mean and you know it,' she said sharply. 'Maybe you should just come round, get to know each other. I'm sure he'd like that, and then maybe you'd see what I see in him.'

'Are you actually being serious?' Olly said, stepping back and running a hand through his hair. 'How do you think it makes me feel seeing him when I know what he's done to you? Do you honestly think I could go and talk to him as though nothing had happened? Wake up Mum, he's hit you before and he'll do it again, what's so hard to understand about that?'

She looked away from him now, fixing her eyes on me, and I could see the pain etched in her face as Olly spoke again.

'Mum, you have to choose, because I just don't think I can see you again while you're still with him.'

She took a step back, and for a moment I thought she might stagger and fall, but she recovered herself and looked at her son, her face set hard.

'If that's how you really feel then I think maybe you should go,' she managed at last.

'Fine,' Olly said after a few moments, shaking his head as he walked away.

I have never felt so powerless as they turned away from each other and left. Watching the only two people in the living world that I cared for tearing themselves apart, and knowing that the woman would be returning to a man who had hit her. I wondered at the anger the man buried at my feet must be feeling if he could see how things had played out, and knowing he was just as impotent to help as I.

I saw nobody again for some time after they left that day. The seasons wheeled through the sky in their never-ending cycle of life, death, and rebirth and all the while I stood, watchful. I lost track of the years. From my lonely position they seemed to blur into one another and roll away from me. The life of the cemetery went on but I paid it little attention. I worried about the woman, and about Olly, often at first and I missed them with an aching loneliness. But without the concerns of the living distracting me I drifted into a watchful slumber, letting the world rush on around me.

It was the familiar sound of tears that brought my consciousness back. They sounded so distant at first but then, as with someone slowly roused from their sleep, I realized it was just in front of me. She had come back at last. The last traces of youth had been driven from her face, and her once dark hair was now laced with white and grey. Had it been so long? The tears rolled down over her cheeks, falling one by one on to the grave. She rested one hand lightly upon me, as she had so many times before, and looked into my face with those same big, sad eyes.

'I've left him,' she managed between the tears, and I felt a swell of pride well up inside me. 'I should have done it long ago. Olly was right, but I was so stubborn or scared I wouldn't listen. I pretended it was all fine, but I knew it wasn't. I was so stupid! And now I've lost Olly too; we haven't spoken for nearly ten years, not since we had our fight here.'

I had not seen him either, though I knew at a certain point in people's lives they become so busy that they are too wrapped up in the present to pay much thought to the past and had put it down to that. I wondered at how painful this must all be for the dead man's spirit to look down on; to watch the little family he left behind fall apart. With all the strength I could muster I willed her to go to her son.

'I know I should just call him,' she spoke again as her sobbing began to subside. 'But I don't want to get in his way. We'll see. I am sorry I haven't been able to come here for a while, I hope you can forgive me. Life just became so complicated. I think a part of me was too ashamed for you to see me like that, I know it seems ridiculous now.'

Her tears had stopped and she was talking to me much as she used to, though she still seemed so tired, and her eyes had lost their sparkle.

'Oh!' She suddenly exclaimed looking at my feet. 'Look at the state of those flowers! I really have been neglecting you haven't

I? Well, let me take these away now and I'll bring some fresh ones again next time. I still miss you, every day.'

She lifted the dead, brown flowers and carried them away with her, looking back over her shoulder at me briefly before disappearing.

After that she returned like clockwork on every anniversary, as well as on what used to be James' birthday in May, and around Christmas. The Christmas visits were the ones I always looked forward to the most. The whole world just seemed so peaceful then, and even the graveyard wanderers that I glimpsed through the year seemed to find a certain happiness around that time. She even started bringing a small gift to lay at my feet along with the usual flowers and I felt I could have burst with the excitement of it all.

She even brought a card to show me on one occasion. Her eyes brimmed with tears as she held it, but her mouth was fixed in a broad smile.

'I sent Olly a card this year,' she said, opening the card and reading the contents to herself again as if she couldn't quite believe them. 'And he sent one back. He lives in Queensland now, he moved there for work not long after our fight. We spoke on the phone last night, not for long, and it was a little strange after so many years, but I think we might be alright. I've missed so much of his life; he's getting married next year and I've never even met her! I don't think I would ever have forgiven myself if I'd missed that too.'

I had never seen her so full of life. To know that they had at last reconciled was the greatest Christmas gift that I would ever receive and it warmed me during the long, cold nights of that whole winter. She was, of course, invited to the wedding and travelled to Australia by herself for it. There were more trips over there as a couple of grandchildren came along and often now she brought photo's to show me whenever she came.

So the time crept by. I stood almost unchanged despite being battered by the weather, but I watched the years collecting in her face and body until she was bent and wrinkled, her eyes the only trace of the young woman I first met. She still kept coming, though now I watched with a twinge of sadness as she made her painfully slow way along the path towards me. Then came the first anniversary of James' death that she had missed for many, many years. I waited eagerly all day, always watching the path that led from the small car park to see her tottering along it. The pale morning brightened as the noon sun shone down brightly; the afternoon slowly faded into evening; and then the cold of night crept back in around me. She hadn't come. I let myself wonder what could have delayed her. I came up with a hundred reasons, and convinced myself that I would see her tomorrow, or the next day, but deep down I knew what had happened.

In the first light of morning the hole was dug next to me and another stone placed at its head. I caught a glimpse of it as the workmen moved it into position, it read: *Here lies Olivia Mary Dawson, beloved wife of James and mother of Oliver. May she rest in peace.* It was only then I realized that I had never known her name. I felt a shudder of sadness run through me as I read it and then looked down at the grave awaiting her, and I knew that I would miss her forever. At the same time I felt deeply content that she was at peace now and that she and James would be together again, as they were always meant to be.

As the sun came up the small congregation arrived. Some were young, but most were old. Looking hard I recognized some of them from James' funeral so many years ago, though time had taken its heavy toll on them all now. As they waited for the ceremony many of them glanced around themselves with a look I knew well by now. I saw it often in the cemetery, it was one that meant they were doing their best not to consider their own impending mortality.

After the coffin had been committed to the ground the black-clad group stood and cried around the headstone beside me. And then they walked away, the young helping the old, until only one familiar face remained. He was greyer around the temples, and was carrying a little more weight, than when I had seen him last, but I still knew Olly even at a glance. On either side of him, with their small hands in his, was a child. A little behind him stood a woman, tall and pretty, her dark mascara a little smudged.

'Hi Dad,' he said with a little sheepish smile. 'I'm sorry I haven't been here for so long. I guess I just never really believed in all this stuff. It was really hard for me when I lost you too, I guess I didn't really know how to deal with it.'

It was funny, I thought as he talked, how death and the dead could turn even a grown man back into his awkward teenage self. I knew this must have taken a lot of courage though, it was the first time he had ever actually spoken to James since he had died.

'Anyway,' he continued, looking down at his own children. 'Before she died Mum made me promise that I would come here and introduce you to your grandkids, so, here they are. This is Jack, and this is Amelia.'

The two children hid themselves slightly behind their father, peeking out at me shyly.

'Hello Grandpa,' they said after a little encouragement from Olly, then ran to their mother.

'And that's my wife, Charlotte,' he said looking over his shoulder. 'I wish you could've been around for all of this Dad. I hope you're somewhere looking down on us at least. You'll have to get used to Mum nagging you again now she's on her way to meet you.'

He smiled, then said a sad goodbye to both graves and turned with his little family and walked away.

As they left I noticed a little sparrow land on the gravestone next to me. She hopped around to look at me curiously for a moment, then flew off, way above the trees until she was lost to my sight. It struck me then how swiftly life moves on. It would not be long before there was nobody left to remember the two lovers lying at my feet, and then nobody would stop by to see me any more. Then I would truly be alone, but I would continue to watch over them forever. I settled back and the world rolled on.

Left On the Shelf
Amy Hickman
Fifth Place

Nolan threw me against the wall again this morning. I know when to expect it now; it's happened every week for months. There's always a sign: his face burns red, his eyes narrow and begin to glisten, then the angry words begin to flow.

Today I hope it's the last time as I lay motionless, bent, splayed open and afraid until Natalie finds me in the corner.

Natalie has picked me up time and time again. There was a time when she would whisper kind words as she stroked my back gently, holding me against her chest. Now she simply returns me to my rightful place with a sigh, sadness in her eyes.

I used to make Nolan so happy. He would hold me carefully in his hands each night, his eyes lighting with joy as my stories fuelled his dreams. I don't know what went so wrong. All I know is that it all changed after the blonde lady stopped coming into our room.

For a few days I didn't see anyone. I told myself that they must have gone away and forgotten to take me. That was okay. They had done it before. But I remembered that each time they had gone away, the blonde lady would neatly pack Nolan's clothes into a big case, and Nolan would always beg to take me with them. Sometimes she would laugh and agree, wrapping me up in one of Nolan's shirts before tucking me in among his clothes. Other times she would tell him he would be far too busy, and that he wouldn't have time for me. Those times I simply sat and waited for Nolan to return. I waited to see his happy face.

This time it was different. An older lady came into the room, tears staining her cheeks as she stuffed clothes into a bag. No neat folding, no wrapping me up. Then they were gone.

The house fell silent for days.

When Nolan returned, wearing black, eyes red and puffy, he turned to me for comfort once again. He held me, ran his fingers lightly over me as he sobbed until the tall man came into the room.

Their hushed words—distorted by tears—seemed alien to me; all I had known was happiness, tales of brave princes and beautiful princesses, so far from these words of loss, anger, grief.

Nolan had placed me back on the shelf, taken the tall man's hand, and left me in the darkness.

Nolan didn't come back that night or the next. He would briefly come into our room to pick up a toy. Sometimes he would glance over at me, but he would leave without a word.

The tall man brought Nolan into the room one night. He was already asleep with no need for my words. I watched as the tall man wrapped Nolan in the dinosaur-covered blanket and switched on the lamp that cast star shapes over every surface. Nolan murmured something familiar: "Story." But the tall man looked at me and shook his head, telling Nolan it was too late for stories.

It was a few days after that night when Nolan first hurt me. He seemed happy for the first time since everyone disappeared. He picked me up and wiped away the stains his tears had left, a smile on his lips as he began to open me. Then came the anger-- the pure hatred in his eyes. The first time, he only threw me on the floor, screaming at me that it wasn't fair before he ran out of the room.

Since the day the blonde lady had brought me home, I'd never felt such cruelty, but it didn't stop there. Nolan would glare at me for hours. For a few brief moments he would be content with me in his hands, but the anger always came the moment he opened me, as though something inside me disgusted him and filled him with rage.

Over time I began to fall apart; a dent in my cover, the glue loosening along my spine, my corners bent and torn. I wondered what I had done wrong and why Nolan didn't simply toss me away like he threatened to with every outburst of anger, but still I remained on the shelf, waiting for the next cruel attack.

"Why do you keep throwing that book on the floor? If you don't want it, throw it away or put it with Mum's things." Natalie's voice came from beyond the bedroom door.

"I can't," Nolan replied, his voice gruff with the usual anger that was always directed at me.

"Oh come on, Nolan. Don't you think you're a little old for fairytales? It's not like you've read it in years anyway, at least not since…"

"Not since Mum died," Nolan replied.

It was then that I understood all of Nolan's tears, all his anger. The blonde lady was his mother, and she was gone.

"You know, I feel sorry for that book. It's stupid to hang onto something that makes you so angry. I get that Mum used to read it to you, but let it go." Natalie's voice was soft, like when she used to whisper to me.

"I can't," Nolan replied again. "Look."

Nolan stepped into the room, looking over at me with swollen eyes. He'd been crying again. He took me from my shelf, ran his fingers over my cover where the fading gold letters were embossed into the card. Closing his eyes, he allowed his fingers to open me before handing me to Natalie.

There, on my first page, her fingertips traced over something that I had long forgotten about. The blonde lady had written something inside me. I remembered the first time Nolan and the blonde lady had cuddled up on the bed, his arm wrapped in plaster, and how he had giggled at those words before they began to read.

"Nolan,
Because you love adventures so much but you're not very good at them, let's keep to fairytales and out of trees!
I love you,
Mum xx"

Biographies

Katie Evans- Katie is a children's author who lives in Southern California with her family and their dog, where they have adventures and tell stories!

Lynne Fellows- A Brit in Spain. Reader, writer, and blogger of all things bookish. A self-confessed word nerd, currently training to be a line editor & proofreader to exorcise the demons of plot-holes and punctuation that can spoil a good story. Writing as L.S. Fellows, you can find her stories in many ebook retailers.

Dominique Goodall- Dominique is an author with an independently published a novella, as well as a co-releasing an anthology for charity, and has won various writing contests over the years including the Lady in the Loft contest with a dystopian entry in 2014. Her interests are varied, and run from gaming, to reading, to singing and dancing with her dogs when no one is watching.

Amy Hickman- Amy is a writer of romance, but enjoys twisting her writing with elements of other genres. While her writing focuses on romance, her tastes in reading material vary between horror, crime fiction, occasional romance, and true crime. Amy is currently the Head of International Operations at the Writer's Workout, a place she feels is a wonderful community of fellow writers where not only is there a great network of support and advice, but where she has been challenged to break out of her comfort zone and embrace different genres and styles. Amy joined the administrative team in 2017.

Javeria Kausar- I write to spread awareness about oft-neglected and overlooked issues. I am a published short fiction writer and I won the Sweek International Microfiction contest and the Damodarshree National Award for my nonfiction essay. I'm currently a student of Literature and I intend to help as many people as possible through my work.

Tony Kelly- Tony Kelly is a mild-mannered history teacher by day, and a mild-mannered writer of fiction when he can cobble together some free time. Born and raised in Orange County, he currently resides in the Sacramento region with his wife, Tiffany, and three-year old daughter, Abigail. Tony is training to be an Olympic curler but has a long way to go.

Danielle Kiowski- Danielle Kiowski is a writer based in Las Vegas, where she lives with her husband. Find out more about her writing at www.daniellekiowski.com.

Oonagh McBride- I'm new to writing but having fun

Mia Neishy- Mia Neishy (nee-she) grew up in Malaysia but now resides in Hawaii. Her writing style has been defined as simple but fluent, slow-paced but detailed. She often takes readers to a destination and have them experience a dreamlike journey with the characters. Her settings are vivid and easily imaginable. Her characters come from a myriad of backgrounds. She is able to bring out the human emotions in her characters through playful dialogues and expressive narrations.

K. M. Shapiro- K. M. Shapiro is a fourth year medical student who loves writing in her spare time. Her favorite genres are thriller, sci-fi/fantasy, young adult, and general fiction. She currently lives in Chicago with her husband and her fluffy cat companion, Dexter.

CE Snow- CE Snow is a classically trained opera singer who took up writing as a mid-life crisis. Whether contemporary or speculative fiction, favorite stories are rich in sensory details and weird twists. A firm believer that people are not always exclusively right- or left-brained, in additional to creative pursuits Snow manages a robotics company and tutors maths and science to at-risk youth.

EB Stark- EB Stark was lucky enough to work in publishing for several years before outsourcing murdered the graphics layout industry. Now she works for the Department of Defense by day and is an editor at Postcard Poems and Prose literary journal by night. Though married to her college sweetheart for over 25 years, she's ever a bachelor—in computers, in digital media, and almost so in creative writing. She pens short fiction when able to distract her inner critic and found her way to print in online venues like Dark Chapter Press and in broadcast with the U.K. film project, Fragments of Fear. Whether it's writing, editing, or creating in Photoshop, she can usually be founding obsessing over commas in her work pajamas while listening to docudramas.

Irina Tyunina- A poet and fiction writer. Has 3 poetic books published and multiple publications in the Russian literary magazines. Lives in Kemerovo, Russia. A linguist. Presently, an interpreter at the University of Medicine.

Pamela Wagner- Pamela Wagner lives in Hamilton, Ontario, Canada. She is working hard to defeat the demons of procrastination and lack of confidence that plagued her in her youth. To that end, she writes stories and poems, mentors young writers, but most importantly for her creative life, she dreams faerie.

Paul Webb- As a child I loved to write. As an adult I dreamed about being a writer but had somehow forgotten that the obvious first step is actually putting pen to paper.

Printed in Great Britain
by Amazon